SMALLS

The South wanted his head.

The North, his heart.

ೞ

By Steve Robertson

.

For my wife Cheryl and my mother, Mollie Floyd,
who encouraged me to fulfill my dream.

The author gratefully acknowledges
the assistance and guidance of Dennis Cannady,
one of the foremost authorities on the
life and times of Robert Smalls.

He is also indebted to his editor, Kelli Keith,
for bringing a first-time novelist's
manuscript to a higher standard.

Foreword

Though this book is a work of fiction, many of the events and people described within its pages have an historical basis. The author has attempted to bring to life the story of a remarkable young black man whose endeavors helped change the course of the Civil War. In doing so, dialogue that some may find offensive was used to capture the era in which the events took place.

Some of the information provided in these pages may not be historically accurate or reflect the actual attitudes, dialogue, descriptions, or events of the person described.

The story of Roberts Smalls, perhaps purposefully relegated to dusty corners of U.S. history for many years, serves as a reminder that the flame of freedom burns bright in every heart, regardless of color, race, or religion.

Prologue
Lighthouse Inlet near Charleston, S.C., Dec. 1, 1863

"Git up," said Moses.

Robert Smalls groaned as he tried to open his eyes. Without success, he slipped back into dreamy darkness.

The woman's voice in his head became insistent.

"Git dem bones up! You ain't come all dis way jes to die, Robert," she demanded in a deep, husky voice.

Robert strained to open his eyes, one at a time and saw a puff of dense, blue smoke. He shook his head, wiped his eyes with the back of his hand, and stared groggily through the haze.

From out of the fog, a face appeared.

Moses?

No. It couldn't be her familiar face.

She's many miles away.

A man mouthed words Robert could not hear over the ringing in his ears. Robert fought a wave of dizziness and struggled to gain his footing. Exhausted by the effort, he dropped back to his knees.

He felt a slight breeze. The smoke dissipated, allowing his eyes to adjust to the light. The familiar wheelhouse looked awry. The door hung loosely by one hinge. Shards of glass littered the wooden floor. Sunshine streamed through a hole in the cabin's roof.

As consciousness returned, the ringing in his ears was replaced by the sound of exploding artillery shells and the whine of bullets.

The man shook Robert's shoulders.

Perplexed, Robert turned toward him.

The voice came closer, "Mister Smalls! Mister Smalls! What we gonna do now, de Rebels be upon us."

Robert took a deep breath to clear his head but was met with a cough that would not quit. With each forward lurch, the back of his scalp sizzled with pain. He reached back and felt a sharp triangle of glass embedded in the tender skin. He grasped it and pulled hard. A hot gush of blood rolled down his neck. The shard slipped from his fingers and shattered on the floor.

Strong arms reached around Robert's waist and pulled him to a sitting position.

A puff of air pushed the remaining smoke out of the cabin. With each new breath, Robert felt the strength return to his body.

"Alfred," Robert bellowed above the noise. "Is that you?"

"Oh, thank you Jesus!" shouted the stocky black man, holding Robert in a desperate embrace. "You ain't dead."

Robert struggled to his feet and leaned against the ship's wheel.

A nightmarish spectacle met his gaze.

Out of the broken window, he saw the barrel of the ship's forward cannon tilted toward the sky.

The ship's bow rested on a sandy beach. Two hundred yards farther loomed a large earthen fort. A Confederate flag whipped in the wind over the ramparts. Orange blossoms of fire, followed by ear-splitting explosions, erupted from the fort and the high-pitched scream of cannon balls passed closely overhead.

He crouched in the remains of the heavily damaged room.

"Alfred," Robert shouted above the battle's noise. "What happened. Why is the *Planter* grounded?"

"It was de Captain," replied Alfred. "He ran de ship on de beach when de Rebels surprised us. You and him was arguin' when de cannon ball hit

4

the wheelhouse. Captain, he not hardly touched. I thought you dead fo' sure! Dat's when Captain say he would take his chances with Johnny Reb."

Robert looked toward Alfred in disgust.

"He was going to give up the ship?"

"Not only dat," said Alfred. "He turned the *Planter* right onto this beach and we been stuck here ever since … catchin' hell, Mister Smalls."

"Where is the Captain?" Robert demanded.

Alfred's eyes widened.

"Dat's jes it, Mister Smalls, he be hidin' down below. Last thing he say 'fo he scatted was, 'give de damn boat to de Rebels. He won't gonna die for a bunch of black niggers.'"

Robert's mind raced as he slumped against the remains of the wall.

Without warning, the Confederate guns fell silent.

Strange … now's their chance to blow us out of the water.

The truth of the situation dawned on him. The commander of the Confederate battery had no intention of destroying the *Planter*. The Confederate steamship turned Union gunship, though bruised and battered by the bombardment, remained operational. The Rebels could board her, wait on the rising tide, and sail back to Charleston.

As if in confirmation of his conclusion, small arms fire erupted. A gray line of Confederate soldiers snaked down the river's embankment and advanced across the beach toward the *Planter*.

Information. He needed information.

"Alfred," Robert said. "Find Sgt. Strong. Tell him to report here at once. Oh, if you see the Captain tell him the firing has stopped. We need him back."

Alfred raced down the steps to the main deck.

Surrender the Planter?

He grimaced at the idea of the ship falling back into Confederate hands.

Robert had commandeered the *Planter* out of Charleston Harbor a year ago while the ship's captain attended a nearby celebration. The Northern press had made a great deal about Robert's courage. President Lincoln, impressed by the heroic feat, even invited him to the White House. The South would howl with delight if he failed.

Surrender?

A wave of fear stabbed at his heart. He and every other black man on board the *Planter* knew what would happen if they became prisoners of the Confederacy. A fate far worse than that of a runaway slave awaited them. Runaways could expect a beating and a short, hellish life of hard labor in a Southern cotton field.

The South had a special punishment in mind for Robert and his crew. The traitorous pack of negroes would beg for death before the Confederacy finished with them. The thought of dying didn't particularly frighten Robert. He had faced death many times in many places. He feared more for his crewmates.

He took a deep breath. With a clear head, he calmly stepped forward to look at the bow of the ship. The Confederate soldiers waded toward the boat through the shallow water, rifles raised to fire at the first sign of resistance.

"By God, I will not go back into slavery! No man will bind me with chains or beat me with a whip. No man will take away my freedom," he muttered.

Freedom.

The word stirred poignant memories. The pursuit of freedom defined his life. From Robert's earliest days as a slave serving Master McKee in Beaufort to the events that had brought him to this beach deep in Rebel territory; the quest for freedom had motivated him to take desperate action.

Robert didn't have time to think about it more. He sprawled across the floor, as a hail of bullets spattered the bridge

.

Part 1

Beaufort, S.C.

○§♥○

Chapter 1

Beaufort, September 1847

By the light of a small lantern, eight-year-old Robert Smalls hurried to finish brushing Master McKee's favorite stallion, Wendigo. The big, black horse whinnied with approval when Robert gave him his morning ration of oats and nuzzled the little boy with affection. Animals and humans instinctively liked Robert.

The slender young boy closed the paddock door and raced through the darkness of the cool September morning to the nearby kitchen. He backed up to a pot-bellied stove, enjoying its warmth. His mother, Lydia, along with Lizzie and Hervie, ladled food onto serving trays. The aroma of bacon and the sweet smell of apple fritters made his mouth water.

"Ma, I got de horses curried and ol' Bess and Gus is already hitched to de wagon. Can I go to de big house and call for de Master?" asked Robert.

Lydia looked down at her son, who was fidgeting with excitement.

"You sits yo' little hiney down here at de table," chided Lydia. "You ain't had a mouthful to eat and it could be a long time 'fo you eats again. Master and his friends just woke up. Hit'll be another hour or two before dey be ready to get on de road."

"Aw ma," whined Robert. "I can't eats nuttin'. My belly's already doin' flips and we ain't even left de yard yet."

Lydia frowned and gave Robert a look that meant there would be no negotiation on the matter. Resigned to his fate, the boy plopped into a chair. Lydia put a plate of scrambled eggs and grits in front of him and stood with her arms crossed.

"Boy, you just don't know how lucky you is," scolded Lydia.

Robert knew what would follow and rolled his eyes.

"When I worked on de plantation there won't no such thing as a breakfast," Lydia continued. "If us got a plate of cold cornmeal mush, we was doin' good. And, that had to stick to our innards for de rest of de day. You best be glad Missus McKee takes good care of her house niggers."

As she talked, Lydia stacked silver serving trays with huge mounds of fried eggs, grits, country ham, biscuits, and pastries.

That's enough for a Pharaoh's army! Robert mused, as he dutifully finished his own meal.

Lydia and her assistants carried the food from the kitchen across the yard to the big house. Thin lines of smoke wafted lazily into the crisp autumn air from the home's six, brick fireplaces. The butler, an elderly black man named Caesar, opened the back door and ushered the women into the house.

Robert's heart quickened when he saw a warm light fill the window of master's bedroom. If Master McKee was up and about, soon everyone would follow, he reasoned.

Lydia and her helpers came back to the kitchen to pack baskets with cured meats, jars of vegetables, and sweet stuffs. She looked toward an impatient Robert and relented.

"Okay boy, go ahead and get Jacob and bring de wagon and carriage to de front of the big house," said Lydia. "No need to be in a big hurry. Dey's just gettin' started eatin' and I 'magine the sun'll be up good before dey comes out."

Robert jumped up to escape the kitchen, but Lydia caught him by the seat of his pants. She looked with earnest into his large almond-colored eyes until he met her gaze.

"Listen here boy," her voice low and intense. "Master say he wants to take you on dis huntin' trip but you listen hard to me. You gots to do everythin' Master say. And all those who be with him. If he say jump, you ask how high? You hear what I'm sayin'.'"

Robert nodded.

"This here be de most important thing of all. When you gets to de plantation house you stays clear of dat overseer. Dat Mistuh Blakely, I hear he got da devil inside of him. You stay close to Master McKee. Don't you never get caught alone with dat Blakely. You hear what I sayin' boy."

Robert nodded again.

"Okay, gives your ol' ma a kiss and be off with you."

Robert jumped into Lydia's arms and gave her a big hug and a kiss on the cheek.

"Don't you fret none," he laughed as he scampered from the kitchen.

Jacob, his ebony skin shined in the light of the barn's lanterns, loaded a wagon hitched to Bess and Gus, two perfectly matched mules. Neatly folded blankets, a picnic basket, and burlap sacks of supplies filled the wagon's bed.

"Gib me a hand with the rest of dis stuff," Jacob ordered as he jumped into the wagon.

Robert passed boxes of ammunition and gunpowder to Jacob, who stowed everything and stepped onto the seat. He snapped the reins and the mules pulled the load to the kitchen door where Lydia was waiting.

Boxes of food went into the wagon along with lanterns, coffee, bags of sugar and rice, and a chest sealed with a strong lock. Lydia grabbed another quick kiss from Robert before he and Jacob drove the wagon around front. Jacob instructed Robert to hitch the mules to a post while he went back to the stables for the carriage drawn by Wendigo.

The first bright rays of sun broke over the horizon bathing the house in golden hues. The McKee home ranked as one of the finest in Beaufort, also one of the newest. Built on a city lot large enough to contain several outbuildings, a large garden, and a small pasture for a milk cow, the McKee house testified to the wealth generated by the family's three plantations. Robert and the other McKee slaves often bragged to their friends about living in the biggest and best house in Beaufort.

Robert jumped when the front door opened and young Ed McKee spilled out of the doorway followed by his brother, Henry McKee, and a distinguished-looking gentleman named Moses Goldsmith. Ed, a strapping young man with jet-black hair, struggled to manage four shotguns and a rifle as he clambered down the steps.

"Let me help," Robert cried, while reaching to catch a rifle slipping from Ed's arms.

"Well done!" laughed Master McKee. "Our hunting trip almost got off to an inauspicious start. Ed, get the rest of the rifles and try to be a bit more careful this time."

Master McKee loomed over Robert. Though only five-feet-eight inches tall, the Master seemed a giant in the eyes of a young lad. He had gentle blue eyes, but deep, hard creases lined his face. His neatly cut whiskers and short beard had streaks of gray. While solidly built, the start of a large belly indicated city life was beginning to tell on him.

"So," said the taller, handsome man standing to McKee's side, "you think this young lad is ready to be in the woods with the great white hunters? I think he may be a bit too young for such an adventure."

"Moses don't tease the boy," chuckled McKee. "If I had to hear him beg again to go on this trip every hair on my head would be gray."

The two old friends laughed. They turned at the sound of a door banging and watched as Ed carefully carried three more rifles down the steps and placed them in the carriage hitched to Wendigo. His sister-in-law, Jane McKee, a tall, stately woman, followed close behind. She watched nervously as Ed secured the firearms onto a valise on the back of the carriage and strapped the lid down.

"Henry, you've got to promise me you will come out of the woods if it starts raining. You know how prone Ed is to catching pneumonia. Thank goodness Dr. Reed will be with you."

"Now, now. You have got to quit worrying about Ed. He is as healthy as an ox," McKee said to his wife. "Speaking of Dr. Reed, where is the old scoundrel? We must be going, or we won't reach Milford by supper."

Mrs. McKee walked back into the house. A few minutes later she returned with a gangly, wild-haired man. Reed buttoned his pants as he walked toward the carriage his shirt open at the collar.

"Sorry old chap," sputtered Reed. "I'm really not used to getting such an early start. I'm famished. Where's breakfast?"

"No time for that. Perhaps we can scrounge up a biscuit along the way," said McKee. "Okay, all aboard that's going aboard."

The four white men clambered into the carriage and Robert handed the reins to Ed. Robert hopped on the back of the supply wagon driven by Jacob, his legs dangling off the back.

Mrs. McKee bid the group goodbye and threw kisses at Henry and Ed as the little caravan lurched into motion. Robert glanced back at the house where Lydia stood to wave a fond farewell, as she dabbed her eyes with the corner of her apron.

The wagon passed stately homes that lined both sides of Cartaret Street as it traveled toward the docks and shopping district of Beaufort. Robert waved at two young boys who gawked at the procession and gave them a triumphant smile.

Saturdays drew big crowds to Beaufort and even at this early hour the streets teemed with activity. On Bay Street, which ran the length of the Beaufort waterfront, farmers came from the countryside to unload produce at outdoor markets. Merchants piled their wares onto the wooden doorsteps to prepare for the onslaught of customers who would soon clog the thoroughfare.

At the wharf, small fishing boats sailed toward the shores of Port Royal and the rich fishing grounds of the Atlantic Ocean. Negro slaves loaded bales of cotton onto tall, three-mast ships moored at the docks. With the holds filled, these ships would sail the ocean to Britain and return with finished goods.

Across the Beaufort River, Robert saw the outline of Lady's Island, home of the McKee's sprawling cotton plantation, Ashdale.

The streets were formed of hard-packed coquina that gave way to dirt as the travelers moved farther from the city. Roads became bumpy and rutted with the tracks of other wagons. Robert held on tight to keep from falling off the back of the wagon.

The coastal road that lead to the McKee plantation on the Colleton River ran along shoreline of sea marsh that extended as far as the eye could see. Dark ribbons of water cut channels through the tall green grass. Robert inhaled the estuary's salty smell as he watched black men, knee deep in mud, pick the oysters that lined the saltwater creek and load them into a small boat. Later, they would be put on ice and served at some of Beaufort's finest restaurants.

Further along the way, men pulled a long seine through the creeks. Shrimp jumped ahead of them in an attempt to avoid capture. Seagulls circled overhead, with a trumpet of raucous cries, in search of an easy meal. The men on each end of the net pulled it to the sandy bank and threw away the unwanted minnows, while the shrimp went into a large croaker sack.

Robert crawled over the bags in the back of the buckboard and snuggled up against Jacob, who puffed contently on a corncob pipe.

"Jacob, I ain't never been to Mi'ford Plantation afore, has you?"

The black man grinned. "Been der? Chile, I was born der. Lived der allus life 'til the massah moved to Boofort. I likes bein' with Massah McKee, but der's times when I miss de plantation. I be's glad to go back der today. See some of my ol' friends, maybe."

"Tell me about Mi'ford," said the boy, eager with curiosity.

"We got's a long ways to go. Might as well," Jacob sighed as he took a puff from the pipe.

"Some folks say life of de plantation 'bout like being in hell but dat ain't de way twas at Mi'ford," Jacob reminisced. "Massah McKee and his daddy John McKee treated his black folks right good. We always had plenty of grub to eat. De work wuz hard. We woke at sun and worked 'til

14

sun leave de sky but if'n you finished yo' task earlier de res' of de day was yo's to do as you like."

Jacob told the boy about the division of labor on the farm and the slave hierarchy. The slaves that worked in the big house considered themselves superior; the butlers, maids, nursemaids, chambermaids, and cooks dressed well, enjoyed much of the same foods as the plantation owners, and slept in better quarters. Next came skilled laborers like the blacksmiths, carpenters, stable men, and gardeners.

"Dose niggers had good houses," said Jacob. "Dey didn't hardly neber get beat."

Near the bottom of the hierarchy came dog handlers, threshers, millers, and rice mill workers. Common field hands labored at the lowest rung of the ranking system.

"A house nigger-man might go sparkin' a good lookin' field hand nigger woman but I nebber seed a house gal matin' with a fieldhand," explained Jacob matter-of-factly.

The paternalistic system of plantation life meant that the owners saw to the needs of their slaves. Twice a year, slaves lined up in front of the big house to receive clothing. Cotton and flax provided material for skilled negro laborers to spin and weave broadcloth. Seamstresses, under the direction of the plantation mistress, provided underwear, shirts, trousers, and coats. They used indigo and berries as dyes, so blue and gray became the most common color for their fabrics—red-dyed fabric was considered a prize. Skilled weavers produced a variety of plaid designs popular with the slaves.

Milford Plantation had a tannery too. A shoemaker attached leather uppers to wooden soles using horsehair thread. McKee kept all his slaves well clad, with the exception of children.

"In de summertime, most 'em of liked to go barefoot," laughed Jacob.

Each slave family had a small plot of land as a garden; what they grew, they kept. Most of their food came from the plantation's commissary. Every Sunday, they lined up to get their weekly ration, which included a bushel of rice, a half-bushel of sweet potatoes, two pints of peas, a slab of fatback, and a quart of molasses—they used the sweet, syrupy concoction, made from sugar cane, liberally.

"Massah McKee say we has a sweet tooth," chuckled Jacob. "Truth be, we put 'lasses on everythin' to try to make it taste decent."

"We et possums, squirrels, rabbits 'bout anything dat has fo' legs," he added. "Lots of folks like possum but I nevah did. Too greezie!" Jacob mused about the right to hunt.

Every morning at sunrise, except for the Sabbath, the slaves reported to the big house where the master and the overseer set the tasks for the day. They required prime hands to do a full day's task. The older slaves and the younger slaves, just learning their responsibilities, got a half day's task. A task normally required ten hours to complete, but during planting season the work day often exceeded 15 hours.

"It was hard work but when you wuz don you wuz done," explained Jacob.

At Milford, slaves worked half a day on Saturdays. They spent the rest of the day washing clothes, tending to their personal gardens and getting ready for Sunday worship.

"Sat'days was de time for de frolics," recalled Robert's riding companion. "Doze was some happy times. All de older boys and gals had big frolics, 'specially in de fall of de year. De frolics be at Mi'ford but sometimes other plantations. If'n we went to another plantation we'd had to have a ticket to give to de 'trollers."

The *patrollers* were white men—white trash—who scoured the countryside for runaways and were feared by slaves. If caught without a pass, they often whipped the slaves before they returned them to the owners.

The frolics offered slaves an opportunity to mingle with other plantation workers. Music, dancing, and games provided ample opportunity for flirtation and romances between the young men and women.

16

"One game called, 'please and displease,' de girl might say, 'What it take to please you?' and de boy might say, 'For us to walk 'round de barn and kiss!'" chuckled Jacob.

The best times came in the fall when slaves assembled to shuck the corn harvest. Gathered around great piles of corn, they sang and danced to fiddle music as they took husks off the corn.

"Soon as de last ear shucked, Massah McKee would say 'whoopee' and start to run from de place, us a chasin' after him. Everybody be laughin'. We catch massah and puts him on our shoulders and makes him set in dis here chair. Den we takes his hat off and throws it in de fireplace, cause it be bad luck to raise another crop with de same hat. Den all us, colored and de whites have a big feast together. Sometimes de massah hide a bottle of whiskey at de bottom of de corn pile and de hand dat gets der first gets to keep it. I got de bottle one year."

Jacob took a contemplative draw from his pipe as memories of Christmas and New Year flooded back. Christmas served a very special time on Southern plantations because it was the only holiday celebrated by the slaves. The McKees filled sweetgrass baskets with extra food rations and clothing and presented them as gifts to the slaves. The male slaves got a bottle of whiskey each. No one had to report to work on Christmas Day. At Milford Plantation slaves had three days of rest but had to work a half-day on New Year because it was unlucky not to do at least some work on the first day of the year.

"Dey was some good times," mused Jacob.

Robert hesitated, "How about whippins'? I hear der be lots of whippins on de plantation."

The man said solemnly, "Yes, chile. Dey was beatins' for doze niggers what didn't do der tasks, or stole, or tried to run away. Not too many at Mi'ford but I hears about plenty udder places. Massah McKee not care much for beatin' a nigger. He put him in de bull house fust, den in de stocks. If'n that don't work. Massah tell de slave 'I puts you on de tradin' block if'n you don't straight up' and dat seemed to do de most good. Most niggers get right after dat."

"What's a bull house," the boy inquired?

The bull house was a structure just tall enough and wide enough to accommodate a grown man. The master forced the recalcitrant slave into the closet-like shed and closed the door. In the summer, they placed the bull house in direct sun. In the winter they put it in the coldest shade. Those confined in the inky blackness had just enough room to turn around or stoop.

"It be so black in der' you can't see yo' hand in front of yo' face," Jacob grew quiet.

"I done talk enough for now," Jacob grew weary after his long narrative. "You be a good boy now. You see all dis for yo'self soon 'nuf."

Robert settled back against a sack of rice and whistled softly to himself. The wagon began a gentle sway as the mules pulled harder to carry the load up a rise. Massive live oaks lined the road, the trees' long branches formed a canopy overhead which engulfed the little party of travelers. Some of the trees grew more than 20-feet in diameter and had branches so long they touched the ground. Gray moss lent an eerie feel to the surroundings. Robert wished he could climb them.

* * *

Soon, after they wound through the grove of majestic oaks, the group came to a halt on the north bank of the Colleton River.

"We'll have to call for the ferry," McKee instructed when the men gathered around the carriage.

Jacob rang a large bell hanging from a tree, pealing out the message that customers awaited transportation to the other side of the river.

A submerged rope-cable rose to a height of six feet over the water. Attached to the rope by an iron eyelet, was a small barge that began its approach from the other side of the river. A well-muscled black man pulled on the cable while an elderly white man with a long gray beard rested on a wooden barrel. The ferry nudged the shore and caressed the road's end.

"Good morning gents," hollered the bearded man. "Oh, it's you Mr. McKee. Happy to see you again. Will you be headed to Milford on this fine morning?"

"Yes, Lucas. We are going up to do a little duck hunting. Hope to bag a buck, or two. Of course, I'll be checking in with Mister Blakely about the condition of things. How have you been?"

The two men exchanged pleasantries while Jacob prepared the team for the crossing. Apprehensive, Henry and Goldsmith looked at the expanse of water, but Dr. Reed snored a peaceful tune in the backseat of the carriage.

"That will be two bits apiece for the carriage and three bits for the wagon," said the ferry operator. "If you want to let the niggers swim alongside the barge there will be no charge. Otherwise, three pennies each," said Lucas.

"Too cold for that," said Master McKee. "I'll pay for all."

With great care, Ed led Wendigo and the carriage onto the ferry and gripped the reins. Jacob put bandanas around the eyes of the mules. Once blindfolded, they followed him meekly onto the long barge. The other men and Robert found places on the ferry. Lucas cautioned his passengers to stay still and then gave the command for the cable man to begin the trip.

The black man pulled the barge against the gentle tug of the river current. The iron eyelet attached to the overhead cable kept the barge on track. Robert watched in amazement.

The ferry was midstream when a loud oath from Jacob startled him and the others.

"Damn you Bess, be still," shouted Jacob.

The bandana over the mule's eyes had slipped and the nervous creature pranced in the traces. The animal lurched forward and collided against the carriage where Ed stood. The ferry's tilt threw the passengers off balance. Ed's arms flailed and he fell backward against the side of the carriage.

Stung by the collision, Bess backed up and the ferry's passengers tumbled in all directions. Ed turned to find a handhold but careened backward again. For a moment his fingers touched the carriage, but he could not hang on. He reached into nothingness, eyes wide with fright, as he began to plummet toward the river.

All of the sudden, a small, black hand appeared in front of him. Ed made a final, desperate attempt to save himself. His fingers locked on to the proffered hand and felt his momentum stop. Robert, wedged behind the carriage wheel, leaned back with all his might to keep from being pulled forward.

Within seconds, the other men rushed to help. Moses grasped Ed's other arm. McKee wrapped his arms around Ed's waist and together they pulled him to safety.

For a moment, it was silent. The men took deep breaths to regain their composure. Robert came from behind the carriage wheel and gave Ed a concerned look.

'You be okay Massah Ed?"

Ed kneeled and put his arms around Robert.

"I am, thanks to you little fella," whispered Ed.

Master McKee and Goldsmith tussled Robert's hair.

"Might better keep that li'l nigger around, Henry," Lucas chuckled.

* * *

The party off-loaded onto a narrow dirt road where McKee instructed Jacob and Robert to serve lunch. While the white men ate, they talked about Ed's close call on the ferry. Ed, still shaken by the experience, took a ham biscuit to the back of the wagon and offered it to Jacob and Robert.

"I can't eat it. Here ..." Ed handed the food to Robert.

"Thanks you Massah Ed," delighted Robert. He tore the biscuit and handed half to Jacob. "Hope it's better than them smelly old oysters we saw a while ago."

* * *

20

On the road again, the hunting party made good progress. As the elevation increased, the fauna changed. Robert looked up at the pine trees that replaced the vast vistas and towered over lowland marshes. He had never seen anything so tall. He overheard Master McKee tell the others that the tallest trees went to the Charleston shipyards as masts for great sailing ships.

Henry McKee settled back into the cushioned seat of the carriage and lit a cigar. Stomachs filled with the heavy lunch, his content companions dozed. In a world of his own, he drove the buggy through the pine forest worried about Milford, his favorite, but most distant plantation.

Henry McKee grew up at Milford Plantation and helped his father expand it from 600 acres of prime farmland to more than 1,500 acres. To clear the land, it required more than 100 slaves and many teams of oxen to cut down forests of pine, oak, and cypress. Even though the blacks did most of the backbreaking work, McKee and his father spent long hours supervising the land-clearing operation. They often came home to the well-adorned plantation house—perched on a bluff that overlooked the Colleton River—dirty and exhausted from the day's labor.

The slaves the McKees brought to Milford built canals for the rice fields. Poisonous snakes and alligators posed a constant threat. However, it was the swarms of mosquitoes that inflicted the largest toll on workers. Malaria ran rampant during the summer months and valuable slaves died in the rice fields. The McKees, not immune to the disease, spent many restless nights with high fevers.

Milford Plantation prospered and after his father's death in 1834, Henry bought two other plantations closer to Beaufort. With cotton prices at an all-time high and rice one of the main commodities of the South, all three properties generated huge profits.

Three years after his father's death, Henry McKee moved his young family to Beaufort, away from the malarial breeding grounds of Milford Plantation, and closer to his other two plantations on Ladies Island. A series of overseers were hired to fill his prolonged absence but resulted in decreased production at the Milford Plantation. Tom Agee, who owned an adjacent plantation, offered the opinion that the slaves at Milford lacked discipline and recommended McKee hire William Blakely, son of a white sharecropper, who had a reputation for "breaking niggers."

In 1846, Blakely arrived to inspect Milford Plantation. To McKee's dismay, they found much of the farm equipment missing or in poor repair; weeds had taken over some of the cornfields; several floodgates in the rice fields were inoperable; and worse, some of the slaves were insolent toward McKee.

"I am not happy with what I'm seeing," McKee confided to Blakely.

"It's nothing that can't be fixed," replied Blakely. "We just need to put the fear of God back into your darkies."

McKee offered Blakely a three-year contract as overseer of the plantation. This marked the second time McKee had been back to Milford since the agreement was struck, one year ago. Increases in the cotton harvest and rice yields during the first year of Blakely's tenure indicated Milford Plantation had made a much-needed turnabout. Nevertheless, troubling rumors about the treatment of the slaves on Milford had trickled back to the big house in Beaufort. McKee, while a strict disciplinarian, always tried to treat the slaves on his plantations with a degree of compassion. The hunting trip would provide the time to mix business with pleasure.

His thoughts turned to Robert—the boy probably saved Ed's life. Had his brother fallen into the river, it would not have taken long to succumb to the icy waters and strong current. It wasn't the first time that the boy had demonstrated a quick wit. Robert excelled at childhood games, eagerly volunteered to help, and, when he learned about the hunting trip to Milford, begged for permission to come along.

McKee relented, but only after a week of persistence by Robert. He had not found it a hard decision to make. McKee enjoyed Robert's company. The little boy had the most engaging smile, which he used to great advantage. Anyone that saw the glee in Robert's face when he smiled couldn't help but like him. Full of energy, he skipped with joy from one task to the next. His mother had taught Robert to always be respectful toward white folks. She instilled "yessuh" and "no suh" and "thank you suh" into his vocabulary at an early age.

Robert also knew how to elicit a laugh, something McKee always appreciated. Observant by nature, Robert could be around someone for a few minutes and acquire their mannerisms. McKee enjoyed the boy's ability to imitate a friend or acquaintance and laughed at the dead-ringer impersonations.

McKee chuckled at the thought of Bishop Mullins' recent visit for lunch. The cleric, known for long-winded sermons, made it a point to have Sunday lunch with his wealthiest parishioners. The wives all competed to see who could put on the biggest and best feasts. Being a religious man, Bishop Mullins showed his appreciation by eating everything put before him. As a result, the bishop's girth became the butt of many jokes around Beaufort.

One visit, Robert helped serve the meal. He ran back and forth between the kitchen and the big house throughout lunch to fetch more food for the bishop. After a satisfied belch, the good reverend thanked his hosts for a fabulous meal, excused himself, and waddled over to the porch where he spied a hammock strung between two oak trees. Bishop Mullins plopped his rotund figure into the rope mesh and used one foot on the ground to start a gentle sway.

The rope hammock groaned under the load and with a sudden snap the cradle crashed down, bishop and all. Henry McKee saw the whole thing and had to turn away to hide his fits of laughter. Mrs. McKee ran over to the bishop and apologized for the flimsiness of the hammock, while she brushed the dust off the preacher. He left in a huff, but not before he accepted a picnic basket of leftovers.

Later that afternoon, McKee, rocking on the front porch, saw Robert playing marbles in the dirt.

"Robert," called McKee. "Come here. I'd like to know what you thought of Bishop Mullins."

Robert rolled his eyes and gave a huge grin. He poked his little belly out and waddled up the steps.

In a deep sonorous voice, he said, "Why Mistuh McKee. It is so kind of you to ask. Thank you, suh, for your kind invitation to dine with you today. The rigors of the pulpit stir up a man's appetite, for sure. I believe I'll has me some of dat fried chicken to starts with and den pass dem mashed taters and send over the butter beans. Um, um, um … that hit de spot."

McKee couldn't help but grin at Robert's imitation of the preacher. That's all the encouragement the boy needed.

"Oh, Missus McKee, yo' sure is a good cook. I'll takes me some more of dat fried chicken and how's about send out for more of dat 'licious greens, be sure der be some fat back in 'em. Fo' sure. And den you can commence with de sweet stuff. I believe I'll have one of each ob dem. Fo' sure."

Robert rubbed his stomach and groaned with pleasure.

"And Mister McKee, you may from now on call me Biscuit."

"Biscuit?" laughed McKee.

"Yessuh, Biscuit," said Robert. "Cause if I eats one mo' biscuit I gonna weigh 400 pounds!"

McKee laughed so hard his wife ran from the house to see what was the matter.

Chapter 2

A loud "hullo" roused McKee and the others from their torpor. A lone rider on a black mare approached, followed by a buckboard wagon drawn by a mule. An elderly black man in heavily-patched clothes drove the wagon and three small black children, their eyes wide with fright, rode in the back.

Some might have considered the Milford Plantation overseer, William Blakely, a handsome man, except for one physical defect. In his mid-fifties, around six feet in height with broad shoulders, Blakely still had the waistline of a young man. He wore a wide-brimmed felt hat plumed with pheasant feathers, great coat over a green vest, white linen shirt, and black cravat. He rode tall in the saddle.

Chills ran down McKee's back when he looked at Blakely's face. A horrid, six-inch scar ran across his left eye, which was covered by a milky, white film. The other eye, a deep shade of green, stared piercingly at the travelers.

"Hello William. It's nice of you to come out to meet us," said McKee, tipping his stovepipe hat in salute.

"Yes, very nice to see you again sir," responded Blakely with reserve.

McKee introduced Goldsmith and Dr. Reed. Ed was already acquainted with the overseer, as was Jacob. Robert peeked from behind a sack of cornmeal at the man on horseback. Like his master, the boy felt goose bumps on his arms when he looked at Blakely. He remembered his mother's admonition and expected to see horns atop the overseer's head. Blakely had no horns, yet the rider projected a feeling of great strength, and danger. It wasn't just the bad eye that scared Robert.

McKee inquired about the children riding on the buckboard.

"I'm sending them over to Fairfield Plantation," explained Blakely. "I've been having a lot of trouble with their dad, Toby Lewis. I've been warning him that I would sell the children if he didn't shape up. Of all the field hands, he's the one giving me the most trouble. Yesterday, the son-of-a bitch attacked me. Mister O'Riley needs some children to work in the kitchen so he agreed to swap these three young ones for a boy that I can use in the fields. It's a good trade. Should teach that nigger Toby a thing or two. The others, too."

McKee grunted in a way that neither condemned, nor approved, what he heard. Even though he owned all the slaves on Milford Plantation, the contract gave Blakely considerable leeway in using them to the best advantage, which included the ability to buy and sell them. Nevertheless, the plantation owner knew Toby well and found it difficult to understand the overseer's dislike for the hard worker.

The buckboard, with Toby's children, continued down the road toward Fairfield Plantation while the hunting party proceeded toward Milford with Blakely in the lead. They arrived a half-hour later with several hours of sunlight left. Robert and Jacob moved carpetbags into the main house while the white men stretched their legs after the long journey.

The Milford Plantation house sat on a high bluff that overlooked the Colleton River. Across the ebony water, rice fields stretched toward the horizon. The fields had been drained of water and slaves had almost completed the harvest. Dozens of black figures worked in the distance to pile golden sheaves of rice into heaps for transport to the rice mill.

Towering live oaks flanked the riverbank where a sheep and two cows ruminated under their watch. The cool, late September day kept flying insects at bay, making outdoor conditions idyllic.

Blakely ordered a stable hand to have four horses saddled and brought to the front of the large, whitewashed house sitting atop an arched brick foundation.

"I thought we would inspect Milford before we retire for the evening meal if that meets your approval," the overseer suggested. "Later, I'd like the doctor to take a look at some of the niggers."

The plan suited McKee and the five men rode away from the riverbank toward the inland fields where the plantation grew tomatoes, peas, beans, yams, potatoes, and okra. Much of the bounty had been picked and stored in preparation for the winter months. Collard greens in various stages of growth filled two acres of land and a much larger field contained tall stalks of corn ready for harvesting.

Blakely led the team back toward the river to inspect the vast rice fields. Once impenetrable swamps, the fields had been cleared after many years of arduous labor. Trees had to be cut, stumps removed, and vines cleared. Slaves dug deep canals to irrigate the fields. They built dikes to dam the water and sluice gates constructed to regulate its flow.

The rice fields of coastal South Carolina towered as one of the greatest agricultural innovations of the South. When tidal forces raised the elevation of the river, slaves opened the gates—called trunks—to the sluices that allowed fresh water to flood the small rice plants. When the rice matured, and the fields needed to be drained, they opened the trunks to allow the water to flow out. The rice fields along the coast of South Carolina produced more than half of the rice in the United States and made millionaires out of their owners.

"Mr. McKee, you will be glad to know we will produce about 600,000 pounds of rice this year," said Blakely. "As you know, we produced only 450,000 pounds last year so I think you will be pleased with the increase."

McKee whistled softly in appreciation. "Well done, William," he said.

Blakely showed the others the slave quarters, rows of neatly-aligned wooden shacks stretching for more than 400 yards. Made of logs, the buildings housed the plantation's 300 slaves. Most of the cabins had fireplaces but no windows or flooring. Chickens ran wild around

27

the,structures and a couple had pigs enclosed in rough wooden fences. Many of the cabins had fire pits in front and small gardens in back. Black children, too young to be in the fields, watched in awe as the riders passed. Shoeless, they wore simple muslin shifts. Two white-haired, elderly black women, nearly toothless, supervised the youngsters.

The group inspected the plantation's livestock and admired the newly-constructed dock where rice would be transported to Charleston later in the year. They also examined the mill where the prized crop would be husked, prior to storage into 400-pound barrels known as hogsheads, for shipment. McKee looked in on the plantation's blacksmith shop, watched a group of six black women weave rough cotton cloth on looms, and then checked in on the skilled black carpenters as they constructed a new rice barn.

"I must say," said McKee, as the group dismounted at the main house. "You have done exactly as you said, William. Everything seems to be in order here. I am delighted with the rice production this year. I congratulate you."

Blakely bowed and ushered the men into the house where the plantation cooks had prepared a feast in their honor.

* * *

After they delivered the contents of the carriage to the main house, Robert wandered around Milford taking in the sights and sounds of the plantation.

"Don't you be straying off," warned Jacob, who sought refuge and a handout from the cooks in the kitchen.

Robert's natural curiosity won over caution.

The sound of children's laughter drew him toward a rickety wooden building separated from the main house by a hedge of Indian hawthorn. He walked through a small passage in the hedge and saw nearly 30 children, that ranged in age from toddlers to those his own age, playing in a grassless yard. One of the smaller children saw him and shrieked. The other children stopped and looked in Robert's direction. Astonishment lit their faces.

Robert turned to flee when one of the older boys shouted, "Hey, who you be? What you be doin' here. Why you dressed so funny?"

The questions seemed more curious than a threat, so Robert approached the children with caution.

"I be Robert," he said. "I be Massah McKee's houseboy. Dis be the first time I been to dis here plantation."

One of the old women watching over the children heard the commotion and walked to where the children had surrounded Robert. He stood uncomfortably still as they touched his woolen jacket, vest, cotton shirt and muslin pants. A few knelt to touch his leather shoes.

"You must be somebody special," said a little girl.

"You chilluns acts like you nevah seen a house negra," exclaimed the nursemaid. "Dis here be da mastah's negra. The massah, he don't wanna have his boy lookin' like no field hand. Dat's how come he gets to wear clothes like da' massah."

"Aunty, how come dees chilluns gots no clothes?" Robert asked.

"Dey don't need no fancy clothes right now," she responded. "Jes a longtail shirt fo' de boys and a calico shift for the gals be good 'nuf til dey get growed."

She looked closer at Robert.

"I declare, I believes dey be some white blood in you boy. Who ya' daddy be?"

"I don't rightly know."

"Well, de proof be in de puddin'." She turned toward the house and ordered the children to follow for afternoon prayers and a nap.

Robert wandered off to explore. He walked past the long line of empty slave homes and was about to head toward the riverside dock when he heard the soft cries of a man inside a tiny outhouse. The structure stood about six- feet tall measured about two-feet wide and two-feet in depth. It had a small door on one side. A long nail held the latch firmly in place.

Robert tapped gently on the door. "Anybody in der?" he whispered.

He heard movement but no answer. Robert stood to one side in case he needed to take quick action, removed the nail from the latch and inched the door open. As it opened, the boy could make out the shape of a man cowering against the back wall. The black man inside turned slowly toward the light and squinted at the afternoon sun. He blinked to adjust his vision.

"Why, you ain't nuthin' but a little boy," said the man, his voice hoarse and strained. "What you doin' at de bull house."

"What's de bull house?" Robert asked.

"Dis be de bull house," the man proclaimed. "Here's where de obersheer puts de bad niggers."

"Is you a bad nigger?" Robert inquired with fear, getting ready to slam the door shut.

"Blakely thinks I is," the man mumbled. "He done sold my chilluns and put me in de bull house for raisin' my fist to him. 'Spect I gets a beatin' tomorrow."

"What yo' name be mistah?"

"I be's Toby."

"Toby Lewis?"

"'Dat me."

Robert rubbed his head and thought about the wagon the group had met on the road to Milford.

"I believe I see'd your chilluns," said the boy. "Dat Blakely fella tells Master McKee he be sellin' dem to de Fairfield mastah."

Toby groaned and put his head in his hands. He stepped from the tiny building and paced back and forth.

"I gots to get my babies back," said Toby. "Dey ain't nevah been without der mammy and pappy. Look here boy, I be leavin' now. You shuts dat door back and forgets you evah seen ol' Toby. You unnerstand?"

Robert nodded. Toby ran across a field into the nearby woods and disappeared from sight. The boy shut the door and put the nail back in place. He looked around to see if anyone was watching.

Frightened by the encounter, Robert ran back to the children's cabin. He sat quietly on a wooden bench and waited for the boys and girls to wake up from up their naps. He said a prayer for Toby.

The sounds of voices singing in unison drifted down the lane that led to the slave quarters. Slaves with hoes balanced over their shoulders came into sight. They walked in groups of three and four. The flow of black men and women thickened as the final rays of sunshine began to set over the horizon and signaled the end of another day of work on the plantation. They sang as they walked:

The Gospel train's a'comin'
I hear it close at hand
I hear the car wheel moving
And rollin' thro' the land
Get on board little children
Get on board little children
Get on board little children
There's room for many a more

Chapter 3

Jacob ran over to Robert.

"Hey boy, de massah be looking for you. You best be gwoin' on up to de big house fast as dose feets can run," Jacob directed, nearly out of breath.

The men were seated around a long dining room table, smoking cigars when Robert knocked on the door. Two black servants hurried to clear the plates and utensils.

"Massah McKee. Jacob say you lookin' for me?"

McKee motioned Robert to come closer.

"I hope you haven't been troubling anyone," he said.

"No suh," said Robert. "I just been walkin' round a bit. You sho' does have a fine plantation here. And you gots a fine crop of little negras down at the chillun's house."

McKee chuckled at Robert, whose eyes had widened in amazement.

"Robert, I want you to sleep with Jacob tonight in Jasper and Maude's cabin. Their children are grown, and they will have plenty of room for you. Try to go to sleep because tomorrow morning we're going duck hunting. Mr. Blakely says he will need your help setting decoys."

Robert could hardly contain his excitement.

"See ya in the mawnin' massah McKee," he said as he skipped out of the room.

Jacob led the boy to a nearby cabin and knocked on the door. A silver-haired black man, stooped over with rheumatism, answered.

"Well hey der Jacob. I ain't see'd you in a coon's age," said Jasper. "Y'all come on in. Maude has de pot on de fire, and we be eatin' sum grub real soon. Marse Blakely told us to 'spect y'all tonight."

The light from the fireplace highlighted Maude's kind face—Jasper's wife for nearly 50 years. The log house had a dirt floor and the cracks in the walls had been sealed with mud. Two mattresses stuffed with wheat straw sat on bed frames made from rough lumber.

Maude pointed to a pot near the hearth.

"We ain't got de rations dis week so we be's a eatin' gruel t'night," she said. She ladled the hot meal into wooden bowls and passed one to her husband, Jacob, and Robert.

The boy sniffed and made a face.

Jacob scowled, "Boy, you best eat what's been put 'fo you. Dis ain't Boofort and you ain't gettin' no scraps from de massah's table dis night."

At the big house, Robert and the other slaves ate any food left over from the McKees' breakfast, lunch, and supper.

He tasted the gruel and spit it out. "Dat ain't fit for hogs!"

"Yo' choice chile," Maude acquiesced.

After the meal, Jacob and Jasper sat on a log outside of the cabin and Robert listened to the conversation from the doorway.

"Jasper, things sho' has changed from de days when I wuz here," mused Jacob. "Seems like folks be a lot worse off den when de master lived here."

"You gots dat right," replied Jasper. "Ebba since dat Blakely got to be de oversheer, hit's been hell 'round here. Fust thing he done was cut de ration. Usn's used to get a bushel of rice every week and a bit of bacon and a bit of molasses. Now de ration be cut in haf. Most all de niggers be hungry at night. Some's even takin' to stealin'. It bad when dey gets caught. Real bad."

"He been doin' a lot of whuppin?"

"Law'd, ya' dassn't know de half of it," Jasper exclaimed. "Dis oversheer beats de po' niggars for most anythin'. Two young bucks got whupped til de blood ran de back las' week causin' dey didn't bring de cows back on time.

"Yes'day, he puts ol' Toby in de bull house. Dis mawning dat Blakely puts all three of Toby's chilluns in de wagon and sends 'em off de plantation. Don't know what's gonna happen to 'dose po' chilluns. Blakely say dey is gonna be lot mo' blood when he let Toby out de bull house 'morrow night."

Jacob shook his head. "You right Jasper. Things sho' has changed."

***

Robert and Jacob curled up on the earthen floor of the cabin, but sleep evaded them. Even though a chill was in the air, pesky mosquitoes hummed about their ears.

"Don't fret chile, dey stop bitin' once dey fill themselves wid your blood," whispered Maude. "It's de fleas and chinch bugs 'dat plague us de most."

Chapter 4

A banging on the door roused the cabin's inhabitants.

"Tell that little nigger to come on out," yelled Blakely.

Fear shot through Robert. He ran to the door.

"Your Master McKee's house nigger?"

The boy shook his head yes.

"Okay, follow me. We got work to do before the sun comes up."

Blakely rode the chestnut mare toward the rice fields. Two dozen wooden duck decoys swayed from the back of the saddle. Robert trotted behind, shivering from the frosty night air. He didn't dare ask the overseer about breakfast.

The boy stumbled in the dark behind the rider. The glow of the moon lit the trail that led farther into the woods. A clearing opened and Blakely dismounted. He took the brace of duck decoys and walked toward a large pond. Two weeks ago, when foretold of the McKee hunting trip, Blakely had ordered one of the harvested rice fields to be flooded. The water and chafe from the rice should lure plenty of ducks to the pond. To guarantee a successful hunt, Blakely had also ordered the slaves to bait the field with corn.

Blakely handed several of the duck decoys to Robert.

"Okay, take these over to there," said the overseer, pointing to a spot 20 feet from the pond's bank.

Robert tiptoed into the water and gasped.

"Marse Blakely, dis water be freezin' cold," he said.

Before he could say another word, Blakely caught the boy by the nape and turned him around.

His voice dripped with venom. "Boy, I don't give a rat's ass if der is ice in that water. You do what I'm tellin' you to do or I'll whip every bit of skin off your little black hide. You understand me boy?"

Robert fought back tears. He shivered, but not from the coldness of the water. For the next thirty minutes, the boy followed Blakely's directions in placing the decoys in a pattern. The black water of the rice paddy inched up to his waist. Robert couldn't feel his feet and his teeth chattered painfully. When he put the last decoys in place, Blakely allowed Robert to get out of the water.

"You stay here. I'll fetch the others," barked Blakely.

The weak rays of the rising sun did little to warm the boy. In desperation he covered himself with piles of pine needles. Slowly, circulation returned to his lower extremities.

Blakely returned with the hunting party 30 minutes later.

McKee spotted Robert in the pine straw.

"Robert, what are doing over there? Are you asleep again?" he questioned.

Robert jumped up and brushed the pine needles from his damp clothes.

"No suh, I be ready to hunt now," he grinned, with a great deal of effort.

The duck hunting turned into a great success. Flocks of mallards and summer ducks flew into the baited field and within minutes the hunters had brought down dozens of them with their shotguns. After the hunt, Robert loaded the wagon with heaps of the brightly-feathered fowl.

"Be sure to give some to the negras," McKee said to Blakely as they passed by slaves headed to the fields.

* * *

After lunch, Blakely asked Dr. Reed to accompany him to the plantation's sick house. McKee ordered Robert to go with the doctor and carry his satchel of medicine. The three walked a short distance to a small cabin. A groan of pain came from inside. The boy timidly followed Dr. Reed and Blakely into the shack. Six black men and four black women lay on bunk beds that lined each side of the structure.

An elderly black nurse greeted Dr. Reed.

"I'll open de shutters so you can sees better Doctor," said Liza.

She gave a quick rundown of the various afflictions. Two with swollen faces had severe abscesses in their teeth; a wagon wheel had crushed one's foot; another had a broken arm; and the others complained of stomach pains.

Dr. Reed administered castor oil to those with fever and stomach pains, reset the broken arm, and wrapped a poultice around the crushed foot. Screams of pain filled the building when the doctor pulled the abscessed teeth with pliers. He took special interest in two of the black women who protested the most when poked and prodded.

After a thorough examination he turned to Blakely. "Sir, I find nothing wrong with these two. I suggest a good whipping will be the best medicine."

Blakely nodded in agreement. "I suspected as much."

He snatched the two young women out of the bunks by their hair and threw them out of the front door as they shrieked in terror. Unfurling a whip, he began to lash both girls. The rawhide cut through their calico shifts.

"We will need an audience for this," he concluded, more to himself than anyone else. "Get back to your tasks. I will deal with you later."

He smiled at Dr. Reed. "Do we need to administer any more medicine?" he asked.

Chapter 5

The excited barks and yips of dogs woke Robert the next morning. Despite the drama that played out the previous day, the boy's spirits remained high. Master McKee had promised Robert he could go on the deer hunt with him. He brushed the dirt from his clothes, slipped on his brogans, and ran to the kitchen where a friendly cook slipped him a biscuit filled with peach preserves. He was surprised to learn the white men had already eaten.

Stable hands brought horses to the front of the house for the McKees, Goldsmith, and Dr. Reed. Jacob brought the buckboard around and told Robert to hop on.

Isaac, a tall, gangly negro dressed in a dark green woolen jumpsuit, held on to a pack of 10 dogs, eager to trail their quarry. The guide explained the plan; the mounted riders were to go to a designated field one mile from the main house and station themselves about 100 yards apart, parallel to the field's edge. After he set the hounds loose in the thicket that showed good signs of white-tail deer, the dogs would drive the deer toward the hunters on a ridge between two swamps.

"Robert, once we get there, you will go with me to my stand," said Master McKee. "I can use an extra set of eyes."

As instructed, the hunting party spread out over the field's perimeter. Each hunter had a clear line of sight should a deer bolt from the woods. McKee and Robert stayed closest to the wagon driven by Jacob, which had been concealed in the tree line.

"You must remain very still and quiet," instructed McKee. "If you see a deer tap me on the shoulder and point."

Imperceptible at first, Robert heard the quiet bay of the hounds deep within the forest. The howls grew in intensity as the dogs came closer.

"They're on him," whispered McKee, his voice tight with excitement. The dogs came closer.

Robert heard the rustle of leaves and peered into the forest where he glimpsed a flash of a white-tail. He tapped McKee on the shoulder. McKee nodded and raised the shotgun as the wails of the hounds filled their ears.

From behind a tree, a huge buck emerged. The rack of antlers boasted 12 tines. The furtive animal looked from one side to the other, then tensed to make a dash across the field. The report of the shotgun caught Robert by surprise, and he jumped into the air.

"Got 'em," shouted McKee as the wounded deer disappeared into the treeline.

The two walked to where the animal was last seen. A small pool of blood proved the shot was accurate.

"We need to get to him before the hounds do," McKee urged. "Follow me."

Robert tailed the man as he ducked between branches and brushed away vines to follow a trail of blood that lead farther into the forest. They had traveled 50 yards when the trail led to a thicket of briars, far too dense for McKee to enter.

He looked at Robert.

"You're small enough to crawl through there."

He gave the boy a length of rope, a bone-handled knife and pointed to the thicket. A faint path made by the escaped deer provided a tiny passage.

On his hands and knees, Robert crawled through the small opening. He puffed from the exertion but continued forward until a movement caught his eye.

He pushed aside a briar bush and saw the wounded deer lying on its side—a hole gaped above its shoulder and blood spilled onto the ground.

At the sight of the boy, the animal shuddered and tried to stand. After a few feeble efforts, it fell back to the ground. The deer turned toward the boy and managed a pitiful bleat.

"Massah McKee, it still be alive," shouted Robert.

"Slit its throat," McKee shouted back.

Stunned, the boy remained motionless. He pulled the knife from his belt and crawled closer to the deer. The animal's large black eyes, filled with terror, stared at boy.

"Do it," came another cry from McKee.

Robert reached over and hesitated before he put the knife against the deer's throat. He closed his eyes, then pulled the knife blade toward him. A gush of blood covered his hands. The deer shuddered once more then lay motionless.

"He be dead, massah," the boy's voice quivered.

"Tie that rope around its hind legs and then get out of there," yelled McKee.

When Robert emerged from the briars, he saw Isaac, Dr. Reed, John, and Goldsmith gathered around McKee.

They all patted him on the head.

"Well done lad," said the master. Together they pulled the slain deer into the open, field dressed it, and placed the carcass on the wagon.

Two more bucks and a doe joined McKee's prize buck on the wagon before the day ended and they drove back to the plantation in a jubilant mode. Along the way, Jacob unlocked a chest to reveal bottles of whiskey and scotch, which made the rounds among the white men. As the men laughed and talked with excitement, curious slaves looked up as they returned home from the fields.

The celebration ended when the hunting party reached the main house. Blakely rose from a chair on the front porch and rushed over to McKee, his face dark and his good eye flashed with anger.

"We got a runaway," said Blakely.

"Who?"

"That damn black devil, Toby," hissed the overseer. "Someone let him out of the bull house last night."

"Get the hounds," McKee breathed the order.

Chapter 6

Toby Lewis was lost. Caked in mud, face swollen from insect bites, his bare feet cut and bleeding, he knew he was out of options. He sat down in resignation on a cypress stump and buried his face in his hands.

"Lawd, what has it all come to?" he lamented.

Before William Blakely took over as overseer, Toby served as Milford Plantation's most admired driver.

Drivers, the highest-ranked slaves on Southern plantations served directly under the overseer. Toby ran much of the day-to-day operations of Milford Plantation. Field workers, as well as skilled artisans, labored under his supervision. He set the daily tasks, made sure the plantation operated efficiently and kept discipline. The other slaves appreciated Toby's inherent fairness. Whippings were rare. He preferred other types of discipline like extra work assignments.

Toby found it hard to believe his fortunes had changed so rapidly. *Wasn't it just the other day that I first laid eyes on Cassie? When was it? Oh yes …*

***

Six years ago, Toby and three other young black men—Hamp, Sanford, and Curley—got permission from Master McKee to attend a party at the nearby Sneed Plantation.

McKee issued passes to the four men with a stern warning, "Whatever you boys do, don't lose these. I can't protect you if the patrollers catch you without your passes. Keep them in your pockets at all times, you hear?"

The four, clad in red-woolen jackets atop white-and-black-plaid homespun pants, nodded in agreement.

"Thank ya' Massah McKee," said Toby. "I be sure dese wild bucks get back with der hides on der backs!"

The boys turned and walked down the lane.

"Hey," McKee shouted. "You boys take one of the boats. Save yourself an hour of walking."

"Thank you suh!" the men delighted, in unison.

Long before Sneed Plantation came into sight, Toby and his companions heard fiddle music waft over the river. They paddled faster and soon saw the tall white chimneys of the Sneed big house. More than 100 black men and women aged 14 to 40 danced and sang on the banks of the Colleton River. A large bonfire cast a circle of light around the crowd. A full moon further illuminated the gathering.

"Here come de Mi'ford buckaroos," someone exclaimed. A dozen well-dressed slaves broke off from the main group and headed to the river to greet Toby and his friends. Several pretty girls gave friendly hugs and the men slapped each other on the back.

They joined the main group and clapped rhythmically to the music. The banjo players, accompanied by an older black man that played a harmonica, beat out a popular tune called *Bile Them Cabbage Down*. It caused everyone's toes to tap in unison. Soon, couples strutted around the bonfire to dance the "buzzard lope." Everyone laughed as they sang the tune.

> *Went up to the mountain*
> *Just to give my horn a blow*

Thought I heard my true love say
Yonder comes by beau.
Bile them cabbage down
Bake dem hoecakes brown
The only song that I can sing
Is bile them cabbage down.

The song had more than a dozen verses and by the time it ended the dancers collapsed in each other's arms. They grinned and laughed as the other colored revelers applauded the performance.

Above the music, Toby yelled to Curley, "I be back. Gots to find me a tree and make water." He hastened a turn and bumped hard into one of the dancers.

Cassie Handley lay sprawled across the ground, her blue dress flew into the air and revealed white petticoats. She sputtered with rage as she jumped to her feet.

"Boy, don't you watch where you gwoin'?" she scolded.

Two friends hurried to help pat the dust from her dress and provide moral support, should it be needed.

Toby stood with his mouth open.

Sixteen-year-old Cassie spoke to him, but he couldn't hear over the blood that roared through his ears. He shook his head to make sense of things but could only stare as the pretty little thing chided him with all her might.

A fashionable gingham dress couldn't hide the figure that blossomed beneath. The teenager wore a knitted white shawl, a black bonnet, and the reddest slippers Toby had ever seen. She had high cheekbones and a slender nose, full red lips, and eyes as dark brown as the tannin-infused river—those eyes captivated Toby.

He struggled to make sense of her outrage.

"…and de next time you feels like you have to 'make water' go to de other side of the house," scolded Cassie. "Now scat."

She stomped away with her friends and didn't looked back.

44

At once, Toby knew he couldn't let this divine creature escape. He launched forward and tapped her on the shoulder.

"Missy, please accept my most humble 'pologies," said Toby. "'Dat was entirely my fault. I shoulda been lookin' better. Is dere something I could get for you? Maybe some punch?"

Cassie looked at Toby with an appraising eye and sniffed. "Where you call home?"

"Oh, I is from Mi'ford little lady. I be one of de drivers there."

Cassie took a closer look at Toby. Tall and muscular, the young man cut a fine figure in his red jacket.

He ventured a smile.

Not bad. Still, he's mighty young to be a driver. He's probably lying.

"Can't think of a thing you can do fo' me," she announced, and flitted into the crowd, her giggling friends in tow.

Taken aback by the rebuff, Toby searched for Curley in the crowd.

Throughout the night, he kept a constant eye out for the beautiful young woman who had stolen his heart. He relished the sound of her laugh and chatter with other men and women.

From across the dirt dance floor, Toby caught her eye. She looked directly at him, gave a shy smile, then turned away.

His heart jumped.

A fiddler joined the banjo players and the tempo of the music increased. More of the young men and women paired up and Toby had to elbow his way to Cassie's side. He tapped her on the shoulder.

"It be me again." He smiled broadened when she turned to face him.

"Oh, and who might 'me' be?" Cassie asked.

"I'm Toby Lewis. Like I say before, from over at Mi'ford Plantation. May I ask yo' name?"

"I'm Cassie. This here be my home. I work up der at de big house. Ettie Brantley be my missus and I be her body servant."

"You like to dance Miss Cassie?"

"Sho' thing," she extended her hand to him.

The next two hours became the most glorious moments of Toby Lewis' young life. The couple danced to the music, twirled in each other's arms, chimed in on the singing, and laughed in pure joy of each other's presence.

Between tunes Cassie introduced Toby to her friends and he regaled them with stories about life at Milford Plantation.

When the last twang of the banjo rang out, Curley found Toby talking excitedly with Cassie.

"Toby, we gots to be goin," he said. "Massuh be expecting us back soon."

Cassie gave Toby's hand a squeeze and a smile that reached her eyes.

"Yo' can come back and see me if you like," she said shyly.

For the next two months, Toby spent every Saturday afternoon walking through the swamps to visit Cassie. She stood apart from the other black girls he knew—she spoke differently.

Cassie told him later that she and her white mistress, Missus Ettie, had grown up as best friends. They played together and Cassie even slept on a small cot at the foot of the white girl's bed at night.

Toby's frequent requests for travel passes aroused McKee's curiosity and he mentioned it to his wife. Mrs. McKee began to make discreet inquiries about Cassie, with visits to the Brantleys on two occasions. After a third visit, she came back in a great state of excitement, much to her husband's consternation.

At the next daybreak, Toby and the other drivers waited at the backdoor of the big house to receive the day's tasks. The young man were surprised when Mrs. McKee, rather than the master, stood on the back porch.

"Toby, I have something for you," she motioned with her hand.

With a happy smile, Cassie stepped from behind Mrs. McKee.

"This girl says she wouldn't mind accepting a wedding proposal."

Toby and Cassie rushed into each other's arms, oblivious of the surprised looks on the faces of the other's present.

Mrs. McKee grinned, "What's it going to be Toby?"

46

He released Cassie from his grasp.

"Sho' I'd like to marry Cassie," he said. "But she belong to de Brantleys"

"Not anymore," sang Mrs. McKee. "I bought her this morning after learning that Ettie is going to Europe for the rest of the year. It was a hard bargain, but she belongs to Milford now."

Toby dropped to one knee and took Cassie's hand in his own.

"Sweet little gal," he said. "I doesn't have a ring to give yuh. But I can give you my heart. Will you be my wife?"

Cassie wiped a tear from the corner of her eye and beamed.

"Course I will, you silly boy. Us don't need no ring."

It was hard to tell who had the most fun as the wedding's planner, Cassie or Mrs. McKee. However, there was no doubt who was in charge.

On the day Toby and Cassie became one, Master McKee presented Toby with a new suit. The plantation's mistress had arranged an elaborate feast and invited the Brantleys and their slaves to join them at Milford, "For the biggest wedding ever held in the South," the slaves would later recall to anyone who would listen.

The affair was held in front of the big house. The groom stood on a white linen sheet as his bride, holding a bouquet of magnolia blossoms, walked toward him. The isle was flanked by the Milford slaves on one side and the Sneed slaves on the other. Uncle Benjamin, who preached on Sundays at the plantation chapel, performed the ceremony, while the McKees and Brantleys watched from the porch. Toby gave Cassie a mother-of-pearl ring that he had painstakingly fashioned from an oyster shell.

After the couple exchanged vows, Master McKee signaled for Jacob to meet him at the altar where Toby and Cassie stood with entwined hands.

Jacob carried a broom with him.

"Toby and Cassie, it's a tradition for the newlyweds to jump backward over the broomstick. The one that can jump over without touching the handle will be the boss of the family and if both of them jump over without touching it they will live in harmony as husband and wife," said McKee.

He held one end of the broom and Jacob the other. Cassie closed her eyes and leapt spryly over the broomstick. When it was Toby's turn, McKee winked at Jacob and they raised the handle six inches just as he jumped. The groom's boots got caught on the broomstick and he went fell to the ground.

Everyone laughed and hooted.

"Toby, ol' boy, we know now who will wear the pants in this family," laughed McKee.

The newlyweds retired to a cabin constructed for them. Mrs. McKee had purchased them a new bed—quite a luxury on a slave plantation. After an evening of wedded bliss, both returned to work the next day—Cassie in the big house and Toby as a driver.

* * *

Toby's intelligence and desire to please first caught the eye of Master McKee when the black man was in his early twenties. The plantation owner threw many challenges at Toby and each time the slave rose to the occasion. He became one of three black drivers by the time he was 28 and head driver two years later. After McKee moved to Beaufort, Toby remained head driver under the next two overseers—Dwight Lamb and Sean Mathis. A hurricane destroyed much of the crop in 1845 and Blakely arrived a year later to change Toby's life forever.

Trouble brewed the moment Master McKee left for Beaufort and left Blakely behind to run the plantation. The overseer called all the slaves to the lawn in front of the main plantation house and laid down the law. Any person that failed to complete his or her tasks would receive 25 lashes for the first offense, 50 lashes for the second; theft resulted in 100 lashes plus two days in the stocks. Any slave that refused to comply with his commands would spend three days in the bull house.

Rations were cut in half until production on the plantation increased. Only those who followed Blakely's law would have the privilege of maintaining a garden. Only drivers could have livestock of any kind.

Hunting and fishing were allowed only on Saturday, if all tasks for the week had been completed.

The slaves shuffled off to their appointed rounds. Blakely called Toby and the other two drivers to his side.

"You boys understand how things will be from now on, right?"

The black men nodded.

"I'll be watchin'," he turned and mounted his horse.

The first whipping occurred an hour later. The two cooks who brought lunch to the field hands stumbled on a root and spilled the contents onto the ground. From a nearby vantage point, Blakely saw the accident. He rode over to the women, who frantically tried to scoop the rice back into the black, cast iron pot.

He instructed the women to loosen the top half of their dresses and let the garments hang at the waist. Blakely had them hold on to small pine trees while he pulled out a cowhide whip.

Without a word, the whip lashed across the back of the first woman—a thin, waiflike creature. She cried out in pain. With measured strokes, he struck 14 more times, until thin stripes of blood marked the woman's back.

The other cook saw the fate of her companion and begged the overseer for mercy.

None came.

She, too, fell to her knees as blood from the strokes of the cowhide whip dripped from her fragile skin.

Blakely rode his horse through a rice field where prime field hands planted rice seeds. He hopped from his horse and inspected a furrowed row, as he called three male workers over to him.

"These seeds are not the proper depth," snarked Blakely.

He ordered another driver, Big Joe, to bind the men's hands and feet. The driver forced the men to hop over to a nearby split-rail fence. He pulled up their shirts, dropped their pants, and ordered them to lean over the fence, their backs and flanks exposed.

Blakely's whip popped like a gun as it cut through the skin of the helpless men. One tried to escape from the lash, leaned too far forward and flipped head first into the dust.

Blakely laughed and ordered Curley to put the man back on his feet for further punishment.

Word of the whippings spread like wildfire through the plantation. That night Toby told Cassie to be extra careful around Blakely.

"Dis man be bad through and through," warned Toby. "Cassie, stay away from Blakely. I believe he just as soon shoot you as talk to you."

The overseer ate alone at the main house. He preferred simple meals and sent two of the cooks to the fields to work. The chambermaid soon followed, as did the butler.

"I can dress myself," grumbled Blakely.

Only Cassie and her helper, Nelle, remained in the kitchen. Once the old butler left the house, the overseer told Cassie she would serve his meals.

She tried to be in Blakely's presence as little as possible. After she brought in the evening meal and set it before him, Cassie hurried back to the kitchen. She hustled to finish the chores and got back to her cabin where Toby and the children waited.

A few days after his arrival, Blakely finished an evening meal, and leaned back in his chair. He kicked off his boots, loosened his string tie, and smoked a cigar.

Cassie came into the room to remove the dishes.

Blakely appraised her with a hard stare.

The full-length skirt and loose bodice did little to cover the woman's curves. Cassie avoided eye contact and hurried to clean the table.

"You're Toby's wench ain't ya'?" asked Blakely.

"Yessuh, Marse Blakely. We been hitched a right good while. Gots three chilluns."

"I couldn't tell it from looking at you," said the overseer. "Come here."

Cassie obeyed as she stifled a gasp.

Blakely hands explored her buttocks and legs, then he ordered her to turn around. He stood, reached from behind to cup her breasts, then slid them down her flat stomach just short of the juncture of her thighs.

"No, would never have believed you have had three children," he mused.

He gathered his boots and walked toward his bedroom. Cassie trembled with fright as she fled from the room.

Toby rode alongside Blakely the next day astride a jenny mule. The two men inspected the upland fields before heading to the bottomland. Slaves worked diligently when the overseer was near. At the first rice field, Blakely frowned when he saw a slave named Mac worked on a sluice gate designed to regulate the level of water that irrigated the young rice plants.

"Come here Toby," he ordered. "Look at this man's work and tell me what you see."

Toby examined the floodgate. "Marse Blakely, everything looks okay to me."

The overseer pushed him aside and pointed to a loose board hidden behind two sturdier timbers.

"This is shoddy work," yelled Blakely. "One king tide could infiltrate this gate with salt water and kill the whole damn crop. It's unacceptable Toby. Take this man to the millhouse and give him 50 lashes."

Toby looked at Blakely in disbelief.

"Marse Blakely, all it take is one nail and dat' gate be good as new," he bargained.

The overseer glared at Toby. "Are you refusing to beat this man?" he snarled.

Toby swallowed hard and looked again at the floodgate.

"Marse Blakely, I can't hardly beat de man for somethin' so small," he said. "Dis floodgate works fine. De nigger don't need no beatin'. Lets me and you go on to mo' important matters."

Blakely's face turned red with anger. The scar went beet red as he got within inches of Toby's face.

"Nigger, you and me has some business to settle. Get your black ass to the barn," he yelled.

Toby walked toward the mule.

"Oh no you don't mistuh," snarled Blakely. "Dem mules is meant for drivers. From now on you are a field hand."

In a daze, Toby trotted behind Blakely's horse to a large barn near the main house. There, the overseer bound the black man's arms and made him stand on the tips of his toes until the rope overlapped a hook hanging from a beam. Toby dangled there. With great effort he could just touch the floor to relieve the pressure of his weight against the rope.

The overseer left the barn and shut the door. Hours passed. Sweat poured from Toby's body as he struggled against the bindings. His arms raged with a fiery pain until he lost sensation and passed out.

When he regained consciousness, Toby's eyes slowly adjusted to the yellow glow of two lanterns that lit the barn's interior. Ice cold water splashed against his face, everything brought into an instant, sharp focus.

"I wanted you to see this," said Blakely.

Cassie lay naked, spread-eagled on the dirt floor of the barn. Her arms were tied together above her head to a wooden beam. Ropes had been tied to her legs and attached to posts—her womanhood exposed. Tears trickled from her eyes as stared upward, refusing to look at her husband.

"Cassie," cried out Toby.

Blakely backhanded him. "Don't say another damned word or it will be worse," he snarled.

The overseer strode over to Cassie and stood above her. He glanced over his shoulder where Toby dangled from the hook and smiled. He removed his belt and dropped his pants. He knelt between Cassie's thighs, grabbed her buttocks in his hands and lifted her toward him.

"Please, fo' God's sake don't do it Marse Blakely. She's all I gots," cried Toby.

The overseer reached for his belt and snapped it across Cassie's face. She writhed in pain and struggled against the ropes.

"You wanna talk again nigger?" he asked.

Toby slumped against his bindings, shut his eyes tight, and tried to close his ears as Cassie's screams filled the night air.

Toby and Cassie never talked about that night.

The overseer moved her to the fields where she struggled to keep up with women hardened to the hot sun and back-breaking labor. Cassie did not complain, even when the first rounds of morning sickness robbed her of her strength. When she told Toby she was pregnant, he just shook his head as though he had expected such news.

The former driver now worked alongside the field hands he once supervised. Blakely rode him hard, finding fault with every task and administered lashings with regularity. Other slaves helped Toby finish his work and applied turpentine balm to his wounds. He kept going because of his three children, who still jumped into his lap and greeted him with joy when he returned from the fields.

As the last hot days of summer came to an end, Cassie went into labor. An ancient, black midwife named Fannie hobbled into the cabin and shooed away the children and Toby.

"It gonna be a long night," she predicted.

Toby tried to keep focused on his children as he listened to the moans of his wife. On occasion, Fannie peeked out the door and motioned for other women to fetch roots and herbs from the forest. After hours of labor, the solemn old woman emerged from the cabin and motioned for Toby.

"Chile, I got some bad news," she professed. "Cassie gone to the Lawd. De baby, too."

A primeval groan full of pain rose from Toby's throat, that took Fannie aback.

He turned and raced toward the main house.

The first rays of the morning sun bathed the house in golden hues. Inside, Blakely was going over the day's tasks with the drivers, when he heard someone shout behind the front door.

"Blakely, damn you, get out here," yelled Toby, his voice filled with a rage that had grown for nine months.

The overseer, flanked by the drivers, walked onto the front porch. He looked down where Toby stood with clenched fists. The overseer had a puzzled look on his face. No black man had ever talked to him before like this.

"Nigger, either you've been drinking, or you done gone and lost your damn mind," said Blakely. "You best be going on home. Or you want to go on and get your whippin' right now?"

"You done killed my Cassie with yo' bastard," Toby screeched.

He flew up the steps, arms flailing, and struck Blakely in the injured eye before the overseer could raise a hand in defense.

The white man fell to the porch.

Toby jumped on him and smashed the overseer's skull against the floor. He took the man's head in his strong, black hands and fought to snap Blakely's neck. Powerful arms reached from behind and pulled him off the white man.

"You done played hell now," said one of the black drivers that held Toby in a stranglehold.

Dazed, Blakely rose on unsteady feet. He shook his head to clear his mind and wiped a trickle of blood from his mouth.

"Put him in the bull house," he spat.

Chapter 7

The echo of the hounds brought Toby out of his thoughts.

After he bolted from the bull house, he ran deep into the woods to put as much distance as possible between himself and Milford Plantation. He knew that once his absence was discovered, Blakely would put bloodhounds—nigger dogs as the plantation slaves called them—on his trail. If they ever got his scent, Toby knew his fate.

The boy said his children had been sent to Fairfield Plantation, but Toby had only been there once and wasn't sure which direction to take. He thought the swamp would be the best way to lose the bloodhounds; a way to double back on his trail and stay in pools of stagnant water—his one shot to elude detection.

Toby didn't count on the swarms of insects that infected the swamp. He swatted at hordes of blood-sucking mosquitoes and itched from the painful bites of deer flies. In desperation, he covered himself with mud. That helped a little.

As he wandered around the swamp, he lost his bearings. A patch of high ground looked familiar and upon closer examination he saw his own tracks. He had gone in circles.

The bay of the hounds drew closer and Toby knew the dogs had picked up on his trail. Tired, feverish from the insect bites, he continued to splash through the swamp, oblivious to the thorns and briars that tore at his clothes and skin.

He staggered past sharp Spanish bayonet bushes that punctured his flesh. A blinding pain stabbed through his arm before he heard the shot. Toby fell face first into a pool of dark water.

Master McKee and Robert heard the shot reverberate through the air.

McKee snapped the whip at the mule's flank and the wagon shot forward. Moments later, McKee saw a small group of men that stood near a clear area in the forest. He reined the wagon to a stop and jumped down. Robert followed his lead.

"They got him cornered," said Ed.

McKee and Robert walked behind Ed down a narrow, downward-sloped path toward the swamp. They waded a short distance where Blakely stood in knee-deep water, his rifle raised to his shoulder. He pointed the weapon at a mud-covered Toby.

The bedraggled man bled heavily from his right elbow. The arm dangled, attached only by a flap of thin skin. Toby stared at the men, his eyes ablaze with defiant anger.

Dr. Reed and Goldsmith splashed through the water and joined the others.

"Toby, is that you?" asked McKee.

The man didn't respond.

"You answer when the master talks to you," barked Blakely.

Silence.

Furious, Blakely aimed the rifle at Toby's chest.

"God damn you, you black devil. You answer or I will put a bullet through your dark heart."

Toby made no response.

Blakely pulled the trigger and Toby collapsed into the water with a splash. Emotionless, the overseer turned and walked back toward the other men.

"Damn, Blakely," declared McKee, shock in his voice, "did you have to do that? Toby was a good nigger."

"You got to set an example," said the overseer. "You hired me to get things straightened out on Milford and I cannot do that, sir, with rebellious niggers. Toby has been a thorn in my side since I arrived. If you would like to end my contract, so be it."

McKee let the offer roll over in his mind.

"No. No Blakely. I understand what you are saying. But dammit, I paid a lot of money for that darkie."

Dr. Reed broke in, "McKee, if it makes you feel any better, you wouldn't have gotten much work out of him anyway. That shot nearly took his arm off at the elbow."

"Well, we better get him out of there," said Blakely.

He turned to Robert.

"Here boy, take this rope and tie it around that nigger's ankles. I'll go get the mule and then we can pull him out."

A groan came from where Toby lay in the water. The overseer pulled a knife from a sheath on his belt and handed it to Robert.

"You best take this with you."

The boy took the rope and waded through the swampy water.

Toby's body had come to rest against a partially submerged log. Around him, the water was crimson.

Robert jumped back when he saw Toby's hand twitch.

"Master McKee, he's still be alive," yelled Robert, his voice tinged with fear.

"You know what to do," McKee barked.

Robert knelt beside Toby.

A raspy breath came from the man's mouth, his head turned to look directly at the boy.

A flicker of recognition crossed his face, then resignation. "Hey boy."

"Hey Toby," stammered Robert.

Toby looked at the knife in Robert's hand.

"Do what you gots to do chile. I be going home to Cassie. I be free at last."

His gaze held the boy's.

"Do it," the boy heard Blakely cry.

Robert trembled as he reached toward Toby with the knife.

Toby convulsed and with a final gasp his body relaxed, as blood trickled from his mouth.

Robert searched for signs of life.

A peaceful smile spread across Toby's blood streaked face.

The small boy managed a weak, "He be dead now, Massah McKee."

As he struggled to breathe, tears ran down his face. Through his quiet sobs, Robert managed to tie a rope around the dead man's ankles.

A mule pulled Toby's body back to the plantation house, where it hung by the heels from an old oak tree. That evening, Blakely ordered every slave on the plantation to walk past the body.

"This is what happens to runaways," he exclaimed.

McKee returned to Beaufort the next day.

Robert said nothing the entire trip.

* * *

Lydia hummed softly as she plucked a chicken for the evening meal. She looked out the kitchen window where Robert played marbles in the yard with two white boys. Her son crossed racial boundaries as easily as a chameleon changed colors. Tomorrow, Robert may fish in the creek with black children from the Melon's home.

A worry-line creased her smooth brow. Even though Robert remained playful and outgoing, he had changed since the trip. She tried to talk with him about the experience, but the boy shied away from any serious conversation. Lydia worried that Toby's murder impacted her son more than he would admit.

Master McKee also seemed subdued, particularly toward Robert. He treated the boy different than the other blacks in the household. Robert continued to help serve meals at the McKee table and worked in the yard. However, he allowed the boy to roam the neighborhood between chores and rarely scolded him.

And that, Lydia pondered, *presents part of the problem. He's too lenient on the young boy.*

Robert stopped trying to amuse McKee with his antics and instead, distanced himself. He no longer begged to go on hunting and fishing trips and had to be ordered. The boy was dutiful but attended without joy in his heart.

Lydia detected a rebellious streak in Robert. The boy remained courteous to his mother and the other servants, did his chores, but spent more time away from the McKee house than she liked. On at least one occasion, she heard him mutter under his breath when she asked him where he had been.

Jacob, on the other hand, returned from Milford, animated and talkative. News of Toby's death spread rapidly throughout the slave community. When the story reached Mrs. McKee, she flew into a rage.

Lydia and the other slaves in the kitchen looked at each other in disbelief when the mistress confronted her husband in the big house. Mrs. McKee, a genteel lady, rarely raised her voice.

"I can't believe you let that monster kill Toby," she screamed at her husband. "And Cassie, my poor sweet Cassie, she was mine. I bought her with my money to be with Toby. Henry, what in the world were you thinking about?"

A year later, Mrs. McKee was delighted when word came that Blakely disappeared from Milford, his horse found wandering in the woods. The man's household possessions hadn't been touched, which lead the local constable to suspect foul play. Milford's slaves professed ignorance about Blakely's disappearance.

"Maybe he moved to 'Bama," suggested the driver who replaced Toby.

Despite an exhaustive search, authorities never found a body.

Details about Blakely's disappearance hummed through the negro grapevine. After Toby's murder, the overseer's hideous treatment of slaves escalated. Blakely whipped a young girl that dawdled behind when weeding a field, the girl's mother rebelled, and she hacked the overseer with her hoe. Within moments, the other women in the field joined the attack. Blakely rose once on his knees to get away, but a field hand swung hard with her hoe and nearly severed Blakely's head at the base of his neck.

Other field hands hacked at the corpse before their sanity returned. They carefully collected the remains, boiled them in a large iron pot, and fed him to the swine. With all signs of the crime hidden, every slave on the plantation observed a strict code of silence. They understood the awful consequences that would befall them should the truth leak out. But Lydia knew the truth, as did many other blacks in and around Beaufort.

McKee accepted the theory that Blakely had moved on to another part of the country. In short time, he hired a new overseer, but not without the consultation of his wife. The reports of inhumane treatment of the workers at Milford ceased and rice production increased.

Chapter 8

Beaufort, S.C., June 1851

On a hot summer night, Robert, now 12, did not return home for the evening meal. Master McKee, irritated by the boy's absence at dinner, questioned his whereabouts. Distracted by an article in the evening newspaper, McKee did not press the matter.

Later that evening, a deputy knocked on the door, "Mr. McKee, we got your black boy down at the jail."

"Good lord, whatever for?"

"The patrollers picked him up. He didn't have a ticket," chided the deputy. "Fortunately, Sheriff Thompson was in the vicinity and took custody before they could do him any harm."

McKee put on his coat and followed the deputy.

Robert looked frightened when McKee found him in the cell with two older black men. His cellmates looked absolutely terrified as they cowered in the corner to avoid the gaze of the white men. Bloody stripes on their muslin shirts showed where they had been whipped.

McKee motioned for Robert to come closer.

"See those men?"

"Yes suh."

"They are to be flogged again tomorrow for running away from their master," said McKee. "Do you want that to happen to you?"

"No massah McKee. I'm sorry I was late. I was playing baseball with some of the other boys and de sun went down 'fo I knew it. It won't never happen again Massah … not never!"

McKee paid a fine to the jailer. He escorted the boy, who wept with shame and remorse, back to the big house and delivered him to his mother. Her tongue-lashing proved far worse than any beating the boy's master could have inflicted.

"Boy, has you gone mad?" she shrieked. "You knows better den to be out on de streets of Beaufort without a pass. You had all of us worried sick, including de massah."

"But I was jes playing baseball with the McCormick boys," wailed Robert.

"I don't care what 'dose white boys do, I jes care 'bout you," Lydia reasoned. "You ain't no white boy. You c'aint come and go as you please. You be big enough to know that by now. Lawd, when I think what dem 'trollers could have done to my baby!"

McKee restricted Robert to the yard of the big house.

Lydia gave a deep sigh of relief when she found out he wouldn't be beaten. Grateful since his run-in with the law, Robert seemed a bit more like his old self.

His white friends, sympathetic to Robert's plight, came to the McKee's yard and cheered him up. Soon, they laughed and cavorted as if nothing happened. After a week of exemplary conduct by the recalcitrant, McKee unceremoniously lifted restrictions on Robert.

Chapter 9

Robert raced toward the fence at the back of the cow pasture when he heard the crack of the bat. As he sidestepped cow patties, he looked over one shoulder to keep an eye on the ball. He jumped as he reached the fence. The baseball hit the top of his bare hand and bounced over into the neighbor's yard.

"Home run!" he heard someone from the other team shout. He turned to see the batter rounding the bases.

His friend, Hamp, ran to the high fence separating the McKee's home from the Stewart's.

"Give me a boost," said Robert.

Hamp leaned over and cupped his hands. Robert stepped on the makeshift support and jumped. He grabbed the top of the fence with both hands and peered into the Stewart's back yard. Two boys stared back at him, one held the errant baseball.

"Looking for this?" said the taller boy.

"Yeh. Can you throw it back over please, suh?"

The boy spat on the ground.

"Nah, I think I'll just hang on to it. Finders keepers, you know."

The small boy looked unhappy.

"Common Festus," he pleaded. "Let 'em have their ball back."

Festus tossed the ball up and down in his hand, a smug smile on his pudgy face.

Robert sized him up. He was a big, pimple-faced boy with widely-spaced teeth. Robert figured him to be about 15-years-old, the first hints of a mustache on his thin upper lip.

Festus squinted his brown eyes. "I'll sell it to you."

Robert could feel Hamp's grip slipping.

"Us ain't got no money."

"Well, then you don't have a ball," Festus shot back. "Maybe you want to just come over here and take it from me. Me and Alex will be waiting for you."

The younger boy heard his name and entered the fray. Slender, with pale skin, he looked a few years younger than Festus. Freckles ran across his face and blond hair hung almost to his shoulders. His blue eyes creased with concern.

"Festus, we don't want no trouble. We just got here. Let's give them their ball and go play soldiers or something."

Hamp's hold collapsed, leaving Robert hanging on the fence by his fingertips. He dropped to the ground and explained the situation as the others approached. The group of boys comprised of mostly whites, with a few black faces sprinkled in the mix, shared the same look.

"That's the only ball we got," said Bubba, a sandy-haired lout who had hit the homerun causing the ruckus. "Let's go get it!"

The other boys shouted in agreement and marched en masse to a gate between the two properties. They crossed the threshold, then raced toward the ball thieves. Festus, his mouth opened in surprise, dropped the ball and ran to the Stewart home yelling for his uncle Ted. Alex also turned to run, tripped on a root, and sprawled in the grass. He reached for the baseball and clutched it to his stomach.

"Get 'im," shouted Bubba.

The boys fell on Alex in a flurry of flailing arms and legs. One of them got his hands on the ball and ripped it from Alex's grasp.

"We ought to beat the crap out of you," said Bubba matter-of-fact like.

64

"Wait a minute," Robert interceded. "Weren't his fault. He wanted to give it back. It was de other one, the one dat ran."

Satisfied with Robert's declaration, the boys walked back to the gate ready to continue their game.

Robert hung back. "Sorry dey got rough with you."

"Oh, that's okay. That was one whale of a shot. Was it that big boy that hit it?"

"Yep. Ol' Bubba. He mostly strikes out but if he ever connects, best watch out."

Alex brushed the dirt off his clothes. "Festus and I are visiting our Uncle Ted for the summer," he explained.

The boys lived in Cape Cod and had traveled South because their mother and father, Tom and Bessie Rhinds, had gone on an extended trip to Europe. His uncle had invited his nephews to Beaufort for some "Southern charm."

"You like baseball?" asked Robert.

"Yep. We played it all the time up North."

"We need us a couple mo' players. Do yo' brother play, too?"

Alex looked down.

"He's really not the athletic type."

The back door of the Stewart house swung open and an elderly gentleman, followed by Festus, came out shaking his fist.

"You scoundrels stay out of this yard," he shouted. "I know your fathers and if you come back again, I will take it up with them. Leave this boy alone. And his brother. Where is Alex?"

Alex turned to Robert and grinned.

"Guess I'll see you later."

* * *

When the neighborhood boys gathered the next day, Alex awaited them in the field.

"Let's see what yo' can do," Robert said.

Alex could hit and throw better than most of the other boys. When he hit a high, fly ball over the head of the centerfielder with the bases loaded, he cemented a place on the team.

The new Northern visitor could hardly understand the thick Southern drawl of the white boys, and the black boys' dialect, something called *Gullah,* was like a foreign language to him. Alex's lack of comprehension built a gap that baseball filled.

Robert found himself drawn to the boy from Massachusetts. The two developed a friendship that extended beyond the playing field. They met almost daily, after Robert completed his tasks, and walked a few blocks to the marsh fed by the Beaufort River. Barefoot, they waded through the mud flats and found adventure at every turn. They stalked blue crabs lurking in the shallows, probed with pitchforks for flounder and Robert taught his friend to throw a cast net for shrimp. Suppers at the McKee and Stewart homes often contained bounty from the coastal marsh supplied by the two boys.

Fetus asked to come along but complained so much about the heat, the mud, and the gnats, Alex stopped inviting him. This suited Fetus, who preferred playing war games with a set of pewter soldiers in the relative coolness of the Stewart home. Festus loved everything about the military and made it known to all that he would be an admiral one day.

As the first days of summer lengthened, the boys learned to overcome their cultural differences. The first time Alex said "y'all," Robert's eyebrows shot up in surprise.

"You gettin' to sound mo' Southern all de time," he laughed.

Robert also changed, "de" became "the" and "Massuh" became Master. He didn't notice the change, but his mother did. She warned him not to "put on airs" around white folks. Being a natural mimic, he had no problem with the transition between proper English, when he was with Alex, and Gullah when around others.

* * *

The McKee's had a small sailing skiff tied up to a dock on the river. The wooden boat, spacious enough for four people, could be paddled with oars or outfitted with canvas for propulsion on windy days. Though primarily used in the calm waters of the Beaufort River, the skiff's keel made it a seaworthy vessel.

"Would you like to go sailing?"

"Don't know," said Robert. "I ain't never sailed before. Alex, I can't even swim."

"That's the first thing they teach us at the Cape." Alex was surprised. "That and how to sail. Everybody knows how to do that. Com'on, I'll teach you myself."

Alex kept his word and Robert learned to dog paddle after a few hours of practice. Satisfied that they would be safe, McKee gave the boys permission to use the skiff as long as Robert came back in time to help with the evening chores. The boys packed a basket with a jug of water, sandwiches, and apples taken from a neighbor's yard, and set sail.

The moment a gust of wind filled the canvas and propelled the small boat into the Beaufort River, Robert knew in his heart that he was home. He marveled at the motion of the boat as it glided down the waterway and picked up speed when the breeze intensified. He reached over the side, dipped his hand into the water, and created a small wake. Robert laughed with delight.

The boys rode the wind past downtown Beaufort, its church spires sparkled in the midday sun, past the docks lined with the masts of fishing vessels, and then past fields of cotton. Robert reveled in the cool wind. It blew gently over his face as the sound of the little boat sliced through the water without effort. As Beaufort faded from sight, he felt a new sensation. He had never been out of Beaufort without the accompaniment of an adult, white man.

He turned to Alex. "I feel free as the wind."

• * * *

The summer of 1851 was one of the most glorious times of Robert's youth. He and Alex settled into a routine of baseball, playing in the marsh, and sailing the inland waters around Beaufort. The boy from Cape Cod, already an accomplished sailor at age 12, taught Robert the fundamentals of navigating the skiff on the broad river. The black boy absorbed everything his friend showed him as the summer days lengthened, and by July 4th he was almost as proficient at the tiller as Alex.

On Independence Day, Alex wanted to watch the firework celebration from the water and requested permission to take Robert. McKee wrote a pass that allowed the boy to be out past curfew, attached with a warning to "be careful."

Before they left for the dock, Festus appeared.

"I'd like to join you"

Alex responded with a quick, "Sure."

Robert attempted to mask his surprise when Festus took the tiller of the little boat.

"Oh, he's a much better sailor than I," explained Alex.

After an hour on the river, Robert had to grudgingly agree. Festus piloted the skiff with ease and confidence. He knew how to set the sail to get maximum speed and the skiff flew across the surface of the water. They took turns sailing the boat and for the first time, Robert saw a smile cross Festus's face.

As the sun set, the boys sailed the boat close to the Beaufort waterfront and dropped anchor.

"I love the Fourth of July." Alex settled against a roll of canvas in the front of the boat. "Except for Christmas it's my favorite holiday. We have big fireworks celebrations at the Cape. How about here?"

"I don't rightly know how it's done anywhere else," said Robert. "Ain't never been nowhere but Beaufort. But they put on a good show. I ain't sure what it's all about."

"What it's all about?" Festus snarked in disbelief. "July 4, 1776. The day we declared our freedom from Great Britain. Why, it was the most important day in the history of the United States. How could you not get excited about the Fourth?"

"Dat must be a big day for white folks. Not so much for us black folks."

Festus bubbled with derisive laughter.

"Boy, you won't never be free. You and your kind was made to serve the white race. You know that? I'll tell you something else. Alex, this goes for you, too. It isn't right for a white boy and a darkie to be spending so much time alone. I believe I'll say something to Uncle Stewart about it."

Robert started to reply but a tremendous explosion shook the air and ended the conversation. The boys remained quiet as they settled back for the fireworks.

After the show, Alex pulled anchor and told Robert to sail the skiff back to the dock at The Point. He raised the sail and Robert adjusted the jib as a sudden gust of wind whipped across the water and careened the boom toward Festus.

"Duck!" screamed Robert.

Startled, Festus looked up just in time for the spar to sweep across the boat, catch him at his chest, and knock him into the water.

Alex and Robert peered anxiously into black water. Festus bobbed up a few seconds later, choking and sputtering. With two powerful strokes he swam back to the boat and the boys pulled him over the side.

Festus went for Robert with vengeance in his eyes.

"Dammit! You did that on purpose!"

Alex grabbed Festus from behind. The narrow confines of the boat allowed him to prevent his brother from moving aft.

"Stop it Festus. That was an accident."

Festus relaxed in his brother's grip, but Robert saw hatred spew from his piggish eyes.

"Just take me home. We'll settle this later," he said through clenched teeth.

Chapter 10

A few days after Independence Day, Alex appeared at the front door of the McKee mansion and asked to speak to Mr. McKee. Caesar, the butler, escorted the child to the study.

"Hello Mr. McKee. It's a pleasure to see you."

"Why good afternoon Alex. Robert has been telling me a lot about you. He said you've taught him how to sail."

"Yes sir. And he's quite good at it. That's why I'm here Mr. McKee. I'd like to sail the skiff to Port Royal and show Robert the ocean. We could camp out and be back the next day. Of course, I would be responsible for him and see that we get back safely."

McKee considered the request. Robert's behavior had improved since he and the Yankee boy became friends.

"Caesar. Fetch Lydia."

When she arrived, McKee had Alex repeat the details of the trip.

"Massah McKee, if it's okay with you I suppose it will be fine with me," she sounded nervous. "But dese chilluns best be back the next day or you and me will be going down de river, too."

"Thank you!" Alex shouted as he ran out of the house to bring the good news to Robert.

The next morning, Robert stood at the backdoor of the Stewart house with a wheelbarrow full of supplies. Lydia prepared food and drinks, as well as blankets and mosquito netting for sleeping outdoors. Alex bounded down the steps of the house with a sack full of supplies. They stowed everything on the skiff, raised the sail, and let the wind and current carry them east toward Port Royal.

The boys chatted with excitement as a gentle breeze pushed their boat down river. Alex reached in his sack and pulled out a nautical chart.

"What's that?"

"This is a map of Port Royal." Alex pointed to the topography. "See these numbers and lines? They show the depth of the channel and show underwater obstructions. If we follow this route it will take us to the Port Royal docks. There's the lighthouse. And those symbols are for sandbars."

Robert pointed to a symbol on the map.

"What's 'dat mean?"

"Why Robert, that's the number 15. You do know your numbers, don't you?"

"No one's ever learned me my letters and numbers. The white folks don't allow it." Robert looked away, embarrassed.

Alex was astonished. He assumed that black children went to school in the winter months just like the whites. He put an arm around Robert.

"It's okay Robert. I can teach you."

Alex spent the remainder of the day pouring over the chart with his friend. Robert soaked up the information like a sponge. Numbers came especially easy. By the time the Port Royal skyline loomed in the distance, he could count to 100 and had memorized half the alphabet. Alex pointed to river depths on the chart and Robert read them with ease.

Port Royal boasted the best natural harbor on the southeastern coast of the United States and ships from around the world lined the port's docks. Alex pointed out the flags of France, England, and Spain. Robert marveled at their size.

"These ships sailed across the Atlantic Ocean from a faraway land called Europe," Alex explained.

71

The boys spent the remainder of the day sailing the skiff in the large harbor. Alex piloted the little boat to the entrance of the sound, and it bobbed over swells as they rolled in from the ocean. Alarmed at first by the size of the waves, Robert's adventurous spirit prevailed and he encouraged Alex to take them further from the harbor.

Alex taught his friend how to sail the boat into the waves and how to time a turn to coincide with the current and swells. The wind picked up and crowned the wavetops with whitecaps. The canvas sail snapped taut and the boat heeled over.

Alarmed, Robert gripped the gunwales.

"I wish you could come with me to Cape Cod," shouted Alex over the roar of the ocean. "Don't worry, we won't tip over!"

The sun dipped low over the western horizon. Reluctant to end the fun, Robert turned the skiff toward the serenity of the harbor and headed for the campsite they scouted earlier in the day.

Night had fallen when they pitched camp. They enjoyed a hearty meal and bedded down, exhausted from a busy day on the water. The snapping of limbs and the sound of hoof beats woke them from their sleep. They bolted upright and peered out of the mosquito netting. Six men on horseback rode to the edge of the campfire and dismounted. They pointed shotguns at the two boys.

"Get out of dere. Let me se yo' faces dammit," snarled a middle-aged man wearing a thin, yellow cotton shirt and faded jeans.

The boys trembled as they crawled out of their make-shift tent and stood at attention.

"Come over here Jake. Is dis' de nigger we chasin?"

Jake, a stout man with a full beard, pulled a stick from the fire for use as a torch. He pushed it close to Robert's face to examine him.

He spat tobacco juice on the ground and growled, "Nah, this ain't him. The nigger we lookin' for is lots taller and older. This ain't nuttin' but a boy. Can't say I've ever laid eyes on dis white boy."

The older man gave Alex a suspicious look.

"What you doin' out here in de woods with dis black boy?" he interrogated.

Alex's voice quivered. "We sailed from Beaufort and are heading back home tomorrow."

He reached in his pocket and pulled out the letter from McKee, which gave his slave permission to be away from home and in the company of Alex. He handed the letter to Jake, who pretended to examine it.

"Here, Jimmy. Be best if you do de reading on this."

The grizzled man in the yellow shirt took several minutes to read the letter before he returned it to Alex with hesitation.

"Boy, you ain't from around here, is you?"

"No sir," Alex breathed a bit easier now that some of the tension had left the air. "I'm visiting my uncle. I'm from Massachusetts."

Jimmy spat tobacco juice between Alex's legs.

"You not one of dem abolitionist is ya?" he growled.

"Oh no." Alex reassured the men. "This boy here belongs to Mister Henry McKee. He is just traveling with me to help with the chores. Abolitionist? No sirree—not me."

"Damn good thing," Jimmy chided as he turned and motioned for his men to remount their horses.

He turned back to Alex, "If you see a nigger running loose in dese wood whose about twice of de size of 'dat one," he pointed to Robert. "You let someone know. You hear?"

Alex nodded solemnly.

Both boys exhaled in relief as the patrollers rode out of sight.

Robert wanted to strike camp and get back on the river, but his friend deemed the idea too dangerous. At first light they hurried to the skiff and set off for home.

On the long trip back to Beaufort, the boys talked about the visitors of the previous night.

"I was scared," admitted Robert. "They didn't like the idea of a black boy and a boy from up North being alone together. I could see it in their eyes. Alex, that was a close call."

"Yep. My legs were shaking. 'Specially when they started talking about abolitionists. Robert, I lied to them. My dad's an abolitionist and I am, too."

"What be a 'bolitionist?" he stumbled over the unfamiliar word.

For the next hour Alex talked about the movement taking place in many Northern states to abolish slavery. He told him about Frederick Douglasss, a black slave who fled to freedom, pretending to be a sailor. Douglasss wrote a book that told about the terrible plight of black people in bondage in the South. His passionate speeches at churches and meeting halls had stirred many white people to take up the cause of abolishing slavery.

Robert was amazed to learn that some white people considered slavery an abomination.

"My daddy heard Mr. Douglass speak and I believe it changed the way he thinks about slavery."

"Alex, does dey has slaves up North where you live?"

Alex shook his head, "No. We have some black folks living in Cape Cod, but they are free men. They have jobs and lots of them own the houses they live in. They got their own churches, too. There's some white folks that don't like the black ones, but they leave the blacks alone for the most part."

"That's where I'd like to be," Robert stared toward the horizon, dreamy-eyed. "We could just keep on sailing North in this boat 'til we got there."

Alex considered the idea but shook his head again.

"Wouldn't last," he said with resignation in his voice. "The law says slaves that run away to the North have to be returned to their masters if they are found. There's bad people living up North that don't do anything but look for runaways. Your master would be looking for you and he would know just where to go."

•   * * *

With the help of a favorable breeze, the boys made good time, and arrived in Beaufort by mid-afternoon. As they sailed past the waterfront, they noticed a large crowd gathered near the courthouse. Curious, they secured the boat to the dock to investigate.

More than a hundred men, women, and children milled around the courthouse square. Alex and Robert squirmed their way through a sea of legs and skirts until they got a better vantage point. When they reached a small clearing in the crowd, they saw a tall, thin black man with his face to a post; his arms bound above his head.

"Let's go Alex. I've seen dis kind of thing 'fore."

"Wait, I want to see what happens."

Sheriff John Thompson, dressed in a black suit, emerged from the jail next to the courthouse steps. He marched into the center of the square, accompanied by two other white men, and a well-muscled black man. Thompson pulled a paper from his vest pocket and addressed the crowd in a thunderous voice.

"This slave, Terrance Hawley, has admitted to stealing property from his master's home, to wit a horse, saddle and provisions, and taking said stolen items with him in an unlawful attempt to break his ties of bondage to his master. He is guilty of running away and resisting lawful arrest. Since this slave has expressed remorse, it is the sentence of this court that said slave received 150 lashes instead of being put to death by hanging."

The sheriff turned to the smaller man at his side.

"Mr. Floyd, do you concur with the sentence of the court?"

The slave's master nodded. "Yes, I concur."

Thompson motioned for the muscular black man to step forward. In compliance, he ripped the shirt off the back of the shackled man. The sinewy black man unfurled a long, cowhide whip. The whip whistled and cracked against the slave's malnourished body. The runaway cried out in pain, then slumped against the ropes that held him upright.

"Hurrah," came a cry from the crowd.

By the sixth crack of the whip, blood began to drip down the man's back. A cheer went up with each punishing blow. Robert turned away from the scene.

Tears trickled down Alex's face.

"Let's go," Robert mumbled.

As they left the crowd behind, Alex looked at Robert with remorse.

"That's the most terrible thing I've ever seen," Alex whimpered.

"I seen worse," replied Robert, thinking of a cold winter day in a swamp at Milford Plantation.

Chapter 11

Alex sat under the shade of an elm tree. Tears glistened on his cheeks. He held a newspaper in his hands and looked at Robert with sorrow. He wiped his eyes with the back of his hand and motioned for the black boy to sit down beside him.

"What'cha reading?"

Alex sighed, "It's a newspaper my daddy got in the mail called *The National Era*. There's a story in it called *Uncle Tom's Cabin* and it's all about you, Robert, and black folks like you."

He handed the periodical to Robert, who flipped through the pages. He couldn't read it, but he examined the illustrations that showed a black family being sold into slavery, and another of a black man being beaten.

"Is that Uncle Tom?" he pointed to the picture.

"Yep," Alex replied. "Reminds me of that poor soul we saw getting whipped yesterday. Robert, none of this is right—the beatings, the forced labor, the way white folks treat black folks. We were taught at school that all men are created equal. If that's true, how can one race put another race in bondage?"

"That's just the way it's always been round here. The white folks, they take care of us, and we do what they tells us to do. Far back as I can remember that's the way it's been done. Der ain't no other way of doing things."

Alex searched Robert's face.

"You ever thought about getting out of here?"

Robert thought about the question, "I have. But then I remember a black man named Toby. He tried to run for it, but he didn't know where to run. They hunted him down with dogs and shot him dead. Lot of black folks think like that. Where they gonna run to even if they did have a notion to leave their masters?"

"I've been thinking about that," Alex confided. "Robert, we got to get you out of this place. We could take the skiff and sail North. It wouldn't be easy, but if we stayed close to the coast, I believe we could make it. Once we get to Cape Cod, daddy would help us. I know he would. We could go on to Canada where no one could get you."

Robert squirmed.

"That's a grand idea alright, but I gots to give that some thought. Master McKee, he be pretty good to me. And I'd miss my momma if I had to go up North. What if we get caught Alex? They'd beat me. They would probably come down hard on you, too."

With a flip of his hands, Alex dismissed the idea.

"I am not afraid of getting caught. Have to be mighty careful. Do most of our sailing at night. You have been a good friend to me. I am willing to take the risk. Robert, I've been praying about this and I believe God wants me to help you."

Emotions washed over Robert in waves. He feared the unknown yet reveled in the possibility of making a dash to freedom. He recalled with horror and indignation, Blakely's harsh treatment of the Milford slaves, his master's acceptance of Toby's death, and the patrollers who made travel almost impossible.

Robert remembered the laughter he shared with McKee about Bishop Mullins, the warm embrace of his momma, the afternoons spent playing baseball and fishing in the creek. As life went for slaves, his was pleasant, better than the plight of blacks working in the rice fields.

Yet, Robert felt a fear shared by all of those in bondage. At any moment, he could be sold and suffer a much worse fate. He'd seen the terror in the dirty faces of Toby's children as they were sent, in the back of a wagon, to a new master. His mother had told him about her childhood as a slave on Lady's Island. The cries of the black man whipped in the courthouse square still rang in his ears.

One memory rushed forward, one more powerful than the others—the surge of the little boat as it beat against the wind, and the feeling of freedom blowing across his face.

Free, like a bird soaring in the sky.

"Alex," his voice solemn, "promise me this. Don't let 'em catch me. No matter what."

The boy from New England proffered his hand, "Let's shake on it."

Chapter 12

Festus watched as Alex slipped out the back door with a burlap sack in tow. Over the past couple of days, his younger brother acted suspicious. He hadn't seen Alex's little black friend in more than a week. At first, he hoped Robert's absence meant Alex would spend more time with him. He had complained about Alex's relationship with the black boy and figured their uncle must have said something.

Alex studied nautical charts borrowed from his uncle's library. He stayed in his room with the maps or read a book their father sent them about a log cabin. Festus skimmed it, then threw it on the table.

More abolitionist crap.

The days grew shorter as summer drew to a close. Soon, he and Alex would be on a steamer back to Cape Cod. He could not wait. He hated the South with its stifling heat, pesky bugs, and dim-witted blacks.

As Alex slipped out of the fence gate, something caught his eye—Alex waved to someone. Festus peered into the dimmed light of dusk and saw Robert. Both boys carried burlap bags and he watched as they headed north toward The Point.

Festus hurried from the house and followed the boys, careful to hang far enough back to avoid detection. He trailed them to a dock where the

McKee skiff was tied. He sneaked closer, his movements hidden by the darkness of twilight. As he neared the boat, he could hear Alex's voice.

"I think we got everything. You stow the food and water and I'll put the charts somewhere safe. Should be ready to go in just a minute."

Go. Go where? No one told me about a trip.

He stepped from behind a bush and walked toward the boys.

"Where the hell do you think you're going?" Sarcasm dripped from his words.

Alex and Robert jumped at the sound of the voice.

"Oh, hey Festus. Uh, me and Robert are just going for a little sail. We'll be back in just a little bit."

Festus looked into the skiff.

"That's a lot of provisions for a short trip. If I didn't know better, I'd say you and this little nigger are trying to run away. Wonder what Uncle Ted and Mr. McKee would think of that?"

Alex dropped the sack of charts and walked toward Festus with his arms open.

"Festus, please don't say anything to anybody. Robert will get in a lot of trouble if you tell. He'll probably get beat. Or maybe something worse."

"I don't care what happens to the nigger," sneered Festus. "Hell, he tried to kill me Fourth of July.

"Common Marse Festus." Robert stepped forward. "Let's all of us just go back home and forget dis ever happened.'

Festus picked up an oar laying on the dock.

"You come with me now. I'm taking you to the sheriff," he snipped.

Alex and Robert looked at each other in horror. As they began to run toward the woods, Festus swung the heavy oar at Robert.

He ducked and felt the swoosh of the oar going over his head.

"Owh!"

Robert looked over his shoulder and saw Alex's lifeless body on the ground. He scrambled to him on his hands and knees. The oar missed him, and the full force of the blow struck Alex on the forehead. Blood flowed from a six-inch gash, over the boy's face.

"Alex! Alex! Talk to me," he cradled his friend's head in his lap. Alex didn't respond.

"Go get help. Now!" Robert ordered through tears.

Robert prayed while he waited for Festus to return. He bent his ear close to Alex's face but couldn't feel the boy's breath. He tore off his shirt and pressed it hard against the wound to staunch the flow of blood. He used the sleeve to wipe Alex's ashen-colored face.

He rocked back and forth, "Help! Help!"

Through the woods he saw flickering lights and the sound of men's voices.

"Over here," he shouted. "Hurry. For God's sake, hurry."

Festus arrived first, a torch in one hand, followed by Ted Stewart, Sheriff Thompson, and a deputy. Their torches cast an eerie orange light on the scene—Robert hunched over the white boy's body, his arms and hands covered with blood.

"That's him," screamed Festus. "That's the nigger that killed my brother."

Chapter 13

Robert wept uncontrollably as he watched the men place Alex's body on a makeshift litter for transport back to the Stewart house. Alex's arms were limp as they hung off the sides of the stretcher. The men bound Roberts hands and began the short walk to the jailhouse.

Festus sidled up to the sheriff. "Me and Alex were going to go sailing tonight, but when we got to the boat, we found Robert already there. He had stocked the boat with provisions and appeared to be running away. Alex tried to stop him from stealing the boat and that boy hit him with the oar."

"I don't think he was trying to kill Alex," Festus continued his ruse. "They knew each other pretty good. I suspect he was trying to hit me but hit Alex instead. The nigger tried to kill me on the Fourth of July. Pushed me into the river to drown."

"'Dat's not the way it happen at all," Robert shook his cuffed hands.

"Shut up boy. You'll get your chance to talk later. You better hope that boy you hit with the oar don't die. You in enough trouble as it is."

McKee arrived before the party returned from the docks. He listened dispassionately to Robert's account of the accident. The explanation fell on deaf ears and McKee left without a word in the boy's defense.

The sheriff put the child in the cell, blew out the lantern, and left the boy in darkness. Terrified, Robert stayed awake all night. When dawn broke over Beaufort, a thin beam of light pierced through the window of the jail cell, Robert heard voices through the door that lead to the sheriff's office. A few minutes later a dark shape appeared and approached Robert's prison door. The sight of Festus shocked him.

The stout boy whispered, "Come here. I got something to tell you."

Robert stepped closer, careful to stay out of Festus' reach.

"Just thought you ought to know it looks like Alex is going to live. The doctor doesn't know if he will ever be able to walk again. Too early to tell. I don't know what you have been telling the sheriff, but you better get your story straight. Because if it comes out that Alex was trying to help you escape, they'll put him in prison too. You keep Alex's name out of this. Mine too."

Robert plopped down on the burlap sack he used as a bed and put his face in his hands. He hadn't thought about what they would do to Alex. He considered his limited options. No white man would take the word of a slave over Festus. Master McKee had made it obvious he would not defend Robert. So far, no one knew Alex intended to participate in the escape. Robert knew he would get punished regardless of what he said.

Dejected, he looked at Festus.

"Just go. Alex ain't got nothin' to worry about except getting' well," he said. "I'll keep quiet."

* * *

Sheriff Thompson had gone back to the scene of the crime to take a closer look. He found nautical charts and clothing of different sizes stowed on the boat, as if *two*, not one person prepared to flee.

"Robert, I got a pretty good idea that Yankee boy Alex was gonna make a run for it with you in tow," he coerced. "That's the way it was right?"

The boy stared into the earthen floor of the jail as he searched for the right words.

"No sir, Alex ain't had nothin' to do with it. Jes me."

* * *

At the trial, the only testimony came from Festus. The judge found Robert guilty of attempted murder of a white man and sentenced him to receive 100 lashes the following day. Deputies outside the courthouse rushed to hold Lydia as Robert was led back to the jail in chains.

The next day, a large crowd gathered to witness the miscarriage of justice. The men wiped the sweat from their brows, while women with parasols, fanned themselves under the hot, August sun. Church bells signaled the noon hour. Sheriff Thompson and his deputies led Robert to the whipping post in the middle of the square. Robert quivered as the lawmen ran a chain through an iron ring at the top of the poll and attached it to the handcuffs on his tiny wrists.

With little fanfare, he faced the sea of white faces as the sheriff read the sentence of the court. Robert stretched his neck to search the for one black face, his mother's face, but he couldn't find her.

Rough hands ripped the shirt from his small body. The blood pounded in his ears and he gasped for air.

The restless crowd became still as it awaited the sheriff's order to begin.

"Wait. Fo' God's sake wait!"

A muffled alarm came from the spectators.

"What's going on here?" the sheriff roared.

"Sheriff, it's me Alex. We've got to talk. Don't beat Robert. It wasn't his fault. It's all mine!" Alex limped toward the sheriff.

The crowd strained to hear what the child whispered into the lawman's ear.

"Take the prisoner back to his cell," the sheriff shouted.

Cries of protests erupted from the horde.

"That nigger deserves to get whipped," someone yelled.

"Not until the judge hears what this boy has to say," the sheriff shot back.

Robert was confused as his chains were removed from the post. His eyes searched for an explanation and saw Alex, his head bandaged, as he confided details to the sheriff. He saw Lydia.

His mother ran to him through the throngs of people. For a moment, the world around them didn't exist as she reached out and held him in a tight embrace. They were brought back to reality when the deputies ordered her to stand back as they escorted Robert back to his cell.

Alex admitted to the judge, "I talked Robert into trying to escape to Cape Cod. Festus, not Robert, hit me with the oar." He begged the court to forgive Robert.

McKee, Stewart, and Sheriff Thompson met in the judge's chamber for more than an hour before they reached a compromise.

"Alex, you and Festus will be sent back to Cape Cod on the next available steamer. Robert, you will be sent to Milford Plantation and banned from Beaufort," the judge concluded.

* * *

Henry McKee reviewed records of the recent harvest when a tap on the study door interrupted his thoughts.

"Who is it?"

"It be Lydia."

McKee rose from his chair and opened the door.

"Why Lydia, come in. What's on your mind?"

Lydia wrung her hands around an apron's edge as she walked into the room.

Apprehensive, she pointed to the chair. "You best sit down for dis."

McKee sat and turned his full attention toward Lydia.

"Massah McKee, I ain't nebber told no one, not even Misses McKee, about dat time you snucked into my room out back in de kitchen when everybody else be sleepin'. You knows dat don't you?"

He was silent, but his eyes betrayed his astonishment.

"No suh, don't you go believin' it didn't happen cause we both knows it did. You was jes a young boy jes wantin' to know 'bout how things be between a man and a woman. But don't you go sayin' it nebber happened cause de proof be right here in dis house. Dat boy of mine be yo' boy too Massha."

McKee squirmed and looked down at his hands.

"What is it you are trying to get out of me?"

"Jes dis Massah," she pleaded. "Us can't send dis boy to de plantation. You know dat in yo' heart and so do I. It be like a death sentence if'n he be sent der. Dat boy ain't knowed nuttin' but kindness in dis house."

"What would you have me do Lydia?"

"Well suh, I been thinkin' bout dat. You has a sister-in-law livin' in Charleston. Ain't dat right?"

McKee nodded his head in assent.

"Dat's where you should send our boy. Send him der Massah. For de love of God send Robert to Charleston."

Lydia fell to her knees and put her head on McKee's lap and sobbed.

He reached out a trembling hand and stroked the kerchief on her head.

"I want the best for Robert, too."

Tear streamed down her face.

"Thank you Massah. Dis boy gonna make us proud." Love radiated from her words.

Part 2

Charleston, S.C.

ೞ⁊ೲ

Chapter 14

Robert enjoyed a charmed life in Charleston. Mrs. McKee's sister, Elisa Ancrum, welcomed Robert into her home and gave him the same preferred treatment he received in Beaufort. Soon after arriving in Charleston, McKee's friend Moses Goldsmith gave Robert a job at the Planters House hotel and he worked there as a waiter for two years. His quick wit and good-natured smile made him a favorite with the patrons.

Robert sent his wages to Master McKee but kept the occasional tip. Over time, he amassed a small cache of coins hidden under the mattress in the tiny room where he slept. Robert loved the hustle and bustle of Charleston. He got to know every nook and cranny of the port city after he hung up his waiter's apron and headed for his second job as a lamplighter.

In the 1850s, Charleston ranked as one of the few cities in the United States with an extensive street light system. At dusk, Robert carried a ladder and cleaning cloth along his route. He propped the ladder against the street light, cleaned soot from the glass fixture and lit the gas jet. He had fifty streetlights to care for along East Bay Street. Just before sunrise, he extinguished the lights on his way to work at the Planters House.

On East Bay, Robert often initiated conversations with the stevedores and sailors who worked the docks. He codeswitched between Gullah and proper English, which allowed him to converse with both the black men and their white supervisors. The stories he heard about foreign ports of call fascinated him. He recalled the sailing trips he had taken with his friend Alex and longed to be back at sea.

His wish came true in a most unexpected manner.

One morning in 1853, as he extinguished the lights on East Bay Street, Robert listened as a dock supervisor castigated a group of black stevedores. The black men wore puzzled, sullen expressions as the white man's voice rose in volume and his hands gesticulated wildly. A wooden crate, crushed at one end, spilled broken dishes, saucers, and cups onto the cobblestone street.

"You can't be stumbling around like a bunch of monkeys," shouted the white man. "This china came all the way from London and damned if you haven't broken half the set throwing it around like it was slabs of bacon. Look. It's marked 'fragile.' That means be gentle with it."

"Boss man, der be ciphering all over dese here boxes. Don't none of us knows how to read and write. We jes does de best us knows how."

"Holy Jehoshaphat," sputtered the white overseer. "I guess I'll have to stand over you until the whole damned lot is unloaded. And I ain't got time for this! I have two other deliveries of sails to make to the *Argonaunt* before she goes to sea."

Robert cleared his throat.

"Hey mistah, I can help."

The sandy-haired man turned and looked down, surprised to see Robert. Now 14, the boy had grown six inches since moving to Charleston and already sported the beginning of a light moustache.

"Who might you be?"

"My name be Robert Smalls, sir, and I can read a bit. If'n you likes, I could watch over this cargo and point out the crates 'dat need careful handling."

Robert had never learned to read, but he remembered the alphabet taught to him by Alex.

The man rubbed his beard.

"Seems like I've seen you on Bay Street before. Whose servant are you?"

"I belongs to Master Henry McKee of Beaufort but I'm livin' in Charleston with his sister-in-law. I helps wait tables down at the Planters House and I take care of de street lights on Bay Street."

The man's eyes lit up with recognition.

"Yes, I remember you now. I eat at the Planter occasionally. Believe you waited my table once or twice."

"More den likely, suh."

"My name is Simmons. John Simmons. Tell you what boy, point out to these men the crates marked fragile while I run these sails down to the captain of the *Argonaut*. Do a good job and I'll give you two bits when I return."

'Yessuh." Robert smiled, surprised he got the job.

Twenty-five cents were more than he made in tips on his best day at The Planter. Such a handsome sum of money would make a welcome addition to the little collection of coins.

When Simmons returned an hour later Robert sat on a pile of wooden crates, arranged on the back of a wagon. The boy hopped down and flashed a smile at Simmons.

"Not a single plate broken, suh."

Simmons examined the load and with a satisfied smile reached into his pocket for change. He flipped two quarters at Robert, who caught both coins in the air.

The man and the boy scrutinized each other.

Robert saw kindness in Simmons' broad face, uncommon among the men at the rough Charleston docks.

"I like your spunk," said Simmons. "How much has your master hired you out for?"

Robert explained the arrangement with his master.

"Are you happy waiting tables and tending to the street lights?"

"It be okay, mistuh. But I sure do miss de sea. I learned to sail in Beaufort."

* * *

Simmons heard the passion in Robert's voice, and they talked for
another half-hour about their mutual love of boats and the water.

Simmons owned a small shipyard on Bay Street. He was best known as
a sail maker, but he had a finger in many other sea-going ventures. Smaller
ships docked at his pier to load and unload freight. His crew of skilled
carpenters made minor repairs on boats of all sizes He also owned a fleet
of two steamships and a schooner, to transport goods to ports along the
South Carolina coast. Though administrative duties tied him to shore,
Simmons loved to sail. When opportunity allowed, he still went to sea
aboard his ships.

Despite a heavy work schedule that surrounded him by people,
Simmons remained a lonely man. A year earlier, his wife and young son
died during a diphtheria epidemic that swept through the city. Simmons
dealt with his grief through work; he woke well before dawn and retired
late in the evening. The grueling schedule left little time for introspection
and he liked it that way.

The young boy's love for sailing rekindled something in Simmons'
heart. He motioned for Robert to follow him as he walked to the end of the
dock.

"What would Mr. Goldsmith say about you taking a sail with me on
the harbor?"

"I guess what he don't know won't hurt him," Robert laughed.

The two hours they spent sailing in Charleston Harbor, formed a
friendship that would last for many years to come. Simmons watched
Robert work the rigging with ease. The boy leaned over the side of the
small sloop and ran his hand through the water as he glanced back and
smiled, content.

Simmons offered Robert the helm. Timid at first, his confidence grew
as he piloted the sailboat around traffic and toward Sullivan's Island.
Simmons gave advice on how to navigate around the harbor. The wind in

their face and spray of saltwater over the bow, they reveled as the boat sliced through the small waves of the harbor.

They tacked southward toward a large, red mass rising from the harbor floor.

"What's dat big building?" Robert pointed.

"That's Fort Sumter," replied Simmons. "They've been building the damn thing for as long as I remember. The whole fort is built on a shoal. I talked with some of the masons from Baltimore who are putting on the brick facing just the other day. They've only mounted 15 guns so far out of the 135 that are supposed to go in. I doubt if they finish the thing during my lifetime!"

"What's wrong Robert?"

"Suh, the sun is risin' high in the sky. I suppose I best be gettin' back. The Planter opens for lunch 'fo long and Mister Goldsmith be mad if'n I not dere."

Simmons took the wheel and sailed back to the dock.

"Robert, how would you like to come to work for me? I could use a deck hand and I think you have the makings of a sailor."

Robert dipped his cap.

"Suh, that would make me 'bout de happiest black boy in Charleston."

Simmons accompanied Robert to the restaurant to discuss the proposal with Goldsmith. After several couriered exchanges, the men reached a deal. Simmons agreed to pay $20 per month for Robert's services. A $1 bonus was paid to Robert, under the table.

* * *

Over the next two years, Robert learned to cut and sew heavy canvas sails to be rigged onto ships serviced by his employer. He toiled with hot turpentine to caulk leaky boats and continued to help supervise the stevedores. He tackled every task with enthusiasm and worked side-by-side to get the job done with a steady banter of good-hearted ribbing that induced laughter from the other men.

They respected Robert, not only for his work ethic but, for the close relationship the teenager had developed with Simmons. The captain's face lit up with joy when Robert was around. Simmons often used Robert to relay work orders in Gullah to ensure the dockside slaves understood the tasks at hand. Robert moved seamlessly from the harsh world of slavery to the privileged world of whites.

* * *

Simmons invited Robert to sail north to the port of Georgetown aboard the *Hawthorne*, an aging packet ship, as a belated sixteenth birthday gift. Loaded with durable goods, bolts of fabric, and an assortment of hardware, the boat made its way out of Charleston harbor and sailed along the coast in gentle seas.

The second day aboard, Simmons assigned Robert to the helm, where he surrendered the wheel.

"I'm going to catch some sleep. Just keep her on this course Robert," he instructed as he headed below deck.

The ten-member crew stared in surprise. They had never known Simmons to relinquish control of the ship to anyone, let alone a teenage boy. Robert stood proudly at his post, searching the horizon for any signs of trouble. The *Hawthorne* sailed through gentle swells toward Georgetown.

Simmons emerged from his cabin later in the afternoon and looked about the ship with satisfaction. He went to his quarters to see how Robert and the crewmen would react. He was pleased to see everything in order and that his protégé seemed in command of the situation. He liked Robert and planned to train him as wheelman for one of his steamships, the *Commanche*.

The captain's brow furrowed when he looked seaward. A band of dark clouds formed in the sky while he was below deck. Summer storms could turn the placid Atlantic into a foaming cauldron in mere minutes. He called for more sail and took the helm from Robert, ordering him to stay close.

Conditions deteriorated and waves splashed over the bow of the schooner. Simmons hugged the coastline as he searched for the Georgetown harbor channel's lighthouse. Rain fell in torrents and gale force winds snapped the sails tight against the spars. The ship bobbed over massive waves and slammed into the troughs as thunderous clouds of spray and foam covered the decks.

Simmons ordered Robert to tie a stout rope around his waist and then to the ship's wheel. The captain did the same and hung on to the wheel with all his might. Towering black clouds turned the afternoon sky dark, punctuated by flashes of intense lightning.

Robert looked at Simmons who calmly steered the ship while others cowered behind cargo lashed to the deck.

No one saw the rogue wave about to breach the starboard side of the boat until it was upon them. An enormous mountain of gray water blotted out the horizon, towered over the boat, and crashed over the gunwales. Simmons clung to the ship's wheel but lost his grip and slammed headfirst into the ships railing. Robert dived toward Simmons and caught the rope around the captain's waist and pulled him to safety.

Blood streamed from a deep gash on Simmons' head. His eyes were closed, and his body seemed lifeless. Robert bellowed for help and two strong crewmen emerged at his side.

"Take Capt'n to his cabin and put a towel on his head," Robert yelled over the cacophony.

He used the rope around his waist to crawl back to the ship's wheel. The *Hawthorne* rolled from side to side in the raging ocean. Robert ordered the crewmen on deck to tighten the sails until the ship wheeled wildly to port to correct the heading.

Through curtains of heavy rain, Robert saw a flicker of light flash in the distance.

The Georgetown Harbor lighthouse.

The *Hawthorne* resisted the ship's wheel. Robert knew the boat had taken on too much water and another large wave would swamp the vessel.

"Abraham," he shouted. "Find Sherman and go below and man de pumps. Thomas, prepare to come about. We have to ride dis thing out. Won't never make it to the lighthouse in these seas."

The rigging groaned as Robert turned the ship away from land and into the waves. He fought against the wind and blinding rain to point the bow into the breakers. A gust hit the sails broadside and the ship heeled over on its starboard side. Robert grabbed the ship's wheel and held his breath. For a moment, the boat hung in a delicate balance as the masts almost touched the water. Gradually, The *Hawthorne* righted itself and plowed ahead against wave after wave.

Using every ounce of his strength, Robert kept the *Hawthorne* on course for another half hour before he felt the fury of the storm begin to abate. Small patches of sunlight broke through the clouds. The sea began to settle, and Robert exhaled a deep sigh of relief.

Abraham and Sherman emerged from the gangway and joined Robert at the helm. They looked at him with admiration as they slapped him on the back.

"Dat was a close call," said Abraham. "You done a good job. Captain gonna be proud of you."

"How de captain be?"

"He got a nasty cut on de head, but he be alive," said Abraham. "Us believes he be okay after while."

Two hours later, the *Hawthorne* tied up at Georgetown. Observers, lining the dock, looked surprised to see a black teenager at the helm rather than the well-known Capt. Simmons. Word began to spread that the captain was carried to shore and a young man, Robert Smalls, saved the ship and her crew.

* * *

For a year after his calm rescue of the *Hawthorne*, Robert trained as a helmsman under the patient tutelage of Simmons and the fleet's other captains. They marveled at Robert's innate ability to learn seamanship, and his near-photographic memory of the coastal estuaries and rivers he traveled upon.

Robert helped pilot Simmons' sidewheelers as far north as Conwayborough on the Waccamaw River and as far west as Society Hill on the Great Pee Dee. These river ports marked the furthest extent of Simmons' commercial operations. However, the biggest part of Simmons' business involved shipping freight between Charleston, Beaufort and Savannah.

From the great Winyah Bay to the Savannah River, Robert memorized almost every channel, underwater obstacle and shoal along the South Carolina and Georgia coasts. He learned to work the tides and avoid snags that lurked beneath the surface, waiting to damage the bottom of the boat. Most of Robert's experience came on two small sidewheelers, the *Commanche* and the *Edisto*.

Chapter 15

Charleston 1856

Robert had accumulated nearly $60 dollars in coins of various denominations and hid them in his mattress onboard the boat. He didn't spend much money on personal pleasures, with one notable exception—he liked to dress nicely. After he earned the position as a pilot, he had a dark blue uniform made, complete with a naval-style officer's hat. He kept himself clean-shaven, except for a well-groomed mustache. His appearance inspired respect from crew and, more importantly, the white men at ports.

Smalls had a fashionable suit he wore when docked in Charleston, a habit developed while he attended secret church services there. Religious gatherings, for blacks, had been banned in Charleston since an aborted slave uprising in 1822. Charleston officials hanged Denmark Vesey, a former slave who purchased his own freedom, and 35 others after they learned of a planned rebellion that encouraged slaves to execute their owners before they boarded a ship bound for Haiti. Two slaves, loyal to their masters, tipped off the authorities to the scheme. They arrested Vesey, the alleged ringleader, and 131 others before the plan could be fulfilled.

Outnumbered white citizens of Charleston, terrorized by the thought of the bloodbath described during Vesey's trial, formed a militia to patrol Charleston and prevent future uprisings. Authorities required slaves to wear a pass when traveling about the city. Church gatherings came under intense scrutiny, as white leaders believed the Vesey plot had been hatched in places of worship. The Seaman's Act of 1822 required foreign black sailors be put in the city jail for the period of time their ships were in port to keep them from participating in future plots.

Slaves attended white churches and continued to congregate in small numbers. The secret gatherings took place in homes and small public buildings out of sight of the white militia, which turned a blind eye if the number of blacks congregating in one place did not exceed a half-dozen people.

Lydia had instilled in Robert a love for Jesus. Saturday evenings and on Sunday in Beaufort, they joined other slaves in the balcony of the First Baptist Church of Beaufort for worship service, while white parishioners sat in pews on the ground floor. Despite the separation, together they sang favorite gospel hymns and listened to sermons given by a white preacher.

Most sermons shared a common refrain—ministers urged the black congregation to submit to the will of their masters. Using selected passages from the Bible, clergy admonished the slaves to be humble servants. A frequently-cited passage came from the book of *Timothy* in the New Testament.

All who are under the yoke as slaves are to regard their own masters as worthy of honor, so that that name of God our doctrine will not be spoken against.

For many slaves, the Biblical admonition held little meaning, but they took great solace from Christianity because it taught that they would be reunited in heaven with loved ones and be free from the shackles of bondage.

Robert attended services at a variety of churches when he had shore leave and with his gregarious nature, and stature as a riverboat pilot, he was invited to join several secret benevolent societies. These small groups of black men had to be cautious. Charleston law made it illegal for more than four black men to meet without the presence of a white man to oversee the discussions.

As his circle of friends grew, Robert increasingly came under the influence of two free black men, also teenagers. Francis Carozo and Alonzo Ransier befriended Robert at a church social and invited him to meet with the Brown Fellowship Society.

"Actually, our group is only open to free negroes of light complexion," Ransier explained, "But we have been watching you Robert since we heard about that incident in Georgetown. Folks around here admire that kind of pluck. Come on down to Worley's Hardware store tomorrow night. Like to hear more about you. You might find it interesting."

Intrigued by the offer, Robert agreed to attend.

* * *

Three candles on the fireplace mantel lit a small room at the back of Worley's Hardware when Robert arrived. Ransier stepped forward to welcome him. Fifteen other men, all well-dressed, turned to see their guest. An attractive black woman at the back of the room who attended to a pot of coffee and sliced pound cake into individual portions, glanced at Robert and smiled.

"Gentlemen I would like to present my good friend Robert Smalls," Carozo announced. "Robert has made quite a name for himself since arriving in Charleston five years ago. Word has it he's the best pilot in Charleston."

Robert shook hands with everyone and exchanged pleasantries, then found an empty seat as Ransier called the meeting to order. For more than an hour the group discussed an offer from the Catholic bishop of Charleston to buy a cemetery owned by the Brown Society for $500. Opinions split and after a lively discussion the men tabled the proposed sale until the next meeting. The group voted to give $25 to a family whose home had recently burned, then talked about conducting a fundraiser for a man injured while loading cargo on a ship.

"Let's take a break," suggested Ransier.

The men filtered to the table where the woman served refreshments.

Ransier sidled up next to Robert.

"Well, what do think of our society?"

"I think you are doing God's work."

"Yes, and we could do so much more if only we had the right to form our own churches," Alonzo interrupted. "White folks are so afraid of a slave revolt that they won't even think about it. Hell, getting sixteen of us together like this is illegal. Can't be more than four negroes together without a white chaperone you know."

He snorted in disgust.

A bang on the front door caused everyone to freeze.

"You niggers open the door!" a loud voice demanded.

Ransier darted across the room and snuffed out the candles with his fingers as a door at the back of the room opened. Men collided with chairs as they fled into the night.

Disoriented, Robert was rooted to the floor.

A delicate hand grabbed his arm and pulled him toward the door. A soft, feminine voice urged, "This way. Come with me now."

The dim light of the moon cast shadows in an alleyway. He followed the woman's dark shape away from the store and into a maze of backstreets. She ran sure-footed, with an occasional backward glance to see that Robert still followed.

She stopped and darted into a dark recess in a brick fence surrounding a tall building. She squeezed into the small space, pulling Robert in with her.

"Be quiet," she ordered.

The glow of a lantern neared, Robert wrapped his arms around the woman in a protective gesture.

He heard another man say, "Damned darkies gave us the slip. Bobby, you and Davie go that way see if you can find any tracks. Rest of us will

patrol King Street and the alleys. I'd love to get my hands on those
scheming bastards."

Robert exhaled as he heard the men walk away in the darkness. As the
tension eased from his body, he became aware of the woman in his arms.

"Thank you," he whispered.

"Don't move yet. "Dey might come back."

They remained in an embrace. Robert smelled the aroma of magnolia
blossoms in her hair. He felt the rise and fall of her bosom against his
chest. He cursed his body as it hardened against hers.

Silence filled the hiding place and several minutes passed before the
woman shifted away from him. She motioned for Robert to follow her.

"Do you have yo' pass?"

Robert felt for his necklace and patted the medal medallion hanging on
it.

"I'm okay. How 'bout you?"

"Yep," she whispered. "But dey will be looking for any black man they
see on a night like dis. Best not chance getting caught!"

Robert trailed the woman as she glided with certainty through the dark
streets of Charleston. On several occasions, they heard the voices of white
men patrolling the area and they hid in the shadows together. After a
series of twist and turns, they passed through a small wooden gate into the
yard behind a large house.

"Looks like massah still sleeping, I be afraid all dis fuss would have
got him up. Dis here's where I stay," she said, pointing to a cabin in back
of the big house. "Us be safe there 'til mornin' comes."

A pot-bellied stove cast soft glow over four beds in the room. Robert
saw the forms of people sleeping in three of them. A child-like figure slept
on a cot next to the unoccupied bed.

"Dat be Daffney, Hilda, and Marcus," said the woman. "'Dat little
thing over der be my daughter, Clara.

Don't know where her daddy be. Some say he in Savannah. Some say
he be dead."

"What's yo' name?"

"Hannah," she replied. "Us be slaves of Massa Kingsman and his missus."

One of the forms on the bed rolled over. "'Dat you Hannah?"

"Yep, jes me Marcus, you go on back to sleep now."

He rolled back on his side and snored softly.

Robert examined her face in the dim light.

She gave him a shy smile, her almond-colored eyes sparkled with mischief, as she removed the kerchief from her head. Black locks spilled over her shoulders and framed her delicate features. She had full lips, high cheekbones, and an upturned button of a nose.

Robert fought the urge to cup her face in his hands.

Hannah caressed his cheek with the back of her hand, then pulled away. She walked to a nearby cupboard to retrieve a blanket and spread it out near her bed.

"Robert," she said. "You sleep here. You be safe for de night."

He clasped her wrist.

"Hannah," he said, "Thank you again. I believe I would be in jail tonight instead of sleeping here had you not hidden me. I owe you so much. Has we met before? You called me by name."

Hannah shook her head. "No, I haven't had the pleasure of meeting you 'fore tonight but I knows a lot 'bout you Robert. I know people think of you as one of de best pilots in Charleston. I know you has many friends in Charleston who think highly of you. I know you be a Christian because I seen you many times attending worship services. Yes, I've had you in my eye fo' a long time Robert."

"And the meeting tonight. Why was you 'der?"

"Francis asked me to be 'der," she said. "He be my cousin on my mother's side. He free but I be a slave. But Francis always treated me like a free woman. We talk a bunch 'bout a South without slavery. We all be praying fo de day the abolitionists will take power and emancipate all of 'dose in bondage. I want to see' dat happen, Robert. Dat's why I be der."

She got into her bed and pulled a blanket to her chin.

"Der' be one mo' other reason I be der," she giggled.

"Why?"

"Cause I knew you be der."

* * *

The wonderful smell of bacon frying in a pan jarred Robert from a deep sleep. He opened one eye to see the origin of the aroma. Hannah and three fellow slaves huddled around the potbelly stove talking in subdued tones. The first light of dawn peeked through a window. Hannah gestured angrily at the man, whom Robert surmised was Marcus, before turning her attention to the frying pan.

"Mornin' everyone," Robert broke into the discussion.

All three turned to him in surprise.

"Good morning to you." Hannah smiled. "I wants you all to meet my friend Robert Smalls. He be a riverboat pilot.."

"How good a friends is you?" asked Marcus, a note of sarcasm in his voice.

"Shame on you, Marcus," replied Hannah. "Jes friends. We met fo' de first-time last night. Francis had us over to his place to talk about the missionary fundraiser and before we knows it the darkness set it. Thought it best fo' Robert stay here instead of on the street at night. You all knows how bad de patrollers has been lately."

The three clucked in agreement.

"Sho 'nuf getting crazy out dere," said Hilda. "All massah talk about dese days be de South goin' out on its own. If dat happen, he say South Carolina won't be part of the Union no mo'. He say dat will be a dark day for us black folks."

"It's already be a black day for us," said Hannah. "Maybe de Lawd have a hand in all this fuss. Might be it takes a mighty war to make things right. Dis I know. It's ain't right for one man to own another man. Even if he be black. Yep. We all best get ready for troublesome times."

Marcus growled, "If dis nigger don't get out of here soon de trouble be upon us a lot sooner than you might be expecting."

"Marcus be right. We need you to eat and be out of here 'fore massah gets to stirrin."

She motioned for Robert to sit at a small table and brought over a plate with eggs, bacon, and grits.

"I done told Hannah this," Robert said between bites, "but thank you greatly for letting me stay here last night. De patrollers was everywhere. I had my pass but dey could have given me a hard time just de same. I'll be out of here in just a bit. But thank you again for your hospitality. 'Specially you, Miss Hannah."

A few minutes later Robert slipped out the back door of the cabin and disappeared into the early morning fog.

* * *

The weeks that followed the meeting went by in a whirl. Hannah occupied most of Robert's free time and thoughts.

"Mr. Smalls done been hit by de love bug," teased Caroza.

It was true, Robert had fallen deeply in love with the beautiful young woman. They spent Saturday evenings at parties and Sundays, the two attended church. She sat on one side of the balcony reserved for black women while he sat on the side reserved for black men. After the service, they strolled along the docks and enjoyed picnics.

Hannah listened, spellbound, as Robert told her about his journeys to faraway places like Society Hill on the Great Pee Dee River, Georgetown, and the elegance of Savannah while working for John Simmons. He told her about the great storms he had encountered—the storm of 1853 nearly destroyed the fishing village of Murrells Inlet, washing away homes and destroyed plantations.

"De sailors coming off the ships after a long sea voyage pay top dollar fo' de produce I brings back from de plantations," he said. "I done saved up nearly $60 dollars. Got it tucked under my mattress on the boat."

"Aren't you afraid someone will take it?"

"No. There be no better men I know den my shipmates," he shook his head. "I trust dem with my life."

They talked about her job as a maid at a Charleston Hotel, the Mills House.

""Dey pays me $5 a month but I gives it all to my massah," she said. "Sometimes he lets me keeps a bit for myself."

"Master McKee hired me out for $20 a month to Mr. Simmons," said Robert. "But he lets me keep a dollar and I sends him the rest. Massah McKee always been good to me like dat."

Hannah's eyes widened.

"A dollar. Robert you be right well off!"

"Yeh, I guess for a man of color I be doin' okay," he laughed.

He took a deep breath and looked deeply into Hannah's eyes.

"In fact, Hannah, I been doing some figuring and I gots about everything a man could need 'ceptin' for one thing."

"What's that Robert?"

"I gots everything, but you. I love you Hannah. And, I wants to marry you. Will you have me?"

Tears filled her eyes as she wrapped her arms around his neck and kissed him fiercely.

"Robert," she hesitated. "Der be somethin' else you needin' to know before we goes any further."

Robert looked confused.

"Clara not de onliest child I has. I gots another daughter named Charlotte but she got sold two years ago by Massah Kingsman. I ain't seen her since den. Now the massah say he be sending Clara to his cousin next week to be her maid. So Clara be gone soon Robert. It just be you an me den."

Robert held her in his strong arms and stroked her hair.

"It ain't fair Robert dat a man can takes you chilluns away from you like dat,"

"Well, little girl, it sho' don't be fair. But Hannah, if'n you will have me, I'll be yours and you'll be mine."

* * *

Henry McKee sent his valet, George, to Charleston to pick up Robert and Hannah. They traveled to his home in Beaufort where the entire household greeted them.

Lydia took one look at Hannah and proclaimed to Robert, "You did good chile."

On Christmas eve, Master McKee officiated the nuptials at a makeshift altar in the parlor. After the bride and groom jumped the broom, they enjoyed a banquet lovingly prepared by Mrs. McKee and Lydia.

Raising a toast to his master, Robert's face broke into a broad smile.

"I never dreamed as a young boy dat one day Master McKee allow me to marry a wife in his own house," he said. "God blessed me with a good master and missus. You have been kind to me, and I always be grateful for all dey done for me. Thank you, momma, for loving me and raising me to be de man I is. And thank you, Hannah, for coming into my life."

A small negro band played and everyone in attendance, white and black, danced until midnight, united in their happiness for Robert and his new bride.

Chapter 16

In 1858, the Lord blessed Robert and Hannah with their first child, a girl named Elizabeth Lydia Smalls—Elizabeth for Mrs. McKee and Lydia for his mother. Robert's spirits soared when he made a trip home to Beaufort aboard the *Edisto* to share the news.

A small crowd of interested onlookers gathered at the cotton wharf when the steamboat docked with Robert at the helm. He smiled broadly as he surveyed the crowd but was disappointed that his mother and the McKees weren't amidst the crowd.

He secured the boat and requested permission to go ashore to visit with his mother and master.

"That will be fine," said Capt. McKeon, "but we will be shoving off for Port Royal at 18:00. Be sure you're back by then."

Robert whistled a happy tune as he walked to the corner of Cartaret Street. The McKees built a new house, much larger than the one on Prince Street where he was born. Along the way, he surprised several of his old friends and their eyes widened with awe at his uniform.

It was Robert's turn to be surprised when he rounded the corner and saw a large canopy in the McKee's front yard. Underneath, a table was covered with enough food to feed a village. Lydia stood at the gate, arms wide open, and Master and Mrs. McKee stood behind her, their eyes glowing with pride.

"I be so proud to see you," cried Lydia, as she hugged Robert and lifted him off his feet. "Can't believe my little boy be sailing dese big boats."

Robert shook Master McKee's hand and choked up when Mrs. McKee put a motherly arm around him. As he looked around, Robert saw a dozen other black men and women from the neighborhood, among them, a familiar red beard.

"Capt. Simmons," he intonated with glee. "What are you doing here, suh?"

McKee chuckled at Robert's bewildered expression. "Capt. Simmons wrote me a week ago that you would be in Beaufort," he explained. "He told us how pleased he is with you and we wanted to welcome you back home with a little party. We really are proud of you Robert. Capt. Simmons says you have the makings of a fine riverboat pilot."

Simmons, decked out in his captain's uniform, strolled over and joined the conversation.

"Why Robert," a mischievous laugh escaped between words, "I've never known you to be at a loss for words. Spend some time with your folks. The *Edisto* won't leave until tomorrow morning."

Robert enchanted the McKees, Lydia, and the guests with stories about the places he had seen and the experiences his life on the sea provided. Lydia grimaced when he recounted the terrible storm off Georgetown harbor and laughed as he talked about the South Carolina outback's country bumpkins.

Capt. Simmons left at dusk to sleep on the *Edisto* and after several more hours of conversation the McKees retired to the big house. Lydia and Robert walked to the kitchen behind the main house where she slept.

She fixed a cot for Robert and with motherly affection, she pulled the covers up around his neck. She paused on the edge of the bed, concern etched her face.

"Robert," tenderness in her voice coated the fear. "I so happy dat you found something in life dat makes you happy."

"Me, too," he replied. "Momma, I feel so alive when I pilot de boats. Capt. Simmons been mighty good to me. De other captains, too. And I gets along fine with de black men. De Lawd has certainly smiled 'pon me."

Lydia lowered her voice.

"Dey is something else Robert that worries all us colored folks in Beaufort. I hear dey be a lot of talk, 'specially in Charleston, dat de white folks in the South be mighty upset about the white folks living up Nawth. I even hear talk dat de white folks thinking about going out on der own and not being part of de Union no mo'."

"Yes, momma, I be hearing de same thing most everywhere us goes," said Robert. "I don't know all de 'ticulars but it has somethin' to do with de North folks not wantin' de white folks out west to take der slaves with 'em. And lot of de Southern folks be mighty upset about slaves runnin' away up North and dem not gettin' returned to 'em."

His thoughts turned to the conversation he had with Alex Rhinds as a young boy about the anti-slavery movement in the North.

"And one other thing," he said. "Der be a bunch of white folks callin' themselves abolitionist stirring de pot. Dey think slavery be a bad thing and dey want to do 'way with it. One of dem got de white folks in Monks Corner so mad dat they tarred and federred him and rode him out of town on a rail. Been hearing a lot about a fellow from up North called Abe Lincoln. Abolitionist think he be de right man for President, but all the white folks 'round here think he be de devil."

Lydia pursed her lips.

"Dese be troublesome times Robert," she warned. "Hear what I gots to say to you. Us blacks people has to be more careful den ebber to mind what we say to white folks. I wants you to jes keep your thoughts to yoself 'til all dis mess blow over. You jes mind yo' own business, steer the ship and do what Capt. Simmons say."

Robert nodded in agreement.

Lydia kissed him on the cheek. "Good night my good boy," she admired him a moment longer, then blew out the candle.

Chapter 17

Bucksport, S.C., September 1860

The steamboat glided effortlessly through the inky black water of the Waccamaw River. In the wheelhouse, Robert scanned the water for logs and other obstructions. He took care to stay in the middle of the river to avoid snags. Though a placid river, underwater obstacles made the Waccamaw a treacherous waterway to those unfamiliar with its many oxbow turns.

His excitement mounted with each bend in the river, even though the long supply run aboard the *Commanche* had been routine. The sternwheeler dropped off supplies to prosperous rice plantations along the southern part of the route. The crew loaded barrels of turpentine at Conwayborough, the northernmost point of the trip, as well as six passengers. At every stop, eager bands of people clamored for news about South Carolina's anticipated secession from the Union. The passengers spent hours debating the upcoming election and a long-legged scoundrel from Illinois named Abraham Lincoln.

Robert's excitement had nothing to do with politics. Soon, the steamboat would tie up at the Bucksport docks to take on firewood for the boilers. The next morning it would depart for Charleston, where he would join the crew of the *Planter*, a brand-new boat twice as large as the *Commanche*.

Alone in the pilot house, Robert hummed a happy tune. Sundown had always been his favorite time of day on the dark river. As the scorching September sun faded behind tall cypress trees, the soft light gave the river a mirror-like finish. Lush, green forests of tall pines and feathery cypress lined the water way and reflected onto its surface. The cool river helped the heat dissipate as the sun disappeared. Ducks zipped across the treetops looking for roosts. The steady splash of the paddle wheel spun at the stern and the throb of the engine added to Robert's serenity.

Nine years had passed since Henry McKee sent Robert to Charleston. Now 21, the boy had grown into a man with a reputation for being one of the best steamboat pilots in the South Carolina low country. Of medium height, Smalls cut a neat figure in his navy-blue uniform and naval hat. He had an athletic build, enhanced by years of loading ship cargo as a teenager, and intelligent, brown eyes. A neatly trimmed mustache and goatee accentuated strong, white teeth. He had learned while serving tables in Charleston that his smile charmed people and he used it to full advantage.

As the *Commanche* approached the evening's berth, Robert blew the steamship's whistle twice and saw a mixed collection of whites and blacks gather near the ship. Passengers on the boat waved from the promenade deck to acquaintances and prepared to disembark. Capt. Bob Daniels emerged from his cabin and took a position beside Robert.

"Did you rest okay?" asked Robert.

The elderly captain looked at him with tired blue eyes.

"No, I made the mistake of playing poker with John Holmes and a couple of other passengers and all they wanted to talk about was Abe Lincoln and taking South Carolina out of the Union," said Capt. Daniels. "Same damn talk we been hearing ever since we left Beaufort two weeks ago. I've about got a belly full of it."

Robert carefully guided the boat toward shore as Capt. Daniels bellowed orders to the deck hands. The black men prepared to lower the gangway into place as soon as the *Commanche* touched the pier. Passengers scurried ashore amid the captain's exhortations to be back aboard by sundown.

From his perch in the wheelhouse, Robert surveyed the scene. Bucksport fascinated him.

Thirty years earlier, Henry Buck of Bucksport, Maine, moved to South Carolina and purchased more than 20,000 acres of prime timberland on the banks of the Waccamaw River. He came in search of the towering pine trees and the virgin stands of gigantic cypress, both of which were in high demand by shipbuilders.

Since then, Buck had carved an empire out of the swamps and lush forests of pine, maple, and oak. A town, named in his honor, had sprung up and boasted a boarding house, turpentine mill, cotton gin, three restaurants and a large commissary owned by Buck. The New Englander operated the largest steam-powered mill in the South and shipped lumber internationally.

He brought Yankee craftsmen to help operate mills run from three plantations and purchased 300 slaves upon arrival. Robert learned the plantation owner not only built good lodging for his slaves, but paid them wages, something unheard of anywhere else. While this did little to endear him with other plantation owners on the Waccamaw River, black families working for him considered themselves blessed.

A tall, barrel-chested man stood on the dock and shouted through cupped hands, "Capt. Daniels, will you dine with me tonight?"

Daniels peered into the crowd and his eyes crinkled with delight.

"Mr. Buck, thank you kindly sir," he replied. "I'll be along soon as we get things settled on the boat."

"Delighted," replied Buck. "Bring your boy Robert with you. We have a lot to catch up on."

Robert and Buck formed a friendship after a raft of logs jammed in one of the broad oxbow bends further up the river. Without success, Buck and his crew worked to clear the jam. When the *Commanche* rounded a bend,

Robert obtained permission from Capt. Daniels, then offered to push the logjam with the boat. Buck quickly agreed.

Robert used the prow to move several key logs. With a splinter of encouragement, the jam freed itself and the logs floated dutifully toward Buck's Upper Mill Plantation. Since then, Buck made it a point to stop and speak to Robert whenever the *Commanche* was in port.

Buck's home was located on a bluff that overlooked the town. The men enjoyed a hearty meal of fried catfish, collard greens, grits, and cornbread before retiring to the parlor for cigars and polite conversation.

Robert marveled at the invitation—Buck was the only white man who had ever invited Robert to dine at his table. The young man wondered if all Northerners had the same disposition toward blacks, but Buck assured him that was not the case.

"Robert, there are white men in New England who hate blacks just as much as some Southerners," he explained. "I measure a man's worth by his character and I think highly of you. Living in the South, I must abide by local custom so I couldn't ask you to sit at my table with other white men. But I am glad to have you dine with me and men like Capt. Daniel in the privacy of my home."

Buck offered cigars to Robert and the captain before lighting his own stogie and exhaling a cloud of blue smoke.

"So, tell me captain, what happened in Charleston at the Democratic Party Convention? I hear they raised the roof."

"You heard correctly," said Daniels. "We weren't in port the whole time, but I've never seen folks in Charleston so mad. It all goes back to the mess in Kansas. Everyone thought President Buchannon and the Democrats would watch out for the slavery interests of the South but that little bantam, Stephen Douglas, has upset everything."

Daniels explained that Douglas, the lead candidate for the Democratic Party's nomination for President, had split the party into factions over his stance on slavery. As new territories joined the Union, Douglas favored the allowance of each to decide whether to allow slavery. That position was diametrically opposed by Southern factions, which felt the *Dredd Scott* decision issued by the U.S. Supreme Court had settled the matter when it affirmed the right of slave owners to transport slaves into the Western territories.

"The Northern Democrats," he continued, "agree with Douglas but the delegates from the South got so mad they walked out of the convention hall. The Democrats were forced to end the convention.

"They will reconvene in Baltimore in two weeks," the captain shook his head. "Most folks believe Douglas will get the nomination to run against that damned abolitionist Abraham Lincoln. If Lincoln is elected, Mr. Buck, that's the end of the Union. You can bet your bottom dollar on that."

"Yes, I concur with your opinion," said Buck. "It will be a sad day for the South. But the political situation has the people's blood up. What do you think about all this, Robert?"

Robert looked up, surprised that a white man would want his opinion. Everything about Henry Buck was different than Southern men.

He thought about his mother's admonition before he chose a response.

"Mr. Buck, what the white folks do or don't do ain't got much to do with me," he said. "Us black folks just have to go with the flow. There isn't much we can do one way or the other."

Buck eyed Robert pensively.

"I suppose you're right about that," he mused. "Slaves aren't going to have a say in how this conflict is settled. I wish you well Robert. But my advice to you is move North if the opportunity arises. There's a mighty big storm brewing. One you won't want to get caught up in."

Almost in unison, the three released a heavy sigh.

"Come on, Robert. We best be getting back to the ship," urged Daniels.

"Thank you for your hospitality and the meal," Robert shook hands with Buck. "I'll never forget you suh."

118

Chapter 18

Charleston Harbor, October 1860

John Ferguson maundered across the wheelhouse of the *Planter*. From his perch, he witnessed the waterfront come to life on the crisp October morning. Black men wiped sleepy eyes as they reported for duty on ships lined up at the Shem Creek docks. Whiffs of smoke wafted from the smokestacks, a signal they would soon be underway.

Ferguson pulled a watch from his pocket.

"Six o'clock. He should have been here by now," he growled.

A strong voice hailed from below.

"Capt. Ferguson! Permission to come aboard sir?" shouted Robert.

"Ahoy there," said Ferguson. "Get your gear on the boat. We're burning daylight!"

Robert leaped onto the *Planter*, making his way past crew to take his place in the wheelhouse. A large crowd of inquisitive observers, as well as a reporter from the *Charleston Mercury*, gawked as lanterns bathed the magnificent stark white, double-paddle wheeler in light.

At 147-feet long and a 30-foot beam, the side-wheeled *Planter* dwarfed the other ships moored at the dock. Her design specifications came from Ferguson's years of experience delivering cargo in shallow waterways. A marvel of engineering, fully loaded with more than 1,400 bales of cotton, the *Planter* drew no more than three feet, nine inches of water, which allowed her to navigate to almost any destination along the coast.

Ferguson worked with the designers to ensure speed and agility. Two independent paddle wheels gave the *Planter* a projected top speed of nearly nine knots, about 30-percent faster than any other boat in Charleston. The twin paddles worked independently, which allowed her to turn on its axis. In the tight confines of some rivers and creeks, this maneuverability would serve the ship well.

Her sturdy frame, built of live oak, gave the *Planter* great strength. Ferguson spared no expense; the bottom was sheathed in copper to protect against sea worms and barnacles. A working ship built to haul many types of cargo, there were also cabins for passengers, a cabin for the captain, berths for a nine-man crew, and a small galley. The wood-burning boilers meant it could resupply with fuel almost anywhere along the routes she sailed.

Cigar smoke and excited chatter greeted Robert when he opened the door to the wheelhouse. The *Planter* needed to pass its sea trials in Charleston Harbor before Ferguson took possession from the F.M. Jones Shipyard. Francis Jones, owner of the shipyard, Dupree Cagnon, an experienced steamboat pilot from New Orleans, and Captain Ferguson crowded into the small wheelhouse on the second deck, leaving little room for Robert.

"Gentlemen let me introduce you to Robert Smalls," announced Capt. Ferguson. "I got him from John Simmons a few weeks ago. He tells me Robert is one of the finest pilots on the coast."

Ferguson liked what he saw in his new wheelman. His friend, Capt. Simmons recommended Robert for the position soon after hearing about Ferguson's plans for the *Planter*.

"John, he's the finest pilot in South Carolina," Ferguson repeated Simmons's words. "I don't know how he does it, but he remembers everything. He can tell you every snag in every river between Savannah and Conwayborough. Every sandbar and shoal. He doesn't read much, but he can navigate with charts. Best of all he's cool under pressure. He's been in some tight spots during the time I've known him, but he works his way out of them. I don't know of any man who knows Charleston Harbor as well as Robert. That includes me, and you know how long I've been sailing these waters. You won't find a better man for the job."

Jones gave Robert a dismissive look but Cagnon, a large man with a fiery red beard, snorted with contempt.

"We won't be needing your darkie today," he growled.

Startled, Robert gave Capt. Ferguson a look of concern.

"I beg to differ, sir," Ferguson rebuked. "We must have Robert close by. I hired him to pilot this ship and he needs to be here for the trials. He may prove useful to you."

"It's your ship," replied Cagnon. "But damn if I'd put a darkie at the helm of my boat."

Robert said nothing and shifted toward the back of the wheelhouse. From there he maintained a vantage from which he could clearly see Cagnon.

"Watch this," said Cagnon.

He bellowed orders for the ship to be untied and pushed away from the dock.

With the *Planter* in the middle of Shem Creek, Cagnon signaled the engine room to reverse the starboard engine and engage the port engine. As the paddles spun in opposition directions, the *Planter* made a slow, majestic turn in the channel. Onlookers on shore shouted hurrahs and clapped while waving their hats to salute the feat.

With the bow pointed toward the entrance of Shem Creek, Cagnon relayed orders to the engine room for half-speed ahead and the beautiful white boat glided majestically into the main body of Charleston Harbor.

During a brief lull in the shouting of orders, Jones waved his arms expansively.

"I must say, Captain Ferguson, this is the finest boat my shipyard has had the pleasure of constructing. You won't find a better boat of its size on the water," said Jones. "This is exactly the kind of packet ship needed for these waters."

* * *

Robert joined the eight crewmen on the *Planter* two weeks prior. While the ship was being built, Ferguson scoured the Charleston docks for the best deck hands available. He selected three of his own slaves for the new crew. Alfred, who had served him well on other ships, became the engineer. His natural mechanical inclination could fix just about anything.

Stephen, an enormous black man with broad shoulders, worked alongside Alfred to fuel the wood-fired boilers. Four other black men, Melrose, Wexford, Gabriel and Abraham Jackson rounded out the crew.

Although he was the newest member of the crew, Robert had already forged friendships. From his experience on other packet ships, he realized Capt. Ferguson had assembled an excellent team for the new boat.

The *Planter* dwarfed Robert's previous ship assignments. Every day since first seeing her, he explored every nook and cranny. The impressive ship's hold, nearly ten-feet in depth, ran the length of the boat. However, the engine room amazed Robert the most.

Capt. Ferguson's design called for a state-of-the-art propulsion system. Two gigantic engines rotated enormous pistons that turned the paddle wheels on either side of the boat independently. A maze of pipes, dials, and gauges had to be carefully monitored by Alfred. The engineer spent days explaining the mechanics of the engines to Robert, whose curiosity for knowledge seemed insatiable.

"Robert, jes point de ship in the right direction and let me worry 'bout gettin' you der," laughed Alfred, as he watched Robert crawl over a drive wheel to get a better look at the starboard paddle wheel.

Robert smiled back.

"I've always believed de pilot should know his ship at least as good as de engineer," he said. "But don't worry, I won't be getting in yo' way

Alfred. I gots plenty to do topside to keep me busy. She be a beauty though, ain't she?"

Alfred nodded in agreement.

"Capt. Ferguson knew what he was doing when he designed her. And I'm glad to see de new pilot is curious about how things work 'round here."

* * *

On the open water of Charleston Harbor, Cagnon sent orders to the engine room to increase speed. The *Planter* slid through calm waters as the twin paddles churned rhythmically. Robert watched from the corner of the wheelhouse with great interest as Cagnon put the boat through its paces, alternating from a near crawl to full speed as rapidly as possible.

The *Planter* responded like a thoroughbred to the whip, bolting through the water when called upon. Great plumes of black smoke belched from her smokestack as the *Planter* answered the red-haired pilot's commands with ease.

At half speed, Cagnon piloted closer to the docks of Charleston. Crowds of interested spectators waved from shore as the ship passed by Castle Pinckney and toward the Battery. Cagnon signaled back by sounding the ship's great steam whistle.

"Let's take her out to sea and see how she does," Cagnon suggested to Capt. Ferguson.

He turned toward the harbor's mouth and signaled for full steam. The paddlewheels turned the ocean white with foam as it forged ahead. Robert watched as Fort Sumter loomed in the distance. The red, white, and blue of the United States flag waved proudly over the fort. Soldiers manning the ramparts saluted as she sped by.

"Let's take her out through the southern passage," Ferguson shouted above the engine's roar. "Then we can beat north and take her back in through the main shipping channel."

"Captain," Robert hesitated to voice his concern, "Might not be a good idea to take her too close to Lighthouse Inlet. De last big storm that came through moved de channel southward. I 'bout got de *Commanche* stuck on a sandbar last month."

"Tell your darkie not be to such a ninny." Cagnon disagreed with the assessment. "The boat will go anywhere I want to take her. There's nothing to be worried about."

The words barely left his mouth before the boat shuddered and came to an abrupt halt. The starboard paddle wheel kicked up a geyser of mud and sand. The portside paddlewheel continued to spin, driving the *Planter* firmly atop a shoal less than two feet under the water.

The impact threw the group of men against the glass enclosure of the wheelhouse. Capt. Ferguson slammed against Cagnon. The pilot's head hit the glass, hard, causing it to shatter. One of the shards sliced into the man's neck. Blood spurted from the wound.

As Capt. Ferguson and Jones tried to regain their feet, Robert sprang over the top of them and pulled Cagnon from the broken wheelhouse window. He put his hand over the wound to staunch the flow of blood.

"Captain give me your shirt," he commanded.

Capt. Ferguson returned a blank look before he peeled away his jacket and unbuttoned his shirt. He handed it to Robert, who took his hand off Cagnon's throat.

"Hold it der," he pointed to the wound.

Robert rose to assess the situation.

"Alfred, stop the engines!"

The command came too late. The engineer had already disengaged the port side engine, stopping the ship's forward motion. The piston that turned the starboard paddles cocked at an unnatural angle. Steam pouring out of broken pipes hissed angrily.

Robert burst into the engine room and realized the seriousness of the situation.

"We've got to get dat boiler out and release pressure," Alfred shouted above the ear-splitting sound of machinery.

124

Alfred provided instructions to Robert who turned valves on the boiler. Stephen struggled to remove wood from the boiler to a firebox.

"Something be blocking de main release valve on de boiler," he warned as fear painted his words. "She could blow at any moment."

Robert shimmied up the maze of pipes. He strained to see through the mist of steam and the darkness of the hold. Crawling higher, he traced the pipe leading from the top of the boiler.

The boiler clanked out its final warnings.

"Hurry Robert!"

Heat from the boilers and steam had made the ship's hold unbearably hot and perspiration dripped from Robert's body as he wormed through the maze of pipes in search of the release valve. He wiped away the sweat with the back of his hand. Through the haze, the turn handle came into focus. The lever had bent downward during the collision. Robert reached for the handle but recoiled in pain.

"Alfred, it's too hot to touch," he yelled. "Get me a wrench."

The engineer hurried to the ship's toolbox and rummaged through it before finding a large wrench. He tossed it to Robert who snagged it mid-flight. Through a cloud of steam Robert managed to lock the tool onto the bent handle. Using all his strength, he struggled to move the relief valve into its original position. He grunted as the handle bent upward.

"Got it," he shouted to Alfred. "Stand back from de boiler!"

With one last twist of the wrench he opened the relief valve and a shrieking noise filled the air as steam rushed through an emergency exhaust pipe. The throbbing of the engine ebbed and the starboard paddle wheel slowly ground to a halt.

Alfred and Stephen joined hands and danced in a circle as Robert extricated himself from the web of pipes. They slapped him on the back and hollered with relief when he joined them.

"You saved de ship," praised Alfred.

No," replied Robert. "Us all saved the ship."

He threw his arms around both of his shipmates.

"Now, let's get de hell out of here."

The three men climbed to the top deck in time to see Cagnon being carried out of the wheelhouse on a stretcher, his throat swaddled in clean bandages. The hurt man saw Robert, lifted his fingers in an awkward salute, and mouthed the words, "thank you."

Chapter 19

Back in drydock, workers scurried to repair the *Planter*. To Ferguson's relief, the damage was not as extensive as he feared. Within a week of the sea trials, the ship proved seaworthy and the captain proudly took possession from the builders.

News of the *Planter's* speed and maneuverability spread along the South Carolina coast. Goods of all types filled the ship's holds and Ferguson could not constrain a happy smile as he watched Robert navigate the nearby coastal ports.

Robert developed an attachment to the ship and its crew of skilled seamen. He loved the responsiveness of the *Planter* as he piloted the vessel through treacherous waters filled with submerged logs and hidden sandbars. The ship proved nimbler than any he had steered before and Robert marveled at its ability to rotate while hovering over one spot.

Capt. Ferguson frequently praised the pilot's quick action on the day of the sea trial. During many trips up and down the coast, Robert manned the wheelhouse by himself. The captain had complete confidence in Robert's ability to handle the ship.

His gregarious nature and ready smile endeared Robert with his black crewmates. At Alfred's suggestion, they called him "Mister Robert" in deference to his heroic actions to save the ship.

At ports, after unloading goods and putting new cargo on board, Robert and the crew spent time together over the evening meals. They sang familiar songs, mostly of a spiritual nature, and shared stories. They took delight in Robert's imitations of people they encountered at various ports and plantation landings.

They howled with glee when Robert poked his belly out as far as he could and strutted around the deck speaking in a Scottish burr that could easily have been mistaken for the captain's.

"It be a fine mess you made for ye'self' lads," said Robert, stroking an imaginary beard, "Ye blackguards toke me whiskey from me cabin. Ye'll ha've to account for this yet! Look in me face Alfred. Ho, ye little scoundrel! You impudent rogue. I know it be you who toke me whiskey 'cause you be de one dancin' like an arse."

During the day, they docked at numerous plantations dotting the rivers and bays on the coast to deliver supplies and pick up loads of cotton, corn, soybeans and turpentine to brokers in Charleston.

With Capt. Ferguson's approval, Robert began his own side business. He bartered with black slaves for fruit, produce, straw baskets of every size and description, and the occasional raccoon hide. In Charleston, the young entrepreneur enjoyed a brisk trade with sailors along the waterfront, street vendors, and restaurants.

Robert got permission from Hannah's master and Master McKee to rent two small rooms above a livery stable on East Bay Street in Charleston as the couple's first home. He struck a deal to clean the stables in lieu of rent. Although slave owners frowned upon the cohabitation of married slaves, Robert's reputation as a skilled riverboat pilot helped seal the deal.

Robert continued to pay $20 of his $21 monthly wages to McKee. Hannah paid the $5 she earned to her master but kept any extra money. She proved to be as industrious as her resourceful husband. Hannah, a gifted seamstress, altered clothes, darned socks, and took care of the innumerable demands of sailors either returning from long sea voyages or those getting ready to depart.

Hannah turned the dusty, cold rooms above the livery stable into a cozy home. She gave the apartment a good cleaning and happily went about the task of decorating it with colorful curtains, a worn, but still usable rug, and old furniture the hotel had thrown out. Robert contributed a potbelly stove and mattress he bought with his savings. They settled into their blissful life.

When Robert returned home after a weeklong trip to Camden, Hannah met him at the door of the apartment with tears streaming down her face.

He kissed her, "What's wrong?"

"I been waitin' all week to say dis. You gonna be a daddy Robert," she beamed.

Robert let the news sink in, then gathered Hannah and little Elizabeth in his arms.

"I sho' do hope it be a baby brudder," the child said as she jumped into Robert's arms and enveloped him and Hannah in a tight embrace.

* * *

Eight months later, Elizabeth nestled in bed between Robert and Hannah to get a better look at her new brother, Robert Jr.

As Robert watched the little girl play with the baby, a new concern popped into his head, and his lips quivered.

"What's wrong?"

"I don't know. 'Jes thinkin' 'bout these chilluns and you," he replied. "You and dem be de most important things in my life Hannah. We doin' okay. Got us some good massahs. But we still be slaves Hannah. And dem chilluns be slaves, too. If things got bad, you could be sold. You couldn't do nuthin' to keep Charlotte and Clara with you and der ain't a damn thing I could to save Elizabeth and Robert, Jr."

"Dat's 'jes the way things are baby," Hannah cooed.

"No. Der gots to be a better way," mused Robert. "I done save 'bout $300 dollars. I'm wondering if you massah might be willin' to sell you to me!"

Hannah stared at her husband.

"You want me to be yo' slave?"

"No. Dat not what I wants," said Robert. "If'n Massah Kingman agree to sell you, den you be free. And de chilluns be free, too."

Hannah cast a longing gaze at the children.

"Our chilluns be free?" her voice shook with emotion.

Robert took her in his arms.

"I will talk with Mr. Kingsman tomorrow," he stroked her hair and rocked her gently from side to side.

As promised, Robert visited Samuel Kingsman the following day. He stood nervously in front the white man's desk but spoke confidently about a business arrangement to buy his wife's freedom.

Kingsman, a plump man with graying hair, listened intently as Robert made his proposal.

"So, let me get this right," said Kingsman. "You want to buy Hannah for $500?"

"Yessuh," said Robert. "And de chilluns, too."

Kingsman clasped his hands and put them under his chin as he pondered Robert's request.

"Well Robert, you know Hannah is quite valuable to me. I thought I was being quite kind to her when I agreed for her to live with you at your own apartment."

"We certainly do appreciate dat," said Robert. "Mighty kind of you, suh."

"I don't see how I could possibly let her go for $500."

Robert's heart sank.

"But I tell you what Robert. If you can come up with $800, I believe we can strike a deal."

Tears sprang into Robert's eyes. He reached across the desk and offered his hand to Kingsman.

"Mistah Kingsman, us gots a deal," he managed to gasp.

Chapter 20

Charleston, March 1861

A few days after the secession of South Carolina December 20, 1860, Major Robert Anderson used the cover of darkness to move federal troops from Ft. Moultrie to Fort Sumter. The troops spiked the cannons and burned the cannon carriages before evacuation. The smoke from Fort Moultrie could be seen for miles, the indication of changes to come.

Throughout winter, Capt. Ferguson transported ammunition, guns, and troops. The *Planter* still took the occasional packet run to Camden and even went as far south as Savannah on a couple of trips. The ship was at sea on January 9th, when cadets from The Citadel fired upon the *Star of the West*, a federal ship loaded with provisions for the Union troops at Fort Sumter.

The months following the secession of South Carolina from the Union became a whirlwind of activity for the *Planter*.

When the *Planter* returned to port in February 1861, Charleston, once gentile, turned into an armed camp littered with tent cities, and grey-clad officers that roamed the streets as South Carolina mobilized its militia. The flag of the Confederacy flew over Moultrie, Fort Johnson, and Castle Pinckney. In opposition, the U.S. flag waved atop Fort Sumter as a reminder of what once was.

Ships of almost every size and description filled Charleston Harbor. The docks teemed with activity. The air was filled with frenetic energy as the white deck hands shouted at the black stevedores to load and unload the ships at a faster pace.

Newspapers blared headlines about Mississippi, Florida, Alabama, Georgia, Louisiana, and Texas as they joined South Carolina in secession. New editions of *The Courier* sold out at street corners before the ink had time to dry.

* * *

Robert supervised as the men unloaded bales of cotton. His heart sank as he watched Capt. Ferguson approach the dock, trailed by three Confederate officers, and board the *Planter*.

"Gather up boys," called Capt. Ferguson. "Got some news."

The workers formed a semi-circle around the captain and the newcomers.

"I received orders today that the Confederacy is commandeering the *Planter*. Effective today," he held up a piece of paper. "This is Capt. Relyea. He will introduce his men. You are now in the service of the Confederate States of America. I expect you to provide the same service to Capt. Relyea as you have given to me. I wish you well."

Ferguson shook Capt. Relyea's hand and disembarked.

"I've heard some good things about you boys and about the *Planter*," said the new captain. "Nothin's really changed 'ceptin we will be in charge from now on and we run a tight ship. That means every one of you will pull his weight or be put to use somewhere's else. Like pickin' cotton or somethin' along those lines."

Capt. Relyea, a man of medium height, broad chested and formal in bearing, strutted along the ship's deck, a suspicious stare eyed each crewman. His grey uniform had yellow stripes on the sleeves, signifying his rank as a naval captain, and a straw hat cocked to one side.

He pointed to the two other white men.

"This here is Lieutenant Samuel Smith, my first mate, and Chief Engineer Zerick Pitcher," he bellowed. "When they tell you to do something, it damn well better get done. We got a lot of work to do so get this cotton unloaded immediately. Anybody have questions?"

Robert hesitated before raising his hand.

"Who are you and what do you want?" barked Capt. Relyea.

"Robert Smalls, sir," in his most humble voice. "Been piloting the *Planter* since she was launched. Just wondering what it is you'd like me to do now."

He looked as Robert with interest.

"So, you're Smalls? Heard quite a bit about you. Ferguson says you are top notch. We'll see about that. For now, go on over with those other boys and get that damn cotton unloaded."

Life aboard the *Planter,* under the command of Capt. Relyea, took on a military demeanor. The crew didn't have to salute, but the new captain demanded strict obedience and very little idle talk. The crew was confined to the boat at all times except Saturday evenings and Sundays.

"I suppose you niggers need to spend some time with the Lawd," he drawled. "But if you hear this ship's whistle blow, you best be back within the hour or Lawd knows we will take it out on your hide."

Capt. Relyea frowned upon Robert's side business. Smalls' steady stream of coins from selling fresh vegetables and fruit dried up overnight, putting a strain on his and Hannah's plans. Robert was bothered by the decrease in income more so than being placed on the ship's labor detail.

Within a week of assuming command of the *Planter*, the new captain found it simpler to shout orders from the comfort of his chair while the black crew did the majority of the work. Robert resumed his position behind the wheel of the *Planter*. The oscillating engines presented too much of a challenge for the new engineer, so he joined the captain topside, while Aflred resumed operation of the engine room.

* * *

The month of April brought orders from Gen. Roswell Ripley to arm the *Planter* with cannons. When the South Carolina militia seized the federal arsenal in Charleston, Gen. Beauregard tasked Ripley with putting the procured weapons to use and the *Planter* was armed with a 24-pound Howitzer taken from the armory. It took a week to modify the aft deck of the ship to hold the big cannon and its wooden mount.

Earlier, federal troops spiked the touch-hole of a 32-pound, rifled cannon before Confederate soldiers could take Fort Moultrie, hoping to make it unusable. Confederate engineers repaired the piece within days of its capture and mounted the behemoth to the fore deck of the steam ship. Thus, the *Planter* became one of the most heavily-armed gunboats in Charleston Harbor. Despite the addition of the cannons, ammunition and powder, she remained as spry as ever. The ship could turn rapidly and bear fire on its target with ease. If necessary, the gunners could fire the fore cannon on a target, spin 180 degrees, and fire upon the same target with the aft mount. This resulted in the ship, now Gen. Ripley's official barge, stationed in front of his headquarters at the Charleston Battery for frequent trips to the Confederate forts protecting the harbor.

The situation at Fort Sumter became desperate for Anderson and his Union troops. The fort had not been resupplied in weeks, despite attempted negotiations from Gen. Beauregard under the white flag of truce. Anderson refused to accept terms, accepting starvation as a suitable alternative.

* * *

April 12th, Before dawn.

A gigantic blast awakened the crew. They rushed topside in time to see a ball of flame erupt over Fort Sumter. People streamed from nearby houses fronting the harbor, still dressed in their nightclothes. Some climbed to rooftops to get a better view.

"Believe it's started," said Alfred, who stood at Robert's side as more cannon balls erupted from nearby forts, streaking across the sky like comets before falling on Fort Sumter in a shower of fire and smoke. "The South's been spoilin' for a fight and now dey has it."

Fascinated by the pyrotechnics lighting Charleston Harbor, Robert grunted an assent.

"Yep," he said. "And it looks like we be right in the middle of it."

Shortly after the bombardment of Fort Sumter began, Capt. Relyea and his two officers returned to the ship in a high state of excitement. They whooped and hollered while patting the men on the back. Capt. Relyea even danced a jig.

"Fire up the boilers," he shouted with glee. "We need to be out of here within half an hour."

A shell fired from Fort Sumter sailed high over nearby Castle Pinkney, a reminder they needed to set sail as quickly as possible.

Throughout the night and into the next morning the *Planter* made slow, lazy turns through Charleston Harbor to avoid the crossfire between the Confederate forts and Fort Sumter. Clouds of acrid smoke occasionally blocked the morning sun.

The constant roar of artillery continued throughout the day. Despite the obvious danger, huge crowds lined the Charleston waterfront. Each time a shell exploded over Fort Sumter a roar of approval from the onlookers echoed in response.

From a vantage point in the harbor, the crew saw the fort take a direct hit. A pillar of black smoke signaled an intense fire burned within. The Confederate batteries at Fort Moultrie and Cumming's Point had been lobbing red-hot cannon balls against Yankee positions for several hours. The sky was littered with fiery projectiles in search of a target. The Confederates poured more than 2,000 rounds into Fort Sumter, yet, the Stars and Stripes flew proudly, though tattered and riddled with holes.

Relyea itched to get into the fight as he drew the *Planter* up to Gen. Ridley's headquarters. Orders came to join a flotilla near Fort Moultrie and participate in action against Fort Sumter. An artillery squad boarded to man the two cannons. From the wheelhouse, Robert watched in fascination as the Confederate soldiers prepared the ship's cannons for action, the first of the war for the boat.

The *Planter* set anchor near Fort Moultrie at a spot that provided excellent sight lines to Fort Sumter. The blast of the forward cannons rocked the steamship backward against its moorings. The shell arced toward the fort, hit the masonry siding and sent a shower of broken bricks into the air.

To his astonishment, Robert felt a sense of pride at the *Planter's* accomplishment.

Capt. Relyea growled, "Smalls, get your black ass down into the hold with the rest of the darkies. You're not needed up here anymore."

Robert spent the remainder of the bombardment seething with resentment.

"You can't let yourself get too upset Mr. Robert," Alfred looked around the gloomy confines of the ship's hold. "Dat's jes de way things is. No need to take it personal like. Dey treat all us black folks like dat. Jes cool yo' heels. Dey be needin' you soon enough and you be back on top steering dis boat."

Alfred's words proved prophetic.

* * *

"Time to get to work Robert," Capt. Relyea said curtly. "Just got orders that Gen. Ripley wants us back at the dock. I'm bettin' them Yanks will be raising a white flag shortly."

It had been over twenty-four hours since Robert was sent to the hold. He breathed the sea air, laced with sulfur and smoke, and steered the ship toward Accommodations Wharf. Ft. Sumter looked like a broken chimney in the distance. Black smoke billowed in a continuous stream from the once proud stronghold.

Must be hell in there. The fort cannot stand much more of this beating.

The once colossal flagpole, which supported the massive U.S. flag, had fallen. Capt Relyea laughed with glee when the tiny white flag went up on the fort's makeshift flagpole. Word came, early that afternoon, Anderson had officially surrendered the fort to Gen. Beauregard.

In celebration, Gen. Ripley and more than 200 Confederate soldiers streamed aboard the *Planter*. A small Army band followed and struck up a rousing rendition of *Dixie* as the boat sailed toward the beleaguered fortress. As they neared, cannon fire erupted. Relyea prepared to beat a hasty retreat, but Gen. Ripley placed a calm hand on his shoulder.

"Don't fret gentlemen," he told those on the bridge. "Gen. Beauregard gave permission for the fort's garrison to have a 100-gun salute, one of the few conditions of the surrender made by Anderson. It's the proper thing for us to do as victors. The men in that fort fought gallantly and bravely."

Capt. Relyea brought the *Planter* to a halt and for the next half hour those on board listened to the reports from the cannons. A loud boom interrupted the cadence and the salute ceased.

Gen. Ripley waited a few minutes, then ordered Relyea to bring them closer to the fort's dock. Although it had been damaged during the bombardment, the dock remained serviceable. The ranking Confederate cadre saluted a posted Union officer that led them inside the shattered fortress. A few minutes later, the remainder of the Confederate troops were ordered to disembark. Soon Union soldiers, many of them covered in soot from black powder, trickled out of Fort Sumter and onto the boat. Sixty in number, they all looked gloomy and dejected.

Maj. Anderson trailed his platoon, the battered United States flag, neatly folded in his arms. At the end of the gangplank, he turned toward the fort he and his men defended in the face of unbeatable odds and rendered a final salute.

"The salute was cut short," Gen. Ripley explained as he reboarded the ship. "Damn shame, too. No one died during this battle until one of the cannons being used in the salute misfired. Killed two Union soldiers. Well, it's done now. Let's get these men out of here."

The *Planter* backed away from the wharf and Robert carefully navigated the ship toward the mouth of Charleston Harbor, where a federal relief boat, the *Baltic*, awaited. An eerie silence filled the air as the crew and her captives steamed eastward. Neither the Union or Confederate soldiers said a word. The throb of the engines and splash of the paddle wheels were the only break in silence.

Robert stole a glance at Maj. Anderson. The tall, distinguished man looked tired, but resolute. The Union officer turned and stared into Robert's eyes. He saw a look of defiance that could not bid well for the Southern forces that had driven him from Fort Sumter. Anderson turned away and cast his gaze upon the Union ship just a few hundred yards away.

Chapter 21

President Lincoln ordered a blockade of Southern ports after Fort Sumter fell, so the race began to get as much cotton shipped out of Charleston as possible before Union ships arrived off the coast. The first few months of the War of Northern Aggression, as Southerners liked to call it, turned the old city into a sea of excited commotion. The docks teemed with workers, black and white, scurrying to offload ships arriving from foreign destinations. As fast as cargo could be unloaded, the ships were reloaded with bales of cotton, which towered in long rows along the waterfront. Ships of every size clogged the harbor at times, making navigation dangerous.

War correspondents from the North and from abroad filled hotels and boarding houses. Troops awaiting deployment by train to Richmond kept local brothels busy day and night. Money flowed like honey, keeping shopkeepers smiling.

Now a leased property of the Confederacy, the *Planter* assumed an entirely different role. It spent much of its time ferrying troops from one fort to another. The military installations around Charleston Harbor needed ammunition, black powder, and provisions, a task well-suited to the shallow-draft boat. Robert was the near-exclusive pilot and gained intimate knowledge of every fortification.

As summer approached, word of an impending naval invasion of Savannah by Union forces came from reliable sources: Northern newspapers. The North met a series of defeats during the early stages of the war. However, the U.S. Navy managed to block most of the South's ports from European trade. The blockades put a heavy burden on the South, which relied on the cotton trade for its war supplies.

"Won't be long now boys," Capt. Relyea released a victory shout for the Rebel win at Bull Run. "Dem Yanks is on the run."

To protect against invasion, Charleston Harbor bristled with artillery batteries. Gen. Ripley, who assumed command after Jefferson Davis promoted Gen. Beauregard, went a step further—he ordered engineers to place mines at the entrance of the harbor. Robert made a mental note of the placement as the *Planter* lined both entrances to the harbor with the explosive traps. Other than the Confederate sappers who anchored the mines to the bottom of the harbor, he had more knowledge of the safe shipping lanes than most men in Charleston.

Under Gen. Ripley's direction, Charleston presented a formidable defense against attack. Confederate flags flew over 15 batteries protecting the northern side of the harbor, including powerful Fort Moultrie. Fort Sumter anchored the southern harbor defense joined by Battery Wagner, Battery Gregg, and Fort Johnson. Another clutch of smaller batteries on the Charleston peninsula protected entrances to the Cooper River and Ashley River.

Forts Sumter and Moultrie served as the linchpins to the harbor's defense. Sailing a ship by them required an audible signal, usually a series of whistles or blasts of the ship's horn. In addition, soldiers stationed at the forts made a visual inspection of each ship as it entered or departed the harbor. As pilot, Robert got to know the various coded signals quite well.

* * *

Life for Robert and Hannah evolved into a rhythmic pattern. He worked from sunup to sundown on the *Planter*, staying aboard with the other black shipmates during the week. If in port, the crew went home half a day on Saturdays and most of the day on Sundays. During the brief time Robert had to spend with Hannah, they spoke little about the war.

Robert and Hannah continued to send wages to their respective masters. The small amount of money they were allowed to keep presented the young couple with challenges. Both resourceful, Hannah continued to earn a couple of dollars each month doing seamstress work for sailors and friends, while Robert secretly resumed his trade enterprise so he could buy Hannah's freedom. To date, Robert had $600 hidden under a floorboard in the apartment.

"Another year and you gonna be a free woman. Elizabeth and our new chile will be free, too," he beamed.

"I hope you're right honey," apprehensive, she forced a smile.

"What you worried 'bout?"

"I don't know. Maybe it 'jes be dis war," she sighed. "Who knows what gonna happen over de next year?"

"Capt. Relyea says the whole thing will be over by Christmas," Robert reassured.

"Yeh, lots of white folks at the hotel say dat, too," said Hannah. "Hope dey is right but my gut tells me it won't be so. If dem Yankees starts comin' dis way, what gonna happen to us black folks? It scare me what they might do."

Robert put his arms around her.

"Don't fret sugar. Everything's gonna be jes fine."

And, for a while, it was.

Chapter 22

Port Royal, November 1861

Capt. Relyea ran up the gangplank waving a newspaper to get the attention of his officers.

"It's all right here gentlemen," he howled, "The whole damn Yankee battle plan for the invasion."

The captain sat on a chair in the wheelhouse and read the article aloud, while Robert stayed as inconspicuous as possible in a corner of the pilot house.

The Courier laid out the top-secret invasion plan divulged by the Northern press. An article on the front page of *The New York Times* provided the full operation's order, down to the regimental level. The plan called for a combined ground and sea attack to two newly-constructed Confederate forts at the entrance to Port Royal Sound.

Robert's ears perked up at that announcement.

"Hey Smalls," said Capt Relyea. "Ain't you from that part of the country?"

Robert knew the area well. As a boy, he and Alex Rhinds sailed to Port Royal on his first trip on a boat. As pilot of the *Planter*, he regularly navigated the sound to deliver cargo to Beaufort.

"Yassah," Robert replied. "Born and bred right der in Beaufort."

"You know where those forts is?"

"I believe the one they call Fort Beauregard be on de north side of the sound on Phillips Island. Then they have a smaller one called Fort Walker down south of dat on Hilton Head Island," Robert recalled from a previous trip. "If dem Yanks tries to take Port Royal they'll have cannon comin' at 'em from both directions. That's 'bout all I know."

Robert withheld the gossip he heard from Lydia during his last trip to Beaufort—both of those forts were underpowered. Gen. Beauregard had given the opinion that the two forts could not defend Port Royal because of the distance separating them. The South Carolina governor said to build them anyway. Both were still under construction and unprepared to face the might of the Union fleet bearing down on them.

Capt. Relyea had just finished reading the rest of the newspaper report when four teams of mules pulled up the wharf hauling two cannons, casks of black powder, and cannon balls. A Confederate officer saluted the captain and handed over a leather, diplomatic pouch.

"We've got orders to reinforce Fort Walker immediately," Relyea said when he arrived back on board. "Smalls, see that those weapons are stored and prepare to get underway immediately. We're headed to Port Royal."

The *Planter* sailed throughout the night. When they arrived at noon the next day, news of the impending battle had already reached Fort Walker's defenders. Atop the fort, Confederate battle flags fluttered in a light breeze while gunnery crews fired targeting rounds.

The stevedores unloaded the cannons and transferred ammunition and black power to the fort. Morale among the Confederate soldiers seemed high, but Gen. Drayton, commander of the fort, had a look of deep concern stamped on his handsome face.

"I hope these cannons help," said Capt. Relyea.

"Perhaps a bit," Gen. Drayton looked at the fort, worry furrowed his brow. "The Yanks are sending 77 ships against us. We will give it a good fight, but I don't know how long we can hold out against such odds. I would suggest you get your boat and crew out of here as soon as possible. Could you possibly take some our sick soldiers to Beaufort?"

Capt. Relyea agreed, eager to assist with any aspect of the war effort.

Eight soldiers suffering from various ailments settled aboard the boat. The crew lifted the gangplank and Robert set a course for nearby Beaufort.

* * *

When the familiar church steeples and waterfront came into sight, his heart leapt with anticipation. With any luck, Robert would have a chance to see his mother and the McKees before heading back to Charleston.

Chaos ruled the Beaufort waterfront as the *Planter* approached. Word of the impending invasion had spread like wildlife and created panic among the population. Wagons and carriages clogged the streets. Residents loaded the wagons with all kinds of valuables: silverware, fine china, furniture, trunks of clothing, and even mattresses.

Some of the wagons tried to beat a hasty trail out of town, the drivers cursing those who got in their way. White men, accompanied by their wives and children, whipped their horses to keep the carriages close behind their household goods.

On the waterfront, crowds of people clamored to come aboard a fleet of small boats. Men waved fists full of dollars at the skippers, seeking safe passage from Beaufort.

With much swearing and threats of violence, Capt Relyea managed to squeeze the bow of the *Planter* against a wharf. Arming himself with pistols, he joined the ship's small contingent of soldiers at the gangplank. Several men tried to board the ship, but Capt. Relyea pointed his pistols at them, and they backed away.

Alfred ascended from the engine room, followed by Stephen, Melrose, and Gabriel. Robert joined them to gather the sick soldiers. and moved them off the ship. The ship's white crew made a path through the crowd so the party could make its way toward town.

A tall, thick-bearded Confederate officer met the party and pointed to a nearby house.

144

"We've acquisitioned it for a hospital in advance of the impending hostilities," the officer directed Capt. Relyea. "You may leave those men there."

They hastily carried the ill and injured into the makeshift hospital and returned just as fast to the waterfront.

"Stay together, men," the captain shouted over the pandemonium. "You niggers best stay close, too. We wouldn't want to lose anyone."

A familiar voice cried out from the crowd and Lydia rushed toward Capt. Relyea.

"Mr. Captain, I'm Robert's mama. So nice to see you sir, even if things be gotten crazy 'round here. Can I talk to him jes for a minute kind sir?"

"Where's your master?" growled Capt. Relyea.

"Oh, he done skedaddled," replied Lydia. "Him and all the rich white folks gettin' out of town lickety split. Massah McKee and his missus left two days ago. They say de whole Yankee fleet comin' down on Beaufort."

"And, they didn't take you with them?" He eyed her with suspicion.

"Oh no suh," said Lydia. "Not enough room in de wagon after they piled up all their belongins. They said dey come home after all dis foolishness be over. Bunch of us black folks be on our own now."

A look at the confusion on the streets of Beaufort confirmed Lydia's story for the captain.

"Okay, tag along with us. You and Robert can talk as we go back to the ship but make it snappy. We ain't got much time."

Lydia hurried to Robert who waited patiently for the exchange to end.

"Hey baby boy," she whispered in his ear and she engulfed him in a ferocious embrace. "You sho' be a sight for sore eyes. Look at you, all growed up. Quick now, how l'ill Lizzing and dat grand baby."

He laughed.

"Mama Elizabeth be doing fine. Robert be growin' like a weed."

"I can't wait to hold dat little thing in my arms," cooed Lydia.

"I hope that happens," Robert replied. "But the mos' important thing right now is you. You be okay? Do you has a place to stay? Shouldn't you be leaving town, too?"

"Don't you fret about me," she assured him. "The McKees gave me the keys to der house. Me and de rest of the staff staying there. Shucks, I 'spect der won't be a white face in Beaufort in a few hours. Dey all scare to death of dem damn Yankees."

"How about you mama? You not scared of the Yankees?"

"Lawd no," she enthused. "De way I looks at it, dem Yankees be bringin' salvation dis way. We been prayin' all our lives to be free and now the Lawd be answering our prayers. Hallelujah!"

The little contingent had reached the entrance to the dock and Capt. Relyea shouted orders to reboard the *Planter*.

Lydia put her arms around Robert.

"Son, you take good care of yourself and Hannah and doze little uns," she said. "Return home soon as you can. I be waitin' right here for you. And, son, don't be worrying about me. I be fine. Can't wait for dem Yankees to come marching into dis place. God be with you Robert. I love you son!"

She stood at the dock and waved her red bandana as the *Planter* backed into the harbor and faded from sight.

* * *

A storm forced the ship to seek shelter in one of the little coves not far from Fort Walker. The crew woke to a heavy fog that prevented the *Planter* from getting underway. About mid-morning, a stiff breeze lifted the fog.

As the veil raised, the crew gazed at the ocean in amazement at the entrance to Port Royal. The Union fleet filled the horizon.

"Holy shit," swore Capt. Relyea. "I didn't know there were that many battleships in the whole damn Yankee Navy. Get me my spyglass Robert."

Robert reached into a cabinet and retrieved the telescopic device for him.

As the captain scanned the armada, he called out the names of the ships.

"There's the *Susquehanna*, the *Mohican*, the *Seminole* and the *Pawnee*," he said. "Oh, I see Admiral DuPont's flagship now, the *Wabash*. They must have named all their ships after Indians. Hell, there's DuPont himself."

He passed the spyglass to Lt. Smith, who whistled softly to himself as he scanned the flotilla the North had sent to capture Port Royal.

"Now I know why Drayton was so worried," said Relyea. "That's a lot of firepower coming against those forts."

Even without the benefit of the spyglass, Robert could see the federal ships maneuver the steady wind to form a long line. As a group, the fleet sailed into the mouth of Port Royal Sound. Fiery blossoms of orange erupted from their guns and Robert traced the flight of the cannonballs as they arced toward the two Confederate forts. The sound of thunder rolled across the water separating the *Planter* from the action.

As the Union ships neared, the Confederate batteries opened fire. Masts came down on several of the battleships, but the entire fleet continued to press the attack. From the *Planter's* safe vantage, it appeared as if the Confederate forts held up well under the constant barrage.

"Their shells are going over the forts," Relyea noted.

The fleet passed between the two forts, then reversed course toward the ocean. When parallel with the coastal batteries, they opened fire, again with little effect.

One of the ships dropped out of the battle line and remained stationary at the southern end of Fort Walker. Turned broadside, it poured shells into a breach in the wall as Confederate soldiers scurried to defend the weak spot.

"That's not good," Relyea pointed his spyglass in the direction of the stationary ship. "They've found a hole in the wall and have already taken out two-gun positions. Hell, that's the *Pocahontas*. I believe her captain is Percy Drayton. He's Gen. Drayton's brother for heaven's sake."

Soon, other ships joined the productive assault on the fort by the *Pocahontas* as the Confederate gunners tried in vain to return fire. The battle continued for another hour before the faint sound of cheering came from the federal ships.

"Our boys are abandoning the fort," Relyea moaned.

"Robert, can you get us past those boats?" Fear replaced the sadness in his tone. "We need to get the hell out of here."

Port Royal, crisscrossed with islands and channels, offered several possible escape routes.

"Sure captain," he replied. "Jes give me a little time."

Under the cover of darkness, the *Planter* slipped past the enemy lines undetected and made its way back to Charleston.

Robert looked back toward Fort Walker, where hundreds of campfires dotted the shore.

Like it or not, the Yankees is here. I sure do hope mama's right about things working out for the best.

Chapter 23

New York City, December 1861

When Federal troops secured a foothold in the South in late November of 1861, wealthy businessmen in New York City positioned themselves to profit from the occupation of Beaufort and Hilton Head.

Better known as "white gold,' cotton grown on the Sea Islands, which stretches from John's Island near Charleston to the St. Mary's river near the Florida-Georgia border, carried a premium. A single pound sold for thirty-cents, almost double the price of inferior types of cotton grown elsewhere in the South. Manufacturers prized Sea Island cotton for its long strands, up to two inches in length, and the silky feel it gave to fabric. Until the blockade of Charleston Harbor, manufacturers in England had a virtual monopoly on the highly sought-after cotton variety.

With most of the Sea Islands under federal control, opportunity awaited those with vision.

William Reynolds couldn't stifle a smile as he surveyed the textile tycoons and cotton brokers gathered around the dining room at the exclusive Grosvenor Hotel in New York City. He tapped a fork gently against his wine glass.

"Gentlemen, I hope you have enjoyed your meal," he intoned above the hum of animated conversation filling the private dining room. "We have important business to discuss."

Conversations ended and curious faces turned toward Reynolds.

"As you have heard, our Army and Navy have earned a glorious victory against those in rebellion against the Union. Our forces now control all of the Sea Islands with the exception of parts of Edisto Island and Johns Island south of Charleston. It's only a matter of time before they also fall. We not only have a foothold in the South and a deep-water base of operations for the Navy, the Union now possesses more than 2,500,000 pounds of Sea Island cotton."

He paused to let the number sink into the minds of the men assembled.

"If I've done the math correctly, the government is sitting on $750,000 worth of the best cotton in the world!"

One of the men whistled softly in appreciation.

"I bet the mills in Manchester would pay a lot more than thirty-cents on the pound," he whispered to his companion.

Reynolds heard the comment.

"Ah, you're beginning to understand this picture," he said happily.

"As I see it, we have an opportunity to control the Sea Island cotton market for many years. We can use it in our own mills. We can sell it abroad. We can even do both. But this window for action is quite small. We must take steps immediately to secure our rights to this confiscated Rebel cotton."

A distinguished looking man asked in a loud voice, "What is it you need of us Reynolds? Doesn't this cotton belong to the government?"

Reynolds pretended to give deep thought to the questions before continuing.

"Does the government own the cotton? Absolutely, Mr. Whitton. "But it's useless sitting in warehouses or in the fields. I have been assured by my agents in Washington that Treasury Secretary Chase wants the cotton sold and disposed of as quickly as possible. I suspect strongly that we can purchase it below fair-market value. Furthermore, I'm told the government is in a quandary about what to do with the plantations and slaves that came with occupation of the Sea Islands. There's even more opportunity there, gentlemen."

The room erupted into loud shouts as men fought to be heard. Whitton stood and cleared his throat.

"Reynolds, I agree we have a wonderful opportunity to get this year's crop. I'm unsure about the remainder of your statement. Are you saying we could control future crops, too?"

"That's exactly what I propose Mr. Whitton. The Sea Island plantations are without their owners. The government certainly has no expertise in running cotton operations, but many in this room do. The right and proper thing for the government to do is allow us to lease and operate the plantations in order to help the war effort. And, once the war ends, as it most assuredly will, our leases will continue and assure a steady supply of Sea Island cotton for our mills and foreign customers."

The men around the table engaged in spirited conversation, making it difficult for Reynolds to be heard. He tapped on his wine glass.

"If I could have your attention again," he shouted, bringing focus to his position at the head of the table. "I have known all of you for many years. You know my background in manufacturing and in importing and exporting raw cotton as well as finished product. If you gentlemen would allow me the great honor of representing our interests in securing the Sea Island cotton, I would be pleased to offer my services."

He put his hand on the shoulder of a young man sitting to his right.

"Gov. Hague of New Jersey is personal friends with Secretary Chase. The secretary has asked the governor to suggest names of men with experience in our industry to be the supervising agent for the Treasury Department's interests at Port Royal. I don't believe I speak out of turn when I say you would be willing to put my name into nomination, governor?"

Sprague raised his glass of wine toward Reynolds as if offering a toast.

"Gentlemen, I can think of no better man for the job. I will be delighted to recommend Mr. Reynolds to Treasury Secretary Chase."

Applause erupted from those seated at the table and Reynolds received congratulatory claps on the back as the room slowly cleared.

Reynolds and Sprague were the only ones left behind.

The governor turned and whispered into Reynolds' ear, "You didn't tell them about the commission you will get from the government for selling the cotton."

Reynolds smiled.

"What they don't know won't hurt them," he chortled.

Chapter 24

Charleston, December 1861

As winter set in, the number of Union warships at the mouth of Charleston Harbor increased in number. Fast schooners slipped in and out of Charleston with little trouble. Their captains raked in enormous profits while Charleston merchants and customers grumbled about the high cost of basic necessities.

The *Planter* easily evaded Union warships and made regular runs to nearby ports carrying armaments and ammunition. As the ship returned from Georgetown, on Dec. 11, 1861, with a load of cotton, the crew spotted a red and orange glow on the horizon. Still six miles from Charleston, the officers made a of list of possible causes.

"It's definitely a fire," conjectured Capt. Relyea. "The Yanks must have attacked one of our forts."

He ordered the *Planter* to full speed.

The ship neared Charleston and the sky turned an angry crimson. Robert steered the *Planter* around a spit of land at the mouth of the harbor, heedless of a Union ship sailing in the ship's direction and headed toward the city.

To the crew's amazement, a great cauldron of fire consumed the heart of the city. Flames leaped high into the air and expansive, dark clouds billowed angrily into the night sky. Even from a great distance, the seamen felt the heat of the fire on their faces.

"Captain, we've got to get to de wharf. My wife and babies is there," Robert plead.

"Damn right," he agreed. "Get us there as quickly as possible, boy."

As the crew scrambled to make the ship ready for berth, Robert steered the *Planter* toward Accommodations Wharf at a reckless speed, ordering the engines to reverse at the last possible moment to stop its forward momentum. The bow bumped into the dock with a loud bang, Alfred disembarked with a haphazard jump to moor the ship.

Capt. Relyea's eyes shined from the light of the blaze. Without hesitation, he jumped off the ship and ran toward the flames.

"Secure the ship. Got to check on my family. But I will be back," he yelled as he ran.

The other two officers followed Relyea into the crowds on East Bay Street.

Robert stole a glance northward. The fire had not reached his little loft apartment, but the flames were spreading quickly. Alfred and the rest of the crew gathered around him on the foredeck.

"What we gonna do now?" asked Alfred.

"Do we still have steam?" Robert's mind was calculating risks.

"Fo' now."

"Good. You stay here with de boat. If that fire gets to de wharf, back de *Planter* out into the harbor to a safe distance. Can you do dat?"

Alfred gave Robert a confident look.

"Course I can, Mr. Robert. Ain't no problem. Now, you go check on doze chillun's of yours and Hannah. We be right here when you get back."

Robert ran toward the fire. Thoughts of Beaufort's invasion just a few weeks earlier dominated his thoughts as he elbowed through the crowd. People hauled belongings and furniture out of their homes and piled them onto carriages. Women and children cried, black servants scurried about in confusion, and men milled about, not sure what to do or where to go.

A huge wall of orange silhouetted the houses and a southerly wind skipped embers down the streets, setting little fires that bystanders attempted to stamp out.

Robert ran northward along East Bay Street toward his home. Many stores along Meeting Street were afire and a gang of black men passed pails of water from the harbor to extinguish the flames with no discernible effect.

Robert made a desperate sprint past a knot of gawking bystanders. He ran up a flight of stairs and burst into the loft above the stables. Light smoke filled the loft as he searched frantically from one room to the other—no Hannah, no children. His heart sank.

Robert paused, his mind raced with various places Hannah would seek refuge.

The Kingsman's home. She's gone to her master's house to be with Daffney and Marcus.

The Kingsmans lived on Tradd Street, about six blocks from where Robert stood. By skirting the southern edge of the firewall, he could be there in minutes. Robert raced downstairs and fought his way through throngs of people to reach his family.

The roar of the fire grew in intensity as Robert ran south on East Bay and turned west on Market Street. When he rounded the corner at Meeting Street, Robert saw the city's only steam fire engine pumping water onto the flames. Men struggled to move the heavy fire hoses into position. At first glance, he thought a company of slaves was manning the pumps—Robert discerned white men, covered with soot, alongside black men fighting the fire.

Flames licked the Charleston Hotel and the Charleston Theatre. Several familiar churches also blazed, their steeples lit like torches. With great relief, Robert saw the Kingsman house still stood and people milled about the lawn. Still a block away, flames shot through the windows of a nearby stately, three-story mansion.

A familiar face stood at the foot of the front staircase of the Kingsman home. Marcus looked up at the flames, tears streamed down his face.

"Lawdy, Lawdy," he sobbed. "I pray dat Jesus protect us. Dis be de onliest place I ever lived.

He turned and stared at Robert with a blank look before recognition lit his face.

"What you doin' here Mr. Robert," he said. "Hannah say you be in Georgetown."

Robert shook Marcus' shoulders.

"Never mind dat," he shouted above the noise of the fire. "Where is Hannah?"

Marcus pointed numbly toward the back of the house.

Robert sprinted toward a small group of people standing at the rear of the property. He saw about a dozen children, black and white, huddled together comforting one another.

Mrs. Kingsman stood with the children. She clasped a painting to her breast. Robert had seen it before. It was a portrait of Mr. Kingsman's grandfather, who had fought in the Revolutionary War.

"Mrs. Kingsman," Robert cried out. "Have you seen Hannah?"

"All is lost young man. We have given up hope of saving our home."

"But Hannah. Where is Hannah?" he begged.

"Robert!" Hannah's voice came from the house.

She ran toward him, her arms filled with silverware. She dropped the valuables and embraced him with passion.

"Oh my God, I was so worried about you. Are you alright?" Robert asked between kisses.

"Considerin' the circumstances, I be doin' jes fine." She sank into his arms.

"Where is Robert, Jr. and Elizabeth?"

She held Robert's arm and pulled him toward the children. Robert, Jr. lay on a blanket, sound asleep despite the chaos surrounding him. Robert cradled him in his arms. The baby opened his sleepy eyes and smiled before drifting back into a deep slumber. Hannah and Elizabeth put their arms around him.

"What we gonna do, Robert?"

"Where's Massah Kingsman?"

"He be with the other men fightin' dat fire."

Without thought of impropriety, Robert motioned for Mrs. Kingsman to join them. She came to where they stood, shaking with fear.

"Mrs. Kingsman, we must get you and the children away from here. My ship, the *Planter*, is docked at Accommodations Wharf. Hannah knows where it be. You and her must take these chilluns to de boat right now. Alfred will let you board and if the fire gets any closer to the *Planter*, he will take all of you into the harbor for safety. Do you think you can do that?"

She looked at Robert and nodded her head with uncertainty.

"Hannah will be your guide. Just do what she say."

Handing Robert Jr. to Hannah, Robert drew her close and whispered.

"Don't look back Hannah. Get Mrs. Kingsman and the children to the *Planter* as fast as you can. Look like de whole damn city going down."

"Ain't you coming with us?"

"No, my place be here. Every man be needed now."

Robert watched as Hannah led the little band toward East Bay Street and disappeared behind a cloud of smoke.

Another heavy gust of wind whipped the flames on Tradd Street higher. Robert shielded his eyes from the heat with his arms and peered between them. He saw the glimmering form of men a short distance away and he ran to join them.

"Where do you need me?" Robert asked the first man he met.

The man pointed toward to an older gentleman seated in the grass, his head cradled in his hands.

"That's Mr. Kingsman. Ask him."

Kingsman looked at Robert in recognition.

"Robert," he mewled. "It's the end of the world. This is God's judgement on Charleston for starting this damn war. Just look. All is lost."

The walls of flame approached their position, so Robert understood the man's despair.

The wooden buildings presented the biggest danger. They provided an almost inexhaustible supply of fuel to feed the fire. Their proximity to each other made it easy for the fire to jump from one structure to the next.

A thought came to Robert.

"Mr. Kingsman, can you give me three men? We may have a way to save your home," he yelled above the roar of the fire.

Robert explained his plan and hope flooded Kingsman's face and called for three black men to join them.

"Follow Robert and do whatever he says," Kingsman ordered.

He grabbed Robert by his shoulders.

"Hurry lad. We don't have much time."

Robert lead the three black men back to the *Planter*. Within 15 minutes, the men arrived at the wharf to push their way through the crowded pier.

Capt. Relyea was on board with his wife and two young children. Robert looked for Hannah but didn't see her.

Robert explained the situation to the captain.

"Sounds like a fool's errand, but get what you need, Smalls," urged the captain. "Go back in if you must, but I'm staying right here."

"Alfred," Robert shouted. "Have Abraham bring up three casks of gunpowder."

Robert ran to a storage box for the aft cannon and found a long roll of slow-burning fuse.

In less than a minute, the explosives were on deck. Each of the black men picked up a cask of gunpowder and hurried back toward Tradd Street.

Kingsman had several other men waiting for their return.

"We may have just enough time to make this work," Robert panted.

The Kingsman home remained unscathed, but the roof of the house next door was already on fire.

"You know you will lose that house?" Robert pointed to flames licking the adjacent house.

"It's already lost," Kingsman replied. "Hell, I own it. Go Robert. Lay the charges now."

Robert sent the six men assigned to him into the Kingsman residence with instructions to bring back as many blankets at they could find. Meanwhile, Kingsman formed a line of men into a bucket brigade. The men sent into the house came out carrying heaps of blankets. The men in the bucket line shifted toward Robert's position.

"Quickly," Robert shouted to his men. "Cover yourself with blankets and wrap those gunpowder casks in blankets too."

Kingsman ordered the men in the bucket line to douse the men with water, which was drawn from a nearby well. The cold water felt good against Robert's skin, but he didn't have time to revel in its coolness.

"Follow me, men," Robert ordered.

As the men neared the adjacent house, the heat from the fire became almost unbearable. Robert directed the men to the side of the house furthest from the Kingsman home and had them place the barrels of gunpowder at three brick foundation piers. Once in place, he motioned for them to leave. He didn't have to repeat himself.

Robert moved to connect each of the barrels with lengths of fuse. Steam emanated from the blankets protecting the gunpowder from heat. He had seconds before they detonated.

Robert lit the fuse and ran as fast as he could toward the Kingsman house. An enormous explosion ripped through the air and Robert felt a heavy hand punch him in the back. He sprawled in the grass, unable to breathe—everything went black.

When Robert gained to consciousness, he felt cold.

That's strange. I'm in hell and it's cold.

Gentle hands helped him sit upright.

"Robert? Are you okay?" Kingsman's words were soft.

"I think so," Robert replied.

He opened his eyes and saw a great heap of rubble where the home next to the Kingsman's once stood. Men doused it with buckets of water and dirt. He shivered and realized with a start that the concussion from the blast had stripped the clothing from his body. He stood and took inventory of himself. Everything remained in place.

A man rushed over with a blanket and wrapped it around Robert.

He stood beside Kingsman and watched anxiously as the fire reached the rubble of the demolished house. Flames tried to take hold but quick action by the bucket brigade extinguished the small pockets of fire before they could ignite.

The wind shifted and the tongues of the flames retreated.

"I believe you've done it," Kingsman thumped Robert on the back with great enthusiasm. "By God, you've done it."

Robert was exhausted. He could do little more than limp around the Kingsman house for the remainder of that horrible night, sore from being flung 15-feet in the air. Just before dawn, he collapsed on the front porch and fell into a deep sleep.

The smell of a wet dog roused Robert later that day and he tried to push the mutt away from his face. But it wasn't a dog he smelled. Opening his eyes, Robert saw a dense fog rise from the ashes of the once-majestic homes that lined Tradd Street. Tentacles of smoke curled from gray mounds of charred debris. A light rain fell to complete the scene of incredible devastation.

"Mr. Robert," Marcus exclaimed. "Nice to have you back with de livin'. Lawd knows it's been a long, dark night. But we still be here. And de house be safe, thanks to you."

Robert's body ached in places he didn't know could ache. He eased up and the events of the night before flooded back. With a start, Robert realized he hadn't checked on Hannah and the children.

"I got to get to de boat." He gathered the blanket around his body.

"Sho' nuf," said Marcus. "I 'spected dat be de case. Massah Kingsman say it be fine to give you some clothes from de house. Got some ham biscuits too. Knowed you would be hungry, Mr. Robert."

Robert was ravenous. He dressed, using a belt to tighten the too-large pants around his waist, grabbed two biscuits from Marcus, and started to hobble toward the *Planter*.

He joined a thin line of shell-shocked men and women walking slowly in a city ravaged by the previous night's fire. There wasn't much left to see. The old Circular Church no longer existed. Institute Hall, where the Ordinance of Secession had been ratified only a year before, was obliterated. Most of the businesses on Meeting Street had vanished.

Robert shuffled out of the line of survivors at Market Street and made his way toward the harbor. All the buildings that lined East Bay Street across from Accommodations Wharf were gone, consumed by the fire. He strained to see his home further north on East Bay, but misty smoke made it impossible to see if the stable still stood.

"That's him. Dat's my Robert," Hannah's excited shouting made him smile with relief.

Looking toward the *Planter*, Robert was relieved to see his wife and both children, Mrs. Kingsman, and the black crew of the *Planter* waving in his direction from the lower deck. Walking up the gangway, Robert fell into their loving arms.

* * *

The days that followed the great fire tested the resolve of the city's residents. The fire had consumed a mile-wide corridor of homes, businesses, and churches from one side of the peninsula to the other. The fire claimed a single life; a black servant who rushed back into a home to save her mistresses valuables.

Robert's apartment survived the fire. Soot covered everything and despite a stiff wind, the smell of burnt wood lingered for weeks. People poked about the ashes looking for anything of value that might be salvaged. There wasn't much to fish out of the sodden, gray mess left behind.

On Meeting Street, the Mills House still stood, saved by the heroic efforts of many. Gen. Ripley's headquarters and most of the businesses near Southern Wharf made it through the fire with little damage. The fire never threatened the Confederate forts protecting the city from assault.

Capt. Relyea formed a work crew to help with the cleanup efforts. The *Planter's* crewman joined other workers to clear the streets of burned out wagons and carriages. In a few spots, brick facades crashed into the streets, blocking traffic. Whites and blacks worked side-by- side to clear the debris.

Robert heard hooves clatter on the cobblestone street and turned to see Capt. Relyea snap to attention. A distinguished-looking Confederate officer, accompanied by two men dressed in suits, approached in a carriage. It stopped where the crew worked, and Capt. Relyea rendered a salute.

"Hello captain," the white-haired officer said. "How goes it?"

"Gen. Lee, Sir," responded Capt. Relyea. "We have a hell of a mess, as you can see. I believe half of the city has been lost, Sir. But don't you worry. We'll have this mess cleaned up 'fo long. And, yourself General. How are you?"

Gen. Robert E. Lee examined the grim scene.

"I've seen better days," he lamented. "Yes, much betta' days captain. This city suffered greatly. Thankfully, we have a merciful God who will see the people of Charleston through this dark time. Good people, like you Captain, must see that everything here is set right. The Charleston defenses remain strong. Do you agree?"

"Yes sir!" reassured Capt. Relyea. "Don't you fret about that Gen. Lee. Ain't nothin' coming through 'dat harbor 'cept the tide."

Gen. Lee chuckled.

"I believe you're right Captain. Well, carry on. We have much work before us."

Gen. Lee's carriage continued down Meeting Street, with an occasional stop to speak with others assisting in the relief effort. Gen. Lee was in Charleston to survey the city's defenses when the fire broke out. Soon after, he would become head of the Army of Northern Virginia. Robert knew he had been in the presence of a great man during that brief encounter on the ashen streets of Charleston.

* * *

Conditions in Charleston deteriorated further after the great fire and grumbles of discontent came from different directions. Hannah was frightened that her master would move from the city, taking his slaves with him.

Northern forces headquartered in Beaufort secured their foothold in South Carolina. Throughout the winter of 1862 reports of slaves slipping through Confederate lines to the federal forces in Beaufort escalated. Those who remained were under constant surveillance.

The ugly scar left by the fire changed Charleston and its inhabitants. A rumor swirled that two black men started the fire. The unfounded gossip put every black man under suspicion. Gangs of hastily-deputized men prowled the city at night arresting black men and women who didn't have a work pass. Capt. Relyea's mood became as dark as the ashes still piled in heaps around the downtown area.

"You damn darkies best not test me no mo'," he barked. "When we're tied up at this wharf, I don't want to see none of 'ya talking to sailors. Jes keep yo' mouths shut and keep yo' tongues from waggin'."

Robert understood the captain's concern. Much of the news about the world outside of Charleston came from sailors in port. That's how he learned about Gen. David Hunter, head of the Union army that occupied Beaufort. Sailors told Robert the general was an abolitionist.

"Word has it he is trying to form a black regiment," a sailor on a blockade-runner told him. "Would have had one already 'ceptin the folks in Washington ain't so keen on havin' black soldiers fighting white ones.

"They tell me hundreds of slaves are coming into the city every day," he continued. "The army is setting up tents for them and trying to take care of them best they can. All the white folks left. I hear there may be 10,000 negroes left behind just on Lady's Island. The Army don't know what to do with 'em."

Robert asked about his mother, Lydia.

"I was told she's keeping house for a bunch of Yankee officers that has taken up residence in the McKee house," replied the sailor.

Robert reveled in the news. His mother was free, as were thousands of his black brothers and sisters. The Yankees had a safe harbor less than 60-miles from Charleston. A beacon of light beckoned him.

Chapter 25

December 1861, Port Royal

Young, handsome, and energetic, Edward L. Pierce, 33, spurred his horse into a gallop. He had less than an hour to get from Ashedale Plantation on Lady's Island to Port Royal for an important meeting with Gen. W.T. Sherman and Commodore Samuel DuPont.

Since arriving in Port Royal Dec. 20th, Pierce had been busy visiting plantations in the vicinity, to take a census of slaves and observe the living conditions of the black men and women left behind. He would report back with recommendations for handling the 10,000 abandoned slaves looking to the "Linkum sojers" for help.

Pierce showed an ability to work closely with freed black men earlier in the year when Federal forces captured Fort Monroe in northern Virginia. Several thousand black slaves were captured during the battle. Pierce, a private at the time, volunteered to organize the blacks and supervise them in the construction of trenches for Union lines.

It had been a week since Pierce landed at Port Royal with orders from Secretary Treasurer Salmon Chase. Pierce saw a chance to prove to the North, and curious observers in Europe, that negros would not be a scourge if turned loose on white society.

A rather radical idea formed as he rode through the majestic live oak trees:

Commodore DuPont had invited Pierce to join him, Gen. Sherman and other high-ranking officers aboard his flagship, the *Wabash*, for Christmas dinner. As the appointed hour neared, Pierce arrived at the Lady's Island dock where a longboat crew ferried him across the bay.

A ship's bell sounded as Pierced climbed the rope ladder. He brushed himself off, returned the salute of a young sailor, and followed the lad to the Commodore's quarters.

"Hello gentlemen, I hope I have not kept you waiting." Pierce entered the room where the officers were already seated.

Commodore DuPont looked dashing in full dress uniform. He sat at one end of the long table and Gen. Sherman, decked in gold braid, occupied the other end.

"So you've been out taking stock of the darkies, eh?" asked Sherman.

"Yes sir. It has been an amazing experience. I never imagined how wealthy our Southern neighbors were. Some of the homes are simply magnificent. I observed only a few of them had been vandalized. Quite surprising to me."

DuPont signaled for the stewards to begin serving the meal.

"I'll have to say Gen. Sherman's men have been diligent about protecting the property of the plantation owners who left," said DuPont. "The general even offered to allow them to come back without any fear of punishment. Quite generous, I'd say.

"Yes, and not the first one took me up on the offer," growled Sherman. "If I had my way, I would put every one of their homes to the torch. Teach them the meaning of war."

Several of the Amy officers murmured agreement.

DuPont slipped Pierce a reassuring look.

"I don't think it will come to that General," said the commodore. "But we do have some serious problems that must be dealt with before they get out of hand."

"For example?" asked Pierce.

DuPont put his fork down.

"My heart goes out to these people. Shortly after we took Fort Walker on Hilton Head and Fort Beauregard at Bay Point, black refugees began arriving at our camps almost starving and in some cases nearly naked. As you may know, plantation field workers were only issued two sets of clothes a year, both of inferior quality. They are made of such wretched homespun material that they do not hold for the year. And we came before the fall issue of clothing."

The commodore said he found that there was little internal order on most of the plantations. There were no ordained ministers for the negros and no doctors.

"They have no place to turn except for the Army camps," said DuPont.

"We have had about 320 come in so far and offered their services to the Army," said Sherman. "I'd say about sixty out of that number are able-bodied men. The rest are just decrepit old men, women, and children. And for every able-bodied male there are five to six females and children to burden my outfit."

He gave a snort of disgust.

The commodore rose from the table and walked over to cabin window, looking out pensively at the sea. He turned back to the table and his eyes locked with Pierce's.

"As I see things young man, we have an obligation to these people. We came as conquerors but did not have the authority to give them their freedom. Since they cannot fend for themselves, we have an imperative call to provide for their physical needs. They are suffering through no fault of their own. This Army, this Navy and the people of the North owe it to the black race inhabiting these islands that their condition will not be the worse for our invasion."

He sat down and silence filled the room. A naval lieutenant with rose-colored cheeks jumped to his feet.

"It's Christmas day. Let's turn our thoughts to happier things." He broke out into a jolly rendition of "We Wish You a Merry Christmas."

Stewards brought in more jugs of ale and talk soon turned to the women the men left behind and how the war could best be won.

* * *

On New Year's Day, Pierce invited an assorted assembly of black men to meet with him in the parlor of a small plantation house on Kiawah Island. The home appeared untouched after the owners fled inland. A warm fire beat back the chill of the cold, January day.

To understand the plight of the black population better, Pierce invited the plantation foreman, his driver, the carpenter, and two field hands to the conference. The first two lounged comfortably in two overstuffed armchairs, but the carpenter and field laborers fidgeted nervously, their eyes darting about the room

"We ain't never been in de big house 'fo this," explained one of the field hands named Jake. "Dis here be one fine place Massuh Pierce."

"You don't have to call me massah. Your masters have left and now you are in the keeping of the Army."

"What you be wantin' usuns to call you den?"

"Why don't you just call me Mister Pierce."

The five black men looked at each other apprehensively.

"We jes call you Missah Pierce den," said the foreman. The others nodded their heads in agreement.

Pierce smiled. *There isn't much distinction between massah and missah.*

"So, tell me Leroy, what is involved in growing this Sea Island cotton?" He pointed to the foreman.

Leroy explained the process began in February when great loads of manure were applied to the cotton fields to fertilize the crop. Planting began in late March and continued through April. The seeds were placed in raised beds about a foot apart. After the plants had grown a few inches tall, they were thinned. The cotton plants were cultivated with hoes and plows during May, June, and July to keep the weeds out. Harvest began in

168

late August and the cotton was left in the sun to dry before being sent to the cotton gins.

"Ginnin' on this plantation was done with foot gins," said Leroy.

"Every slave can gin about 30 pounds of cotton a day with the foot gin. Some folks has dem steam engine gins dat can turn out 800 pounds ever' day. Once we get a load of cotton, we puts it on de long boat and send it on down to Beaufort. Dey sez it goes on up to Charleston from der."

"How many slaves remained on the plantation?"

"Us usually be about 80 black folks, countin' the womens. Probly 25 little 'uns ain't fit yet to work in fields, Missah Pierce. Some of the men folks be missin' at de moment. Dey is off lookin' for der wives and der chillluns but I 'spect dey be coming back for long to get der rations."

"Dat's right Missah Pierce. All dem niggers come runnin', come time to get der rations. I keeps de key to de larder 'roun my neck on a chain," said Benjamin, a huge, jet-black man designated as driver of the slaves. "All de people get one peck of corn a week 'ceptin the chilluns. Dey get one-fourth a peck. 'Bout once a month dey get some pork, but not lately 'cause dem Lincom sojers come an take all de livestock with 'em. We got's enough corn and molasses to last 'bout one more month. But we ain't go no salt Missah Pierce. And people gots to have der salt. That bein' de thing usuns need de most ... fo sure."

Pierce asked each of the men how they felt about freedom. Leroy, Benjamin, and Noah, the plantation carpenter, expressed excitement about the prospect of being free men.

"We miss our massah. He be mighty good to us niggers," said Jasper, the taller and thinner of the two. He avoided eye contact with Pierce and bowed his head submissively. "He lot betta den some of dem mean massahs down de road from here. I guess it don't matter much if we be free or not. De white man do what he pleases with us. We yours now massah Pierce ... I mean missah Pierce."

Pierce looked pensively at the small group. This wasn't the first time he had heard these kinds of thoughts from blacks. Freedom rarely caused great passion in them. The secluded and monotonous life of a plantation, with its strict discipline and ignorance, had left them with little, if any, self-worth. Even black men in positions of power felt helpless in the company of white men.

Benjamin had explained to Pierce that disciplining the men on the plantation had become more difficult because there was not a white overseer to back up his commands.

Noah timidly raised his hand.

"Missah Pierce, der be something I wish mightily for my chilluns," he said.

"What's that?"

"If Missah Lincon could send some peoples here and teach our chilluns to read and cipher numbers, dat be 'bout the best gift he could send us po' black souls. Dat's what I think Missah Pierce. Dat's what make my ol' heart soar like a hawk."

Chapter 26

Port Royal, March 1862

Mansfield French, minister and leader of the Gideonites, leaned over the railing of the *Atlantic* steamer as it neared the entrance to Port Royal sound. He couldn't believe all that Pierce and the others accomplished in eight short weeks.

Pierce's report to Secretary Chase outlining the conditions of blacks living on the Sea Islands was published in Northern newspapers. The piece fanned public opinion for emancipation to new heights. New York, Boston, and Philadelphia buzzed with excitement when citizens heard of Pierce's proposal to begin a grand experiment in Port Royal. They sought to create a model society of black people using a guided transition to freedom and citizenship.

If the endeavor at Port Royal, where slaves had lived in isolation and ignorance for generations, succeeded, then it could be implanted elsewhere in the South as the flag of the Union advanced.

Pierce found his abolitionist friends in Boston eager to participate. In New York, French told about the desperate situation the Sea Island colored population faced. They stressed the importance of meeting the physical needs of the former slaves and asked for clothing, food, and farm implements. The National Freedmen's Relief Association sent out a call for suitable teachers to instruct the freedmen in industrial and mechanical arts, in the rudiments of education, and the Word of God.

Everything came together with lightning speed. Now, only eight weeks after Pierce and French first met at Port Royal, they were back, bringing with them missionaries, teachers, nurses, and highly skilled craftsmen instilled with a God-given mission to lead the former slaves to self-reliant citizenship.

Two hours before the *Atlantic* docked, Pierce asked Mansfield to bring the men and women to the ship's deck—forty-two men and twelve women.

The minister looked with pride and humility at the faces of the volunteers of this great experiment. They were young, full of good intentions, and excited to go about their work.

"Ours is, indeed, a new, untried mission. The final results of which may decide the fate of the poor slaves of the nation. To do our work, and do it properly, requires such wisdom as only God can give," instructed French. "You will find the negros of the plantations, in some cases, idle and roaming about—husbands searching for wives, parents for their children. We must make allowances for them as we go about this sacred work.

"They will receive you as friends, but they will not only carefully weigh your words and action, but they will try your spirit. They are sensitive, acute observers, and readily distinguish between a patronizing friend and a real one," he continued. "To have an influence over them, you must first convince them that yours is a brother's hand and heart. First prove to them that their interests are yours, and you will acquire power to elevate and improve them."

The volunteers applauded the two leaders, then kneeled for prayers and hymns before going below to make final preparations for departure at Port Royal.

Pierce turned to French and gave him a quizzical look.

"Do you think they can do it?"

"I'm excited about the possibilities but we have much to overcome Edward. I fear that some of them have come with the honest intent to do good work, but they will find it difficult to adapt to this new environment. We must endeavor to encourage them. They will meet many challenges and obstacles dealing with the colored race. We must show them that progress can only be made when they learn from their failures."

The two men embraced. Then they, too, went below to prepare for the start of the "Port Royal Experiment."

Chapter 27

Charleston, March 1862

On a cool winter day in March of 1862, Capt. Relyea ordered the black crew to stay aboard the *Planter* while he and the officers went into the city. The captain confined the black workers more often since the fire. Disappointment brewed among the crew who had families waiting at home.

After supper, the black men gathered to smoke pipes and enjoy the absence of the white men. Abraham played a ditty on his harmonica while Alfred danced a jig. All laughed at the sight of the big man high-stepping around the deck.

On an impulse Robert grabbed the straw hat, Capt. Relyea left lying on a bale of cotton, and put it on his head.

He puffed out his chest and began to strut around the little group of men.

"Now listen here you niggers," Robert tried his best to imitate Capt. Relyea's Southern drawl. "'bout had enough of y'all lollygaggin' around dis here boat. Won't stand for it no mo'. No sir, it jes won't do. Yo' be the laziest bunch of ninnies I ever seen. Got half a notion to keel haul de whole lot of ya."

"Capt. Relyea," laughed Alred, "You know you has de best crew of niggers in Charleston. Admit it."

"Won't do no sech thing," Robert mocked. "Hell, truth be knowed, you probably de ones dat set that der fire."

They all laughed.

Alfred pondered, "You know somethin'? In de darkness with you wearing dat hat, damn if you couldn't pass for Capt. Relyea hisself."

Robert stopped his antics and froze in place.

"What you mean by that?"

"I jes saying," explained Alfred, "In the gloom of de night you look jes like the captain. Same height. About the same body size. Put dat hat on you and you is de spittin' image of him."

Robert flung the hat off and threw it on a bale of cotton.

"Last thing I want to look like be Capt. Relyea," he laughed.

But Alfred's comment planted a seed in Robert's mind.

* * *

The number of Union patrol ships grew since the invasion of Beaufort and Port Royal. The number of runners making it through the blockade dwindled to just one or two a week.

The week before Christmas, 1861, Alfred roused Robert from his berth on the *Planter*.

"Gotta' see this Mr. Robert," he hissed.

Robert dressed quickly and went to the pilot house where Capt. Relyea and Lt. Smith peered through spyglasses at the entrance of the harbor.

"What the hell you think they doin'," growled Capt. Relyea.

"Damn if I know," said Smith. "But that's a lot of damn ships they've brought with them."

Without the benefit of the spyglass, Robert watched as a dozen ships sailed toward the mouth of Charleston Harbor. Gun batteries from Fort Sumter and Fort Moultrie lobbed shells toward the intruders.

"Well I'll be damn," said Capt. Relyea. "Looks to me like they are scuttling their own ships."

The forts ceased fire as it became obvious the ships were being sunk at the mouth of the harbor by the Union forces.

Throughout the morning ship after ship settled to the bottom of the harbor. Their masts and spars poked out of the water forming a forest in the middle of the channel. As unbelievable as it seemed, the Union forces had sunk their own ships to stop navigation of Confederate ships into, or out of, Charleston.

"Damnable thing to do, "muttered Capt. Relyea.

The sunken Northern fleet was de-masted by waves within a week. A month later, a series of storms broke up the so-called *stone fleet*—old whalers filled with stone and dirt. The runners bypassed the blockade through the southern channel until Mother Nature cleared the rest.

Capt. Relyea was so delighted by the failure of the federal's efforts to block the harbor that he gave the crew liberty to go ashore. After tying up at Southern Wharf, Robert made a beeline to his home. The progress of cleaning up the charred city remained slow. The streets had been cleared allowing for the movement of traffic to the various loading docks lining East Bay Street. A scaffold had been erected at the North church, but for the most part heaps of burnt timbers and ash still marked the area of downtown ravaged by the fire.

At the bottom of the rickety, wooden stairs Robert smelled the aroma of bacon cooking.

Hannah is home.

Hannah stood at the kitchen stove. She cooked with one arm and held Robert Jr. in the other. At the squeaking of the door, she turned in surprise, and burst into tears. She set the child on the floor and ran into Robert's welcoming arms.

"Oh, baby," she cried, "It be so good to see you. I've missed you so much."

"I missed you too, darling," Robert he squeezed her hard and gave her a kiss. "How's my girl?"

176

Robert unfolded Hannah's arms from around his neck and walked over to where Elizabeth sat. The little girl looked up in wonder at this familiar man in the house. Robert picked her up and held her in his arms, surprised at how much she had changed over the past few months.

A little hand stroked Robert's face.

"Hi Pappy," the four-year-old girl said.

It felt good to be home. Robert enjoyed the company of his crewmates. He loved piloting the *Planter*, but none of that compared to the happiness he felt watching Hannah while he frolicked on the floor with his little girl.

After supper, Hannah put Elizabeth down with Robert, Jr. for the night. Robert washed and went to bed. Hannah slipped behind the burlap curtain separating the bedroom from the rest of the apartment. She hummed a gospel song as she prepared for bed. A candle on the nightstand cast shadows from behind the curtain, silhouetting her body.

With a giggle, she rushed from behind the curtain, jumped into the bed, pulled the covers over herself and snuggled up against him.

They spoke in muted tones, so as not to awaken the baby and Elizabeth. The couple lay in silence for a few moments. Then Hannah turned her face to Robert and stroked his cheek.

"Robert, I be worried about some things."

"Tell me what be bothering you, honey."

"Since de fire, things has changed in Charleston," said Hannah. "Lots of families lost everything, their homes, their possessions and their businesses. Lots of folks don't know how dey gonna make it. Last week, Mr. Kingsman's friend, Mr. Howell, say he be leaving town. His store burned to the ground. He had a slave merchant meet him where his house used to be and he sold 10 of his slaves dat very mornin'. One of 'em be my friend Daisy. She had three chillun's at her side and dat slave man chained them all together and marched 'em off to I don't know where. Most everyone I talk to say dey will most likely be goin' to Georgia or Alabama.

"Mr. Howell not the onliest one. Lots of slaves being sold by white folks needin' de money."

"Has Mr. Kingsman said anything about you and Jacob and the rest of his servants?"

"No, I ain't heard nothin' 'bout him sellin' any of us," she said. "But he lost his store, too Robert. Marcus say he hear Massah talkin' to Missus 'bout maybe going back to der plantation in Georgetown. If dat happens, I 'spect he be taking me and Elizabeth, and Robert, Jr. with 'em. Lawd knows what would happen to us den. How much more do you owe's massah Kingsman for me and the chilluns?"

Robert told her they had about $650 in gold coins, leaving $150 left on the $800 price agreed upon nearly two years earlier.

"Not enough to get a clear title to you," he said. "But if Massah Kingsman be hurting for money it might be enough, but even if we do buy your freedom, der ain't a chance that we can get to the North."

She clutched Robert tightly.

"Will you ask him," she implored. "Robert, I'm so scared he and missus will take us away from Charleston and we will never see each other again."

Robert assured her that he would have a talk with Kingsman the next day.

"Hannah, have you heard about slaves running away to Beaufort?"

"Oh yes, seems like we hear about mo' slaves makin' a run for it every day," said Hannah. "It be risky business though. Last week de patrollers caught two black men trying to get across de Ashley River to de Yankee lines. Dey took 'em back to the jailhouse and beat dem to death with rawhide whips. I hear de Confederate army be building trenches all 'round de city to keep de Yankees out and us black folks in. But Robert, der's plenty slaves done risked der lives to get to the Yankee army."

"Why you ask?" she worried.

Robert told her about a plan he devised since the night aboard the *Planter* when he imitated Capt. Relyea.

"I don't know if I should even be talking about it, but a powerful notion's been stirring inside my head. It be mighty dangerous though. Might even be a deadly kind of thing, Hannah."

178

"Go on honey," she urged.

"Well, 'most every day we go around de harbor taking freight to dem Rebel forts. When we get to Fort Sumter, we so close that I can see men working on the Yankee ships. I reckon it be only 'bout a mile from the fort to the Yankee's blockade fleet. On a calm day I can hear de Yankee soldiers talking and laughing. Dat's how close we be to them."

"I belives I'm startin' to get your drift," said Hannah. "You wantin' to get over to those Yankee ships, ain't you?"

"Well baby, I'd be lying if I said the idea aint' crossed my mind a time or two," Robert admitted. "But just thinking about it makes my head spin 'round and 'round."

He tried to explain in greater detail the many flaws in his plan. For starters, he couldn't just take over the *Planter* with the white crew on board. Relyea always carried a pistol, as did his two assistants. During the daylight hours Charleston Harbor was filled with other gunboats that could intercept the *Planter* if the crew tried to make a dash to the federal ships.

Of course, his biggest concern was Fort Sumter. The big guns would blow the *Planter* out of the water long before she broached the mouth of the harbor if something was amiss. The same guns that kept the Yankees out could surely keep the Confederate boat in Charleston.

"And Hannah, don't forget this. If we got caught, we would die. Every last one of us," he said. "They might even kill de children."

Robert felt Hannah's body recoil. The tension eased when she snuggled closer to him.

"I only have one thing to say 'bout that," she whispered in his ear. "Don't you worry about talkin' to Massha Kingsman tomorrow. 'Cause we gonna be needing that $650 once we get to dem Yankee ships."

Chapter 28

Capt. Relyea gave Robert a hard look when he boarded the *Planter* the next morning and his heart lodged into his throat. He feared someone overheard his conversation with Hannah the night before and relayed his plans to the captain.

"Dammit Smalls," Relyea growled. "I told you to have those cannon balls moved aft before you left the ship yesterday. Can't trust you niggers to do nothin' right."

Robert gulped hard out of relief.

"Oh, yessah Capt. Relyea. Dat' be my fault. Should have done it myself," he replied humbly. "I'll get de boys to hop to it right away, suh!"

"Let it happen again and I'll have the whole bunch of ya flogged," Relyea said, before he stomped to his cabin.

Must have had a bad weekend with the missus.

He navigated the *Planter* away from the wharf and toward Fort Sumter with a load of flour, beans, hard tack, and black powder. The captain didn't come back to the bridge until after the *Planter* had moored. He didn't say a word, just strapped on his sword and left with Smith and Pitcher.

After the white officers disappeared behind the fort's sally port, Robert ducked down to the engine room, where Alfred adjusted dials.

"Where's Abraham?"

"Gave him a breather Mr. Robert," the engineer replied. "It be hot work down here."

Robert gave him a knowing look.

"Alfred," he began. "Der be something I've been wanting to talk with you about."

Alfred turned toward Robert, interest showed in his eyes.

"What be on 'yo mind Mr. Robert?"

Robert looked around to make sure the engine room was clear of others.

"Alfred. Remember the other night when you say I looked kind of like Capt. Relyea."

Alfred nodded.

"Kind of got me thinking," Robert hesitated. "Thinking about something mighty dangerous. Something that scares me to even talk about."

"What dat be?" Alfred was curious.

Robert blurted it out. "I want to take the *Planter* and sail it to the Yankees. I want to get out of Charleston."

He immediately felt better. The thought had been bottled up inside him all day. He had to tell someone other than Hannah and he trusted Alfred more than any other man he knew.

Alfred's response surprised Robert.

"Good Lawd Mr. Roberts," he said in a hushed tone. "Been thinkin' de same thing myself but couldn't get up the courage to talk with you about it. Hell, when I saw you parading around like you was de captain, I thought to myself den dat you could sail us right past dem guns at Fort Sumter. Dem folks at the Fort wouldn't know no better if it was dark outside."

He reached out and drew Robert into an embrace.

"When we going Mr. Robert?"

* * *

181

Two nights later, Alfred followed Robert home where Hannah had prepared a small meal for the three of them. After supper, Hannah, rocked Robert, Jr. to sleep, closed the door, and threw a sash across the windows. They huddled in the middle of the room and spoke in whispers.

"Hannah, I talked with Alfred and he be ready to take his chances with us," Robert said.

She looked at the engineer.

"Alfred, you know what happens if we don't make it to the Yankee ships don't you? Once we get started, der aint no turning back."

Alfred returned the gaze. His voice quivered.

"Hannah, I know exactly what would happen. But I also know dat if we get to dose Yankee boats I be a free man. All my life I have dreamed of being free. God has given us a chance to throw dese shackles of slavery off. I know we be taking a mighty risk. I got a good idea what dem white soldiers would do if 'n we got caught. I can't worry 'bout that Hannah. All I knows is freedom is jes a few miles away. And Mr. Robert be de man that can get us der."

They talked far into the night discussing ways to escape from Charleston. Alfred said they had to find out the disposition of the rest of the crew. Did they want to join them? How should they approach the others with the plan? Could they trust every one of them to keep quiet?

"We could sail the *Planter* with just five of us," said Alfred. "I jes don't know how we'd get shed of the others? If all of us don't agree, den what's to keep dem that don't want to go from spilling de beans?"

Robert understood Alfred's position. However, he had been working with these men for nearly a year. He respected them and he believed they respected him. Robert wasn't as concerned about their participation as he was about Capt. Relyea and his mates.

"Ever since de fire dey been keeping a tight watch on de *Planter*," Robert warned. "When the Captain goes ashore, he almost always leaves Smith or Pitcher behind. Ain't none of this gonna work as long as dey on board. I guess we could hit them over the head or something. But that mighty risky, too."

,The three sat in silence.

"Robert!" Hannah jumped to her feet. "What if we do this. Ever since de fire Massah Kingsman been talking about doing something special to thank Capt. Relyea for helping to save his house from the big fire."

Robert looked at her quizzically.

"Oh, I know what you're thinking," she said, "He wasn't actually there but he did give you permission to take dem barrels of black powder to Massah Kingsman's house. Massah say several times how grateful he be to you, but also to Capt. Relyea. Been saying he'd like to do something special for de captain."

"How 'bout I kind of say something to Massah about having a party to thank the captain and both dem lieutenants. Course, he ain't gonna invite none of the black crew no matter how much he likes you Robert."

Robert scratched his head and contemplated. The idea had some merit, even though it was a long shot. There was no guarantee all the white crew would leave the *Planter* to attend a party in their honor. Yet, he couldn't think of anything better that didn't involve violence.

"You think you can pull this off?" he asked.

"Robert, you leave de party to me. You jes worry about getting the rest of your crew together. Dat's de part dat scare me most," she replied.

* * *

His opportunity to talk with his crewmates came two days later. After they made a long run to Georgetown using unpatrolled creeks, the *Planter* returned to Accommodations Wharf. General Ripley's headquarters, located next to the wharf, seethed with activity.

"What's going on?" Capt. Relyea shouted to a soldier standing on the pier.

"Great news," the soldier said. "Gen. Beauregard smashed de Yanks at Pottersville. Got 'em running back to Washington."

The captain gave a whoop and turned to Lt. Smith.

"Get Pitcher and let's go see what all the excitement is about," he said.

The three white men strode to a nearby building where sounds of music and celebratory shouts of victory filled the night air. Only the black crew remained onboard the *Planter*. Robert went below and found Alfred.

"Now's our chance," he said. "Pass de word for the crew to gather below."

A soft glow from the *Planter's* boilers provided the only light as the crew found places to sit in the engine room. Alfred stood close to the porthole, to listen for approaching footsteps.

Robert leaned forward and in a hushed, but urgent tone, made his case. "What I'm about to tell you must be a secret. Can you keep a terrible secret?"

The heads nodded, some with apparent uncertainty.

"Men, me and Alfred been talking, and we believe all of us has a chance to gain our freedom. It's not far from here. Just across to where dem Yankee ships be at the mouth of the harbor. And, de *Planter* can get us der. If we can sneak past de forts, we can be free men. We just give the *Planter* to the Yankees and be on our way."

The men looked at Robert with astonishment.

Stephen asked, "You say Alfred be part of this plan?"

Alfred turned to face the group, resolved. "Yes Stephen. I'm in. Might be the onliest chance I ever has to be free. Mr. Robert can get us there. Ain't no doubt about it."

Abraham, his eyes wide with concern, "What if us be caught?"

"I think we all know what will happen," Robert conceded. "Either we get blown out of the water by de guns or de Rebels will take us and hang us. Hell, hanging might be merciful if us get caught."

"If we get caught, we ought to blow ourselves up," said Melrose, his husky voice deep and solemn.

Wexford stood up, obvious agitated by the idea.

"Look, I wants my freedom 'bout as much as anyone on dis boat," he said. "But things ain't all dat bad. Don't forget what happened to Vesey and all his crowd."

184

"Wex," Robert said. "Yes, I admit der be great danger. But if us all keep quiet about this thing, if us don't let our tongues wag, us can do it. Vesey had too many people who knew about his plans. Dat's why he failed."

Silence filled the hold.

"Before Capt. Furgeson brought me to work on de *Planter*," Gabriel began in his natural soft-spoken manner. "I worked on Massah Richardson's cotton farm in Georgia. Grew up on de farm. Spent my boy days workin' from before de sun rose til 'way after it set. Always tried to do mah best for Massah. He be a hard man. If de slave not do his task, Massah beat him like a dog. Most all of black folks hated dat son of a bitch. One day I be sick wif de gripe. Couldn't hardly raise myself from de bed. But I wanted to do right. 'Bout midday de 'ol sun was beatin' down on me to de point mah head was spinnin' and I couldn't stand no mo.

"I fell down, right der in a row of cotton. Massah Richardson rode up on his big horse and said 'Nigger, you get up from der 'for I cuts you with dis here whip.' I tried my best to get up but everytime I got to mah feet I'd feel like a knife be cuttin' into mah innards and I'd fall back to de ground.

"Massah Richardson didn't say 'nother word. Jes climbed down off dat horse and proceeded to beat me wif his whip. I got up on my knees and wrapped mah arms around his legs.

"Don't beat me no mo Massah, I said.

"But dat white man just kicked me in the belly and commenced to whipping me. Somewhere long the line everything went dark. Next day I woke up in my cabin. Massah came to the door and looked at me. He say I ain't no good for nothin' no mo'. Slave trader came and took me to Atlanta and put me on de block. God looked down on me and smiled 'cause Capt Furgeson bought me and brought me to de *Planter*.

"Shouldn't no man be beat de way I be beat," he stifled a sob. "All dese years I been ashamed of what dat white man did to me. Dat's why I wears dis here shirt all de time."

Gabriel stood in the middle of the small room and slowly unbuttoned his shirt, letting it drop to the floor.

"Look what dat man did to me."

Several of the men gasped. Robert looked and then turned his face away in horror.

He had seen many beatings during his life, but nothing could compare to the deep, dark red scars crisscrossing Gabriel's back, stomach, and chest.

"I told Capt. Furgeson when he bought me dat I would not let a man beat me like dis again. He say he understood and he treat me good. But dis bunch of whities on this boat done threatened to whip me. I tell you dis. I die before I get whipped again.

"Mr. Robert say he can get us to freedom. I say he can. I say to hell with dese white sons of bitches. Ain't nothin' here for us 'cept more of de same. Count me in Mr. Robert."

Wex bent down to get Gabriel's shirt. He draped it gently against the man's shoulders. He motioned for the others to join him. As one, they wrapped their arms around Gabriel.

Nothing was said. Nothing more had to be said.

Chapter 29

There was a spring in Robert's step when he left the boat a couple of days later to visit Hannah. Since the night the crew banded together for the great adventure, the men tried to act as normally as possible. Robert had warned them to refrain from talking amongst themselves whenever a white man was on board the *Planter*, which was almost always. Nevertheless, an undertone of excitement permeated the ship.

If Capt. Relyea noticed anything different about the black men on his ship, he didn't show it. Robert's instincts told him their secret was safe—at least for the moment.

When Robert opened the door to the little loft above the Bay Street Delivery Stables, Hannah squealed with delight and jumped into his arms.

"Whoa, baby," Robert chuckled. "I love you too but let me get inside de door before you knock me down!"

"Oh Robert," she breathed, "You won't believe what I has to tell you." She took his hand and led Robert to a chair at the table.

"Sit down," she directed him to a chair. "Robert, I talked with Missus Kingsman dis mornin' about havin' a party for Capt . Relyea and she say dat one of de best ideas she heard lately. She rushed into Massah Kingsman's study and say 'Howard, I has de best idea. Let's have a party for de captain of de *Planter* and de white officers.' Mister Kingsman jumped on the idea, too. He say, 'Catherine, dats' a wonnerful thought. We owe the captain a debt of gratitude for saving dis neighborhood. Der's some other folks who feel de same say.'

"Den he say, 'It's been too damn gloomy around here ever since de fire. Dis will give us all a chance to celebrate.'

Den Missus Kingsman get all in a titter thinkin' about all she got to do to get ready for de party. She done decided dis will be a gala. Told me to start cleanin' de silver cause she wanted to have a shindig."

Hannah's excitement was contagious.

"When will they have the party?"

"Don't know yet, hon. Missus Kingsman say she got to talk with some of de other ladies and get invitations printed and delivered. But 'spect she be wantin' to have the party pretty soon."

Robert stood and lifted Hannah off her feet in a loving bear hug.

"You sweet, sweet girl," he laughed. "You did it. I'm just hoping we can get de rest of the white crew off the ship as well."

"Leave dat to me," Hannah winked.

So, he did.

The fruit of Hannah's efforts became obvious a week later when Capt. Relyea came aboard the *Planter* skipping with excitement. He held an engraved envelope, which he clasped to his chest. The black crew watched with curiosity as he signaled for Smith and Pitcher to join him in the wheelhouse.

He opened the delicate envelope, withdrew a card, and began to read:

The Captain of the Planter, the honorable Thomas Relyea and his officers are cordially invited to a gala to pay honor to the courageous efforts they, and other members of the Confederacy provided during the Great Charleston Fire. The gala will be held May 12 at Mills House from 8 p.m. until midnight. Given by a grateful city.

He read off a long list of hosts other than the Kingsman who were sponsoring the gala, "The best families in Charleston will be honoring me," boasted the captain.

"Us, too," Pitcher admonished.

Capt. Relyea gave him dismissive look.

"It's about time we got some recognition," Relyea said. "Damn if this ain't the cat's meow. Best tell the missus so she can be getting a new frock. I could use a new uniform. You boys do the same. Got to look our best so the other officers don't show us up."

The captain's announcement was old news for Robert.

Hannah had told him days before that the party she suggested to Mrs. Kingsman took on a life of its own. When Mrs. Kingsman told her friends about the plans for a party honoring Capt. Relyea, they eagerly joined in the planning. Several said they had soldiers they would like to invite. Then one suggested the junior officers couldn't be invited without asking the senior officers, including Gen. Ripley. Soon, a small party to honor the captain of one boat had grown into a gala for more than 120 of the Confederate's finest soldiers in Charleston.

The only place still standing that could accommodate such a large group was Mills House. Gen. Ripley's wife was asked to join the ladies planning the gala, and easily procured the hotel by running the idea past the general. Now, Charleston buzzed about the gala. For the first time since the great fire, a festive atmosphere filled the air.

Robert was excited, too, for an entirely different reason. While Capt. Relyea and Charleston partied, the *Planter* would make its dash to freedom.

Chapter 30

Keeping a secret proved harder than Robert thought. Every day aboard the *Planter* brought new doubts about the successful implementation of escape. Throughout April the *Planter* made supply runs to Fort Sumter and Fort Moultrie and each time Robert stole glances at the Yankee blockade at the mouth of the harbor. The Union ships were close, almost within shouting distance.

Robert's co-conspirators performed admirably and if there was any hesitation, he didn't see it. The routine of the ship helped keep their minds focused. The ship towed coal barrages to surrounding forts, took a load of lumber to Kiawah Island, and transported troops from one location to another.

On a beautiful spring day toward the last week of April, the *Planter* docked at Kiawah Island. The crew unloaded lumber while the officers lounged under a nearby live oak tree, out of earshot. Alfred worked beside Robert, passing lumber to outstretched hands on the dock.

"Mr. Robert," he whispered. "I got somethin' to ask you."

"What?" Robert's eyes were alert.

"You be takin' Hannah and de babies wif' us, right?"

Robert nodded a quick agreement.

Alfred gave Robert an apprehensive look.

"Mr. Robert," he lowered his voice further. "I wants to take my missus and our three chillun's, too. Done talked to her 'bout it. Explained de risk. She say if I go, she go. With the young uns, too. That not all. Some of de others wants to take der women folks, too."

Robert tried not to show his surprise.

"Hold up," he tried to contain his fear. "How many people know about our plans."

Alfred thought for a moment.

"I don't know for sure. But jes about all de crew has people dey wants to take to freedom."

Robert was taken aback. When they first agreed to take the *Planter* to the federal lines, Robert insisted on secrecy. Everyone pledged to stay quiet. But tongues wagged. All Charleston might be in on the escape plans, as far as Robert knew.

"Damn, Alfred," he muttered. "Dis ain't exactly what I was hoping to hear."

"I know," Alfred said miserably. "But we jes like you Mr. Robert. We all has folks we love and wants to take wif' us. We just got to tell all of them dat dis is it. Can't take no mo' with us."

Robert groaned.

Alfred edged a little closer as they labored to move the lumber ashore.

"Mr. Robert, I hates to worry you mo' den I already has but ders one mo' thing us needs to talk 'bout."

"Tell me de good news," Robert said sarcastically.

"Wexford, I don't think he want to come. He say he scairt."

This latest bit of news didn't come as a total surprise. Wexford had always been the most timid member of the crew. A small man, but brawny, he more than contributed to the work on the *Planter*. But he was skittish as a colt. When Capt. Relyea barked an order, Wexford jumped as if someone had spooked him. From the start, he hadn't seemed enthusiastic about the escape plans.

Robert also knew Wexford had a wife and eight children living in Charleston. Several of the oldest children were married and worked in

Charleston. It would be difficult for him to leave so many family members behind.

The thought of a defector so late in the plan caused Robert great concern.

"Do you think we should just call de whole thing off?"

Alfred nearly dropped the load of lumber Robert handed him.

"No!" he yelped.

Capt. Relyea shot a curious glance in their direction.

"What's goin' on over there?"

"Nothin' Captain," Robert maintained his normal visage. "Thought some of this lumber was going overboard but Alfred caught it just in time!"

Relyea turned away with disinterest and resumed his conversation with Pitcher and Smith.

"Damn," Robert whispered at Alfred. "Be more careful."

"Sorry Mr. Robert. It jes surprised me when you said to call off everything."

"I didn't say dat," Robert snapped. "I just wanted your advice. We has to be united if we be going to pull this thing off. We can't be telling other folks about it. I guess I'm scared, too, Alfred."

He remained quiet as lumber passed hand-to-hand. After a few minutes of silence, Alfred edged closer to Robert.

"We all scairt, Mr. Robert, but you can't worry yourself sick 'bout Wexford. We got to push ahead. Do dis thing come de night of de big party. It might be de onliest chance we get. All of us lookin' to you. So you gots to be strong. Do dis Mr. Robert. Take dis matter to God. See what He have to say."

Take it to God

Robert repeated this silent mantra, it's the one thing he neglected. Later, out of view, he got on his knees and sought guidance from the true Master.

Chapter 31

Charleston, May 12, 1862

Gen. Ripley came aboard the *Planter* to order the collection of four cannons from the Confederate Battery on Cole Island, a sandy strip of land that guarded the mouth of the Stono River.

"I've been overruled by that son of a bitch Pemberton," he handed the orders to Capt. Relyea. "In his great wisdom, he has decided to abandon our battery on Cole Island. He says we can use the cannon more effectively at Fort Ripley. But if we do that, captain, we might as well give the Yankees an engraved invitation to steam up the Stono River and have lunch in Charleston."

Robert understood the implications of the general's objection to abandonment of the fort. The Stono River curled south of James Island and then came within a few miles of Charleston. The route would allow federal ships and troops to avoid the gauntlet of cannons on guard in Charleston Harbor.

"I'm a student of history and this blunder has been made before," said Gen. Ripley. "The British came up the Stono during the Revolutionary War and captured the city."

"Then why the hell are we abandoning the fort on Cole Island?" Capt. Relyea's eyes widened with surprise.

"Because that asshole Jefferson Davis put Pemberton in charge of South Carolina and Georgia and he ain't nothing but a Union sympathizer," Gen. Ripley warned. "Don't let me hear you repeat that Relyea. You hear me?"

"Oh, yes sir. Jes between the two of us," the captain bootlicked.

Gen. Ripley slammed his hand down on the rail.

"Making matters worse, he wants those cannons moved today. All Charleston has been getting ready for the gala tonight. Sorry to be the bearer of bad news, but it's got to be done captain."

"Dammit, headquarters knew we had plans for tonight," Capt. Reylea was mad enough to spit nails. "I've got to pick up my new uniform; make sure the missus is dressed and ready; hire a coach; and now de' bastards at headquarters wantin' me to go all de way to Cole Island? I ain't got time for dis shit!"

"Don't seem right Captain," Pitcher agreed. "But if we strike out now, we should be able to load the guns and have them back by sunset. Jes' store them onboard and get them over to Ft. Ripley in the morning."

Capt. Reylea gave his first mate a look of frustration. "Well, t'ain't nothin' we can do about it at this point. Get us underway, Smalls."

* * *

The best route from Charleston to Cole Island took the *Planter* through Wappoo Creek, which connected the Ashley and Stono Rivers. By mid-morning the ship had steamed the five miles to the mouth of the Stono, where a company of Confederate soldiers stood guard over four cannons already dismounted from their carriages.

It was hot, heavy work but shortly after lunch, the crew had 200 rounds of ammunition, a beautiful seven-inch rifled gun, an eight-inch Columbia, an eight-inch howitzer, and a long, 32-pounder stowed in the hold. The captain ordered a full speed return to Charleston and arrived as the sun began to set.

The ship had barely moored before, Capt. Relyea, Smith, and Pitcher hopped off. The sound of band music wafted across the water from the Mills House. As he trotted toward the East Bay Street, the captain turned his head in Robert's direction.

"I'll be back in the morning," he yelled. "Make damn sure nothing happens to dem guns. You hear?"

"Yes sir Capt. Relyea," Robert reassured. "I won't let them out of my sight!"

Robert watched the three white men disappear into Charleston from the pilot house. He looked on the deck where six black faces stared back at him. In that instant, he became aware of the enormous responsibility on his shoulders. The success, or failure, of the next few hours depended on his ability to act cool and confident.

Robert clambered down the ladder to the deck as the men gathered around.

"Okay, we all know what to do," he looked each one squarely in the eyes. "For now, let's eat some supper and try to get some rest. After midnight we will meet below deck and make our final preparations."

He turned to Wexford.

"Wex, have you changed your mind? Would you like to come with us?"

"Mr. Roberts, I wisht I could but I gots to think 'bout my family." A note of regret made his voice quiver. "I done prayed 'bout it and the Lawd keeps tellin' me I should stay here and take care of my chillun's. One day dis war be ending. I hope to see you then suh."

"I understand," Robert consoled him. "You go on home. No matter what happens to de rest of us, you tell them you didn't know nothing about us leaving. Can you do dat?"

He gripped Robert's hand.

"Yessuh, I won't say word," he said. "God bless ya Mr. Roberts. God bless all of you."

He left without another word.

"Reckon we can trust him?" Alfred worried. "He could turn us in and probably get a big reward."

"Believe we can Alfred. We have no other choice, I'm afraid."

Chapter 32

At Alfred's suggestion, Robert convinced a cabin steward aboard the Confederate ship *Etowah* to participate in the evacuation. The little, unarmed steamer was docked a couple hundred yards away at Atlantic Wharf, which was not guarded like the Southern Wharf.

The steward, Davey Jones, was Alfred's close friend and distant cousin. He agreed to take Hannah, Missy, Abraham's sister, Bessie, and the children on board the *Etowah* around 10 p.m. and keep them hidden until the *Planter* arrived. After leaving the Southern Wharf, Robert would send a rowboat to the *Etowah* and transfer the precious cargo onto the *Planter*.

When no armed guards marched down the pier to arrest him, Robert concluded Wexford had kept his word. He summoned Alfred and together they used a crowbar to break into Capt. Relyea's cabin. Relyea had taken his new dress uniform with him for the gala but left behind his regulation captain's coat and the straw hat that rarely left his bald head. A small safe in the corner of his cabin contained Confederate codes and Robert knew the combination.

He dropped to his knees and fiddled with the combination lock. Several turns of the knob allowed the door to pop open.

"I believe Uncle Abe might be interested in these," Robert joked to Alfred.

They joined the rest of the crew on the foredeck and gathered into a small circle, protected from the view of the wharf's sentry. Abraham emerged from the galley with a large, steaming cast iron pot.

"Low country boil to celebrate de occasion," he grinned. He opened the lid to reveal shrimp, sausage, corn on the cob, and potatoes—a treat for a crew accustomed to far less sumptuous meals.

Robert's stomach fluttered with excitement and anxiety. His thoughts were with Hanna and the children. He prayed they had not been stopped by the Charleston patrols. Nevertheless, he put on a brave front for the benefit of his friends and made a fuss over the food.

The moon, almost full, bathed them in a soft light. The brightness of the night sky worried Robert a bit. Even though they would depart at night, a sharped-eyed sentinel could see something amiss. While this added to Robert's anxiety, it did not weaken his resolve.

"Hope the captain be having a large time," Robert laughed as he heard music echo from the Mills House.

He began to sing a gospel song, *Bound for Canaan Land*, that Lydia taught him many years ago. The others joined in on the familiar refrain.

> *Where are you bound?*
> *Bound for Canaan Land.*
> *Your horse is white, your garment is bright*
> *You look like a man of war*
> *Raise up your head with courage bold*
> *For your race is almost run*
> *Where's you bound?*
> *Bound for Canaan Land*

Abraham started another song, *Deep River*, then others suggested their favorite tunes. The music calmed the group and strengthened their bond.

198

Around midnight, the men stopped singing in order to avoid attracting attention from the shore.

"Mr. Roberts," said Samuel. "What's de first thing you gonna do when we reach dem Yankee ships?"

"I believe I'll ask them if they would like a prize, courtesy of Gen. Ripley and Charleston," he chuckled. "Then I'm going to ask them if I can see my momma."

The men gave a good-natured laugh.

"How about you Samuel? Same question back to you?"

Samuel's face became grim.

"Mr. Roberts, I believe I will get down on my knees and thank God for delivering me out of bondage," he said. "And then I'm gonna jump and holler and scream for joy!"

The banter continued past midnight. Each crewman shared his dream of what it meant to be a free man and reaffirmed their commitment to the plan.

"If somethin' happens and we get caught," said Samuel, "let's scuttle de ship. Then we should hold hands and jump into the water."

"I can't swim," said Abraham.

"I know," said Samuel. "Don't believe any of us can."

Robert could swim, but he knew what Samuel meant.

"I like the idea Samuel. We all go to freedom together. Or, we all go down together."

Chapter 33

In the little apartment atop the horse stables on East Bay Street, Hannah placed a white sheet in the bottom of a raggedy carpet bag she salvaged from the hotel. She worked quickly and quietly while Elizabeth and Robert, Jr. played. After packing a change of clothes for each member of the family, she looked about the apartment to see what else might fit. She settled on two apples, diapers, and a small Bible she won in a singing contest at church.

"I'm forgetting something," she muttered to herself. "What could it be?"

She remembered. "Lawdy how could I forget that!"

Elizabeth gave her a curious look.

Hannah walked over to the bed and reached under the mattress to remove a bag of money containing the $710 they saved.

"Mr. Kingsman won't be needin' this anymore," she mused.

Hannah looked through the window at the darkened sky. It was early, only 8 p.m., but she wanted to get to the rendezvous aboard the *Etowah*, where the others would be waiting to be picked up. She fashioned a sling to carry Robert, Jr. close to her body and threw the carpet bag over shoulder. Elizabeth grasped Hannah's hand and headed to the door. She looked once more at the little loft she turned into a home and walked out.

Hannah drew little attention from those on the street. At this time of night, most stores had closed leaving taverns as a destination for those that milled about. The wharf Hannah needed to reach was an easy eight-block walk and she strolled to avoid unnecessary attention. When white men and women approached, she respectfully stepped aside to allow them to pass. They never noticed her and the children.

Still, Hannah was nervous. She did not have a pass to be on the streets. She detoured through back alleys to avoid further contact with anyone. Her eyes darted from one side of the little alley to the next in search of shapes in the shadows.

"Hurry, Elizabeth." She quickened her pace.

Within minutes, they reached Legare Street, a block away from Atlantic Wharf. Hannah turned the corner and, before she could stop herself, bumped into a stout man dressed in a police uniform.

"Whoa there, little lady," the man reached out to keep her at arm's length. "Where you headed in such a hurry?"

Hannah peered around the policeman to see if she could evade him. Three other men wearing badges stood behind him, blocking any hope of escape. Hannah felt the blood rush to her cheeks. Her knees trembled.

"Why, why, I is going to see my missus," she stuttered. "She need some sewing I done for her. You know, for de big party tonight, suh."

The policeman looked at her with suspicion.

"Where's your pass?"

Hannah almost fainted, "My pass? I must have left in back at my place, suh. I was in such a hurry to get dis dress to the missus that I done forgot all about dat pass."

The three other policemen joined.

One of them reached for her carpetbag and snatched it from her.

"Let's see what we got here," he opened the bag and rummaged through its contents."

He finished and turned to the first officer.

"Well I'll be Sgt. Hucks. I don't see no sign of a fancy frock in this here bag. This woman is lying."

"So, no pass, no dress, and no good reason for being out tonight. Missy, you done landed yourself a trip to jail. Guess we gonna have to take those kids from you though."

Hannah took a step backward. She was about to run away from the patrollers, even though she knew she had little hope of escape.

A voice behind the policeman broke the tension.

"Hannah, is that you?"

The policemen pivoted to see who was there.

Against the glare of a streetlight, Hannah made out the form of a short, stocky man.

He stepped out of the light and Hannah gasped.

"Mr. Kingsman, I be so glad to see you," unable to contain the relief in her voice.

"I've been looking all night for you," he replied. "Mrs. Kingsman can't go to the ball tonight unless she gets her dress finished.

The policeman who searched Hannah's bag readied for an argument, "Ain't no dress in her bag Mr. Kingsman."

"Oh, I know. I had one of my servants pick it up earlier today. Hannah probably didn't even know it had been taken. She needs Hannah for a last-minute alteration to the dress."

"She ain't got a pass either," said Sgt. Hucks.

"I'll vouch for Hannah. Really gentlemen, don't you have more pressing business in the city? I will escort Hannah and issue a pass for her return home. Come Hannah. Missus is waiting."

He strode over to Hannah, took her arm and escorted her away from the patrol. He stopped to pick up her carpetbag and whispered, "Don't look back."

The policemen watched in astonishment as the sophisticated gentlemen, a well-known businessman, escorted the black woman and her children toward the docks.

"Where are you going Hannah?" Kingsman asked when they were a safe distance from the patrollers.

Hannah started to weave a story in her mind to explain things but had second thoughts. This was a man who had been kind to Robert and saved her from the police.

"Can you take me to Atlantic Wharf?"

"Certainly. We're almost there."

They walked in silence.

"Taking a little trip Hannah?" he jested.

"Us, yessuh. Dat a good way to put things."

"And, I suppose Robert might be going along?"

"Couldn't go without him."

Kingsman stopped and put his hand to Hannah's cheek.

"I had a feeling that might be the case. Well, good for you. If I were in Robert's shoes, I would do the same thing. It's a brave thing you are doing Hannah. Thank goodness I happened to see you before those rascals could take you away. I think God has His hand in that. And I think He will be with you and Robert on this trip you are about to take. Give Robert my best regards, will you?"

They reached the gangplank of the *Etowah*.

"God bless you Mr. Kingsman," she was a mix of emotions. "Thank you for what you done for me and Robert ... Bye now."

She scampered up the gangway, waved goodbye, then disappeared below deck.

* * *

Kingsman gazed at the ship for a long time.

"Safe travels," he whispered, slipping silently into the night's dark embrace.

Chapter 34

None of the conspirators aboard the *Planter* slept. Around 3 a.m., Robert drew in a long breath and in a hushed tone told the crew to get ready.

Alfred and Abraham went below to stoke the boilers. Robert went to the captain's cabin and put on Relyea's uniform, it fit him well. He put on the captain's straw hat, pulling it low over his eyes so the shadow covered his face.

Robert's eyes scanned Southern Wharf. The headquarters were dark with no sign of life. A lone sentry had his back to the ship.

The engines broke the silence of the night. Clouds of steam and smoke billowed from the *Planters'* stacks. A few minutes later, Alfred called up to Robert that the boat had a full head of steam. All was ready for departure.

Robert gave orders to untie from the pier. Gabriel and Stephen pushed the ship away as Robert backed her from the wharf. He looked out the window of the wheelhouse to make sure the Palmetto flag and the Confederate flag had been raised. Everything looked in order.

He glanced at the sentry. The guard turned to look at the ship and Robert held his breath. The guard gave a lazy wave of his arm, turned away, and resumed watching the street.

The paddle wheels seemed to thrash enough to wake the city. In truth, the noise was unnoticed by anyone on shore. No lights flickered in windows to cause Robert concern.

The *Planter* turned into the tide. In the pale moonlight, ships docked at neighboring wharfs looked ghostly. Off the bow Robert saw a lantern being swung side to side from a ship docked at the Atlantic Wharf.

His heart raced with joy. *Hannah must be there.*

A hundred feet from the *Etowah,* Robert ordered William to row the dinghy to fetch their cargo. In the moon's soft light, he saw shadowy shapes walk down the gangplank.

"Only six," he thought frantically. "There should be eight."

Robert squinted, then relaxed. One of the figures held a tot on her hip and a bundle swaddled in a sling.

William rowed the dinghy back to the *Planter* where Gabriel and Samuel waited to help the new passengers aboard. Robert saw Hannah look up and give him a quick wave before she disappeared into the hold with the children. Robert was surprised to see the tall, lanky figure of the *Etowah's* steward step onto the *Planter*.

"Mr. Robert," Davey's voice was quiet and humble, "I'd like to come too."

"Go down below and watch the women and children," he whispered back. "Glad to have you."

The passenger pick-up took longer than anticipated and the tide ran against them.

Alone in the wheelhouse, Robert could hear his heart beating. He scanned the harbor for signs of danger. The only lights came from two nearby Confederate batteries, Castle Pinkney and Fort Johnson. Robert fought the urge to make a mad dash to the harbor entrance, but kept the *Planter* going forward at a slow, steady pace.

"I mustn't raise suspicion," he muttered to myself.

As he passed the forts, Robert gave a signal on the ship's whistle and the boat passed without challenge.

Fort Sumter loomed over the starboard side of the ship. The Confederate flag waved from a bastion. Lanterns silhouetted the shapes of several soldiers on guard. The brick walls of the fort bristled with cannons. All were sighted-in on the entrance to Charleston Harbor, where the *Planter* was headed.

On the horizon, the first pale rays of a new day cast light on the ship and her crew. Robert maintained his position in the wheelhouse, feet wide apart and arms crossed in the way he had seen Capt. Relyea do many times. He pulled the brim of the hat down further and said a silent prayer.

When the *Planter* came within hailing distance of the Fort Sumter sentinels, Robert casually gave two long pulls on the ship's whistle, followed by a short pull. He watched as a tall, uniformed man gazed through binoculars at the *Planter*. Robert's knees began to tremble, despite his best efforts to stay calm. The uniformed man turned to talk to a soldier beside him.

A voice from the fort rolled over the water.

"*Planter,* cleared to pass."

Thank You, God.

Robert waved to the men atop Fort Sumter.

A quick glance out of the wheelhouse window showed Fort Sumter receding behind him. Robert kept the plotted course, careful not to change arouse suspicion. Even though the ship had cleared the fort, she remained well within gunshot range.

A loud knock came at the wheelhouse door and Robert's heart skipped a beat.

Abraham stood there.

"Mind if I come in Mr. Robert?"

He welcomed the company.

William and Gabriel soon joined them, and Robert could sense their excitement.

Careful to avoid mines the *Planter* laid in the months earlier, they crossed the bar and Robert ordered full speed. She responded immediately and spray hit the wheelhouse window as the ship plowed through the waves.

The ear-splitting roar of a cannon caused the men to flinch. As one they glanced backward and saw a plume of water erupt. Signal lights flashed from the Fort Sumter rampart.

"Dey is on to us! Dey be signaling Fort Moultrie," Robert yelled.

A cannon ball exploded on the starboard side, sending a shower of seawater across the wheelhouse and soaked Abraham, who leaned out of the window to keep an eye on Fort Sumter. "Dat was a close one." He grinned and wiped the water from his face.

Another cannon report sounded. The projectile plunged into the water far behind the *Planter*.

Robert turned the wheel sharply to avoid a mine. Then, he put the ship on a heading for the mouth of Charleston Harbor, where sailors aboard the federal blockade ships could be seen scurrying into action.

"We're home free," Robert shouted in jubilation and the wheelhouse erupted into cheers. "Mr. Roberts," said Gabriel, clutching his arm. "Dey gonna fire on us. Look!"

The early morning light showed sailors scramble to the cannons on the Union ship.

"Oh my God!" It dawned on him that the *Planter* still flew the Stars and Bars and the South Carolina state flag.

"Get those damn flags down!" he shouted.

Gabriel sprang into action.

While they brought down the flags, Robert gave the wheel to Abraham and scrambled down to the hold.

"Hannah," he screamed. "The sheet. Give me the sheet now!"

An arm reached out of the hold grasping a white sheet.

Robert took it and dashed to the front of the boat.

"Hoist it up Gabriel," he urged.

The momentum of the *Planter* during the mad, last minute dash carried the ship closer to the federal fleet. Twelve portside cannons were aimed at the *Planter*.

To come this far only to be blasted out of the water by the people we thought would save us.

He ordered the ship to a crawl. They drifted toward a ship named the *Onward*. White faces stared through portholes and three officers stood behind the guns. The Union men peered through the morning light, confusion written on their faces.

"Don't fire," Robert shouted. "We are the *Planter* out of Charleston. We desire to surrender this ship to Uncle Abe."

A voice shouted back, "Hold your position."

An officer leaned over the rail and four black men looked back. His mouth dropped in amazement.

"Where's your captain?"

"I don't rightly know, sir."

"Mr. Robert be de captain now," Gabriel pointed to Robert.

The *Onward's* captain turned to confer with the other officers.

"Okay, you may approach," he said.

Robert piloted the *Planter* closer to the *Onward*. He ordered Abraham to drop anchor and they came to rest a few yards away from the federal ship.

Sailors covered the decks and rigging of the *Onward* to get a better look. Robert signaled below for Alfred to stop the engines. William, Davey, and Missy emerged from the hold. Hannah came last with the children in tow.

She looked at Fort Sumter in the distance, then at the Union ship. She raised Robert, Jr. above her head in Victory.

"We be free baby. Free at last!"

Chapter 35

Chaos ruled in the minutes following the *Planter's* escape from Charleston.

The crew and passengers streamed onto the main deck shouting for joy, tears streamed down their faces. Several dropped to their knees and offered thanks to God. Others embraced. Alfred and his wife, Missy, held hands and jumped up and down, unable to contain their glee. Blue-clad sailors aboard the *Onward* whooped, hollered, and waved their hats to celebrate the Confederate gunboat was now in Federal hands.

Robert rushed to Hannah, where Elizabeth held a firm grip around her mother's legs, a look of confusion on her young face. The babies slept peacefully in her arms. He gathered all four in an embrace and kissed Hannah with ferocity.

Hannah's eyes gleamed with pride.

"We made it Robert," she grinned. "Sweet Jesus, we be free. We done been delivered from bondage, jes like de good book promised."

His voice choked with emotion and couldn't reply. He rejoiced in silence, savoring the moment.

A voice from the *Onward* broke the reverie.

"Prepare to be boarded!"

Robert turned to see a young officer from the *Onward* approach the *Planter* in a longboat that was lowered with incredible speed.

He turned to face the officer.

"Hello captain. I am Robert Smalls, pilot of the *Planter*, at your service," he said with as much confidence he could muster. "Welcome aboard, sir."

The naval officer introduced himself as Lt. Frederick Nickels, Captain of the *Onward*.

"You're a lucky man," said Nickels. "I was about to order my crew to fire on the ship when you raised that white flag. I thought you were trying to ram us! Now, tell me, what the hell is all of this about?"

Robert laughed. The guffaws rumbled from his chest in an explosion of relief. The knots that were in his stomach since this morning disappeared, replaced by a sense of liberation. Tears rolled down Robert's cheeks. He wiped them away with the back of my hand and caught his breath.

"We mean no harm to you or your ship," he told the officer. "In fact, sir, I am proud to surrender the *Planter* to you and Uncle Abe. As for me, my crew, and my passengers, we slipped under the noses of the Rebels to gain our freedom. We are free, ain't we?"

The captain seemed unsure of himself.

"Well sir, for the moment you are considered contraband, property of the United States government," he replied curtly.

He softened. "But yes, you should no longer consider yourselves slaves. You won't be sent back to your masters. That's for sure!" He appraised the *Planter*.

"This is a fine ship Smalls. One that I think will be quite valuable to the United States. But how did you get past Fort Sumter with it?"

Robert told him about how he planned the escape, how the white officers left the ship to go to a party, and how he had masqueraded as Capt. Relyea.

"Then you knew the signal to pass Sumter?"

"Oh yes. I know the signals for all of the forts in Charleston."

Nickels gave an appreciative whistle.

"That's not all," Robert said. "Come look at this."

He ushered Nickels to the deck and pulled back a canvas cover to show him the four cannons.

"That one," Robert pointed to the rifled cannon, "was at Fort Sumter before the Confederates took over. I'm glad to return it to its rightful owner. We were supposed to deliver all of dem to Fort Ripley dis morning. I hope Uncle Abe will find dem useful."

Robert reached into his coat pocket and handed Capt. Nickels one of the items he had retrieved from Capt. Relyea's safe.

Nickels opened the book and flipped through the pages.

"Oh my God. This is a Confederate code book!" his eyes widened.

"Yessir. It has all the signals and codes being used by the Confederate army in Charleston, including flag signals."

He reached out and shook Robert's hand.

"Smalls, you have done the Union a great service that won't be forgotten. I've got to get you to Capt. Parrott. He's going to want to hear what you have to say."

Nickels looked again at the guns, at the black men and women still celebrating, and at the ship that had carried them to the federal blockade.

"Unbelievable," he shook his head in amazement.

Robert and Nickels boarded the longboat and the crew rowed to a larger ship, a sidewheeler named *Augusta*. The officer explained that he was taking Robert to see Capt. Parrott, commander of the naval blockade squadron.

"He will be wanting to hear your story Robert. Don't leave anything out," he coached.

They transferred to the flagship and two officers led them to the commander's quarters. Sailors gawked at the sight of a black man dressed in a captain's uniform marching through their midst. Despite his nervousness, Robert smiled.

Capt. Parrott, a portly man with curly brown hair and a full mustache, rose from a desk in his room to meet Robert. He extended his hand and shook it. Robert marveled, *two handshakes, from two white men on the same day.*

"Capt. Parrott, this is the negro who brought the *Planter* to us," Capt. Nickel acknowledged. "It's a fine prize, too."

Parrot invited Robert to sit down and for the next half hour Smalls recounted the tale of the *Planter's* escape from Charleston, complete with details about the ordinance aboard. Parrott interrupted Robert several times to ask about the signals he used to pass the various forts. Lt. Nickels placed the codebook on the commander's desk. The older man flipped through the pages and his eyebrows shot up in surprise.

"We've got to get this to fleet headquarters at once," ordered Parrott.

He looked at Robert with admiration in his eyes.

"Young man, this may be the most remarkable naval feat I've seen since this war began," he praised. "I'm going to send you, your crew, and your passengers to Port Royal to report to Admiral DuPont. Nickels, transfer two members from your staff to the *Planter* and get Smalls to Port Royal as quickly as possible. Meanwhile, send this codebook to Port Royal by the fastest packet ship we have available."

Robert rose from the chair and thanked Parrott for his hospitality.

"By the way commander," Robert added, "I guess you have heard that de Rebels abandoned Coles Island yesterday."

Capt. Parrott looked at Robert in astonishment, seemed to lose his balance, and plopped into his chair.

Chapter 36

Midday, on May 13th, the passengers and crew of the *Planter* enjoyed a fine lunch prepared by the chef of the *Onward* as they said goodbye to Charleston. Two Union officers joined Robert in the wheelhouse with orders to report to Port Royal as quickly as possible.

"Do you want to pilot her?" Robert asked Lt. Joe Hucks.

"No, Smalls," he replied. "You've done quite a job getting the *Planter* this far. She's all yours for now."

Robert called for the crew and passengers to assemble on the foredeck. When they gathered, he ducked back into the wheelhouse and emerged with a package.

"Dis be from Lt. Nickels." He placed the package into Abraham's hands.

The crewman carefully stripped the wrapping paper and, with a shout of surprise, unfurled a United States flag.

"Run it up the flagpole," Robert ordered.

The Stars and Stripes flew proudly as the *Planter* turned toward Port Royal.

Robert hadn't slept in more than 24-hours and wasn't in the least bit tired. Too many emotions ran through his head. As the boat steamed south, the Charleston skyline and Fort Sumter faded in the distance. It was too surreal to believe. Grateful to God, relieved the danger had passed, and simply ecstatic to be free.

My family is free.

He and Hannah could build a life together without the fear that they, or their children, could be sold.

He thought of those wonderful days in Beaufort when he sailed with Alex Rhinds. Robert felt free as a bird riding the waves. That's how he felt now, only as a boy, Robert knew he would have to return to his master's house at the end of the day. On this day, he had no master. The heady feeling of freedom made his heart soar.

* * *

Throughout the journey to Port Royal, members of the crew visited the wheelhouse to share their elation.

"I just can't believe it Mr. Robert," William's eyes danced with excitement. "It all seems like a dream to me."

"I know what you mean," Robert replied. "This time yesterday we were loading cannons and answering to our white masters. Now, we do as we like. It be a great day William, one dat we will be telling our children about for many years to come."

Robert asked the white officers, "What should we expect when de *Planter* reach Port Royal?"

They explained federal troops, under Gen. David Hunter, controlled the area around Beaufort. Commodore DuPont commanded the blockading fleet that ranged from Florida to Virginia. Thousands of blacks had fled to Beaufort since the naval engagement secured Port Royal.

"There's still some confusion about the legal status of black folks," said Lt. Hucks. "Hell, I'm confused. I consider colored folks like you to be free once they get to our lines. But the government says to call them war contraband. That doesn't make any sense to most of us. Gen. Hunter issued an order last week that all the negroes in Florida, Georgia, and South Carolina are now free. It won't stand though."

His statement concerned Robert. He had heard about the general's emancipation order earlier while he was in Charleston. The news spread quickly throughout the city.

"What makes you think his orders won't stand?"

"Ol' Abe Lincoln won't stand for it," he said. "There's still a lot of slave owners in the border states like Kentucky and Missouri. They might swing over to the Rebels if Lincoln allows his generals to free slaves. Wait and see, Smalls. Hunter is about to get taken to the wood shed by Lincoln over this."

Robert was disheartened by this bit of news. Was he a free man or just a spoil of war?

At dusk Robert surrendered the wheel to Lt. Hucks and went below deck. Hannah sat on a soft bundle of cotton that had been left in the hold from an earlier port of call. Elizabeth and Robert, Jr. slept on blankets stretched out on the deck.

Hannah took Robert's hand, kissed it, and rubbed it against her cheek. She smiled sweetly.

"Sit down baby," she patted the cotton. "It' been a long day hasn't it?"

"A long day but a very, very good day," he smiled. "How you holding up?"

"The first time I've had all day to catch mah breath," she laughed. "We all been so excited we couldn't sit still. Been singin', dancin' and a doin' lot of prayin'. Everyone's wondering' what tomorrow will bring. Where we gonna stay, things like dat. But I ain't worried about de future Robert. Whatever comes, me, you, and de babies has our freedom."

A tear rolled down her cheek and Robert brushed it away. He reached over and kissed her.

"Yes, my darling, we are free. God has showered us with His love. We will be in Beaufort soon and everything gonna to be okay. I promise. Now, try to get some sleep. Us still has a long way to go."

Chapter 37

Port Royal, May 13, 1862

Edward Pierce, with Mansfield French in tow, brushed aside two soldiers and burst into Gen. David Hunter's office.

The general looked up in surprise. A blond-haired man sitting with his back to the door peered over his shoulder to see the cause of the commotion. The two soldiers tumbled in behind the intruders.

"General sir, they came in before we could stop them," the smaller of the two men explained.

Hunter gave the soldiers a dismissive gesture.

"Don't worry about these two. I can take care of this. Close the door behind you when you leave," commanded the officer.

He gave Pierce and French a curious look.

"Okay, what's all this about?"

Pierce brushed his fingers through a mop of black hair and thrust a sheet of paper on Hunter's desk.

"You know damn well what this about," he said in a loud, accusatory voice. "Your men are raiding the plantations and taking away our best workers. You are undermining everything we're trying to accomplish here."

"I assume you're talking about the black regiment I'm recruiting?" replied Hunter.

"Oh yes," added French. "But I would hardly call what you are doing 'recruiting'."

"Sit down gentleman and let's talk this out. I believe you are already acquainted with Col. Reynolds." He motioned to the portly middle-aged man sitting across from his desk.

Reynolds rose but Pierce waved him back into his seat.

"Of course, we know Reynolds," Pierce said. "He's been here nearly as long as I have. I just wonder what he's doing in your office at this time?"

"No need to fret gentlemen," said Reynolds in a high-pitched, wheezy voice. "I was just telling the General how much I appreciated his efforts to enlist our black friends into the Union's great cause. It's simply a wonderful idea for the General to take it upon himself to raise a black regiment. I do believe it will be our country's first such army unit."

He gave Hunter an admiring look.

"Quit toadying up to the General," spat Pierce. "We know your true intentions."

Reynolds raised an eyebrow. "And what do you think my 'true intentions' are?"

"You would like nothing better than to see our work at Port Royal fail. Then you and your cronies in New York could sweep up all of the Sea Island plantations at will."

"I think you overestimate us," remonstrated Reynolds. He turned to Hunter, who listend intently. "Gen. Hunter believes forming a black regiment is essential to keeping Port Royal in Union hands. If we can't protect our foothold in South Carolina, then what is the use of trying to civilize these black beasts?"

The general grunted an affirmation. "Washington has denied every request for additional troops that I've made. The situation is grim. I have 16,000 troops at my disposal to face 65,000 Rebels spread out between Savannah and Charleston. They surround us. So, I decided to take matters into my own hands."

French interrupted, "David, our troops have been here since DuPont took the Hilton Head forts and there hasn't been a single Confederate counter attack since then. All of the plantation owners had fled. Who's left to attack? And where did you get those numbers? I can't believe there're that many Confederate soldiers left in this area. Most of their forces are fighting up North and in the West."

"My intelligence officers assure me the assessment of Rebel troop strength is quite accurate," said Hunter. "We are in great danger, whether you choose to believe this or not. If Washington refuses to reinforce my command, then I must utilize local manpower."

His voice took a conciliatory tone.

"Actually Mansfield, you and Pierce should be grateful. Are you not the ones who have been telling me that the black man will fight for his freedom? Didn't I free the slaves in South Carolina, Georgia, and Florida earlier this week with my General Order 11? The two of you have been fighting to abolish slavery for years. I did it with the stroke of a pen. Now, I am giving our black friends a chance to serve their country. How can you find fault?"

Pierce gave Hunter a small smile to break some of the tension in the room.

"General, you showed great courage in issuing the emancipation order for the Southern Command. I hope it will withstand scrutiny from Washington," he said softly and with genuine appreciation. "For too long, those of us who came South to prepare these black souls for integration into society have been unsure of their political status. Giving them their freedom was a bold step and we commend you for doing it."

He took a deep breath.

"But we must protest the methods you are using to form your black regiment!"

"What is it you find so offensive?"

French reached into his coat's breast pocket and pulled out several sheets of paper.

"General, these are reports that have been pouring in from our plantation superintendents. They tell us your soldiers are creating chaos. Your order calls for every able-bodied black man between the ages of 18 and 45 to be conscripted into the Army. They are being taken from the fields where they are working to put in the spring crops and spirited away without a word of explanation."

"We have worked hard to get the trust of the black man and now your men are impressing them into the Army," added Pierce. "Many of their wives believe their men are being rounded up to be sold to the Cuban sugar plantations, just like their white masters warned before abandoning their farms."

Hunter shrugged.

"Well, war always puts a strain on families. I need a black regiment formed as quickly as possible and my staff has advised conscripting the men of fighting age is the most expedient way of accomplishing this purpose."

Pierce stood, put both hands on Hunter's desk and leaned forward.

"But don't you understand General, that you have taken the most able men who work the fields from us? They are in the middle of planting this year's cotton crop. The nation desperately needs this cash crop to help pay for the war effort. If you force these men to serve, their families will face incredible hardship. All you've left behind is women and old men. They won't be able to plant and gather their own subsistence crops, much less 87,000 acres of Sea Island cotton."

Hunter leaned forward. "Be that as it may be Mr. Pierce, I will have my black regiment and I will do my duty as commander of the South to protect us from the enemy. You may sit down, Sir!"

Pierce slumped back into his chair and looked at French.

"Cheer up gentlemen." Reynolds lit a cigar and blew a ring of blue smoke into the air. "If you are unable to bring in this year's cotton crop, I feel sure me and my partners in New York can. We all know these darkies are an indolent type in need proper supervision. Really, not much more than savages from the jungle."

A knock on the door interrupted the conversation.

"Come in," barked the general.

A solider handed a note to Hunter, saluted and left the room. Hunter opened the envelope. His eyes widened with surprise. He turned to his visitors.

"Well, this is interesting." He turned to Reynolds. "Apparently one of your savages just stole a gunboat in Charleston harbor and sailed it under the Rebel's noses to our blockading force. The black pilot just docked the boat here in Port Royal. A man by the name of Robert Smalls."

Part 3

Port Royal, S.C.

ⳤⳤⳤ

Chapter 38

Port Royal, May 13, 1862

The *Planter* sailed from Charleston into Port Royal shortly after 10 p.m. Even in the darkness, Robert saw the changes since he last visited the port. A 450-feet-long wharf jutted into the harbor and a variety of ships, from schooners to steam-powered side wheelers, docked there. Six large warships swung at their moorings. Crews worked by lamplight to unload supplies from a merchant ship.

A sailor, one of six on the new dock, waved a lantern to signal Robert to an unoccupied spot. The black crew, the women and children gawked at the hundreds of campfires and endless rows of tents along the shoreline.

"Commodore DuPont sends his greetings," shouted one of the sailors on the dock. "He requests the company of Robert Smalls."

"I'm Smalls. Give me just a minute."

He clambered up the gangplank and returned a hesitant salute from the sailors, who looked at him with admiration.

An ensign stepped forward. "It is true you brought this ship out of Charleston?"

"Me and the crew."

* * *

Robert instructed the crew and the others to stay aboard the *Planter* until his return., He climbed into a small barge and sailors rowed him to the flagship, *Wabash*, which towered over other boats in the harbor. Commodore DuPont waited on deck.

Curly gray hair framed his weather-beaten face. Robert judged that he was in his 60s, but the man's blue eyes were bright and clear.

DuPont looked Robert up and down with a critical eye.

"So, this is the young buck who took my friend Ripley's boat out of Charleston," he laughed. "I'd like to be a fly on his wall today. I bet all of Charleston is upside-down over this."

"And there's the *Planter*," he observed. "I believe we can use such a ship. Come on aboard Smalls. I want to hear all about this great adventure of yours."

He took Robert by the arm and ushered him aft to a stateroom occupied by five junior officers stationed around a table. They all stood when the Commodore entered the small room. DuPont pulled an envelope from his pocket and produced a letter.

"Gentlemen, I would like to introduce you to Mr. Robert Smalls," he announced. "He has sailed one of Charleston's finest ships from under the Rebels noses along with armament, supplies, and fifteen other blacks. Capt. Parrott tells me this man has valuable information. Let's hear what he has to say for himself."

Robert retold the story of the escape. DuPont and his officers leaned forward, intent to hear every word. Questions about the signals and codes were the only interruption. They spread out maps of Charleston on the Commodore's desk and drew locations in the harbor where Robert helped lay mines. When Robert mentioned the Confederates abandoned Coles Island, the officers exchanged long glances with DuPont, whose voice betrayed his excitement.

"Why in the world would they leave the Stono River undefended?" DuPont was puzzled. "Smalls, are you sure about this?"

"I was there just a few hours ago," Robert replied. "I still have the cannons on board the *Planter* if you'd like to take a look, Sir. As for why, I don't rightly know. I did hear Gen. Ripley say something about a man called Pemberton ordering the fort closed."

DuPont stroked his beard.

"Pemberton, huh—We got word him and Gen. Ripley have not been seeing eye to eye. But it still makes no sense for the Rebels to leave the Stono open to us. Hell, if we act quickly, we can steam right up the Stono and be in Charleston within days."

He appraised Robert.

"Tell me this Smalls. Would you be willing to lead a scouting party back to the Stono. It's not that I don't believe you. I want visual confirmation that Cole's Island has been abandoned. If it is, this could change the entire course of our operations in South Carolina. "

Robert considered the commodore's request. On one hand, he would do anything within his power to bring down the Confederacy. Yet, a trip to Coles Island would take him back to the place from which he just escaped.

"It would be my great honor Commodore." Robert threw caution to the wind.

"I like your spirit Smalls. We could use a man like you," he said in a half-jest.

"Are you offering me a job?" Robert teased.

DuPont's eyes twinkled with amusement.

"You damn right I am. You, and your crew. Those that want to serve, that is."

"Well, in that case, it's back to Charleston for me." Robert grinned.

An officer cleared his throat to catch the commodore's attention.

"Sir, I have a rather delicate question to ask Mr. Smalls."

"What is it?" replied DuPont.

The officer turned to Robert, "I apologize, but can you read and write, Smalls?"

"No sir. I can read numbers on a chart but the opportunity to learn to read and write never presented itself to slaves. I had a kind owner, but I would have been beaten or worse if I was taught to cipher."

DuPont leaned back in his chair and gazed into the air. "I see what you are getting at Dobbs. Regulation states pilots must complete classes in naval training. Obviously, this poses a problem for me and for Smalls."

A junior officer sitting at the back of the room, dressed in Army blue, raised his hand.

"Have something to say young man?"

"Yessir. A thought comes to mind—The U.S. Army doesn't require recruits to be literate. It's just an idea, but I think Gen. Hunter would be agreeable to Smalls enlisting in the Army. Then, he could detail him back to the Navy."

"Doe the Army have any black officers?"

"No sir."

DuPont walked over to Robert and clapped him on the shoulder.

"Congratulations my man," said the Commodore. "You're in the Army. Now, go back to your ship and get some rest. It's been quite a day."

* * *

After meeting Robert, the Commodore sat at his desk to write to his wife.

Dearest Sophie,

She is a fine boat, can carry seven hundred bales of cotton, has a fine engine and draws but little water and will be of the greatest use to us—so for herself she is a valuable acquisition, quite valuable to the squadron. I sent for the hero, Robert, and he soon came, a pleasant-looking darkie, not black, neither light, extreme amount of wooly hair, neatly trimmed, fine teeth; a clean and nice linen check coat with a very fine linen shirt having perhaps been of the wardrobe of the Navy officer who commanded the boat but fitting him very well if they were.

His information is thorough and complete as to the whole defense of Charleston; Stono Inlet is abandoned, they are building a fort on the middle ground in the harbor and making it stronger and stronger, but there is not much land near.

I told Robert I would take care of him and his people, that he was a hero.

Your loving husband, Samuel

DuPont sealed the letter and marked it for dispatch. He addressed another letter to the Navy Department with a more complete report of his conversation with Smalls.

To fleet headquarters,

The bringing out of this steamer, under all circumstances, would have done credit to anyone. The armament of the steamer is a 32-pounder, on pivot, and a fine 24-pounder howitzer. She had, besides, on her deck four other guns. One of the four belong to Fort Sumter and had been struck in the rebel attack on that fort on the muzzle.

Robert, the very intelligent slave and pilot of the boat, who performed this bold feat so skillfully, informed me of this fact, presuming it would be a matter of interest to us to have possession of this gun.

This man Robert Smalls is superior to any who has yet come into lines, intelligent as many of them have been. His information has been most interesting, and portions of it of the utmost importance. I shall continue to employ Robert as a pilot on board the Planter for the inland water, with which he appears to be very familiar.

Samuel DuPont, Commander Southern Blockading Fleet

* * *

Robert reunited with his family following the meeting with the admiral and escorted them to his former home on Prince Street. Lydia nearly swooned when she saw Robert, Hannah, and the children. She dropped to her knees and motioned for the children to come to her. She gathered them in her arms and wept for joy. She reached for Hanna's hand and put it against her cheek.

"You 'uns most be starvin'." Lydia regained her composure. "Come in and bring your friends with you."

As she bustled about the kitchen, Lydia told Robert she was now housekeeper and cook for a company of soldiers who took up residence in the McKee home after Port Royal fell. All the whites in Beaufort had taken an oath to leave if the Yankees came.

"Anyone dat didn't leave would be shot." Lydia laughed. "Only one white man was in Beaufort when the Yankees marched into down, and he was drunk."

She thought the McKees were living near Charleston, but wasn't sure.

"Dey tried to get me to go with 'em but I say I wanted to stay. Dey didn't fuss a bit. Massuh McKee gave me two gold dollars and say he see me after de war be over. Robert, tell me all 'bout dis thing you done."

As Lydia cooked breakfast, Robert told his story once again. In some ways, it still seemed like a dream. But when he looked around the room at his wife and children and the faces of those who accompanied him out of Charleston, he knew it was for real.

"It's good to be home, mama."

Lydia smiled. "Okay, all dose dat is hungry, come and get it."

Chapter 39

Port Royal, May 14, 1862

Robert awoke to the sensation of little fingers tickling his mustache. He grabbed the little hand and nipped playfully at her fingers. He caught Elizabeth in his arms and tickled her until she cried for mercy.

"Stop Papa," she laughed.

Robert kissed her forehead and sat up in bed. Hannah rushed over, kissed him, and placed Robert, Jr. in his arms. His eyes adjusted to the familiar surroundings. He slept in his former childhood home as a free man; his family, together under a single roof.

"You've been sleeping all de mornin', lazy bones," teased Hannah. "Time to wake up and tell us 'bout meeting with the Commodore."

"Well, I think we have a new best friend," Robert was still in awe. "Commodore DuPont seems to have taken a cotton to me. Probably 'cause I know these waters better than anyone on his staff. He gave me a job Hannah!"

A look of concern came over her face.

"What kind of job?"

"You know, being a pilot. Just like I is with the *Planter*."

She scowled.

"Robert, I thought you was getting away from all dat. We left Charleston to be free, to raise our family. Now here you go jumping right back into the middle of things. Don't seem right Robert."

Robert motioned for her to sit beside him on the bed.

"Darling, de way I see it, I don't really have a choice," he reasoned. "Sure, we could go somewhere and try to get way from dis craziness. I'm as tired of the war and the suffering it brings just as much as you. But Hannah, the Navy needs me right now. I know where all de mines are laid, I know all de inlets, de shallows, de creeks, de rivers … all de things de Yankees need to capture Charleston.

"And think of all our friends back in Charleston. If there be anything I can to help gain their freedom, den I has to do it. I can't run from dis duty, Hannah."

She squeezed Robert's hand and leaned her head on his shoulder.

"Had a feelin' you might feel that way," she said softly. "Do what you gotta' do baby. I be proud of you. Glad you be my man."

Alfred knocked on the cabin door.

"Mr.Smalls, dis a fella' wantin' to speak wif you. Say he be a reporter from a paper way up North. Wanna let him in?"

Robert gave Hannah a quizzical look.

"I guess that be okay Alfred. Show him into the parlor."

The newly-enlisted pilot spent an hour with the newspaper reporter. While Robert retold the story of the escape from Charleston and answered endless questions, an artist who accompanied the reported sketched quickly.

"This is the biggest story I've ever covered," the reporter told Robert. "You're going to be famous Mr. Smalls."

A commotion outside of the house caught their attention. Walking onto the front porch, Robert saw several dozen black men and women gathered in front of the home. They waved and shouted with excitement.

"Where's Smalls?" yelled one of the black men in the crowd.

The newspaper reporter stepped forward and pointed to Robert.

230

Cheers erupted. Men waved their hats and several women held their children above their heads so they could see *the* Robert Smalls.

Robert turned to Hannah.

"Not sure what all dis commotion be about," he said sheepishly.

"Who dat?" a black child cried out to his mother.

"Dat Mr. Robert Smalls chile," she replied. "He de' nigger dat stole de rebel boat out of Charleston. Dat be a great man, honey chile'."

Chapter 40

Cole's Island, May 19, 1862

The reconnaissance trip to Coles Island proved Robert had conveyed the correct information to the commodore. Two Union shallow-drafted gunboats, the *Crusader* and the *Lance*, entered the mouth of the Stono River. Robert piloted the lead boat, the *Crusader*, around a shoal.

As the little fleet entered the Stono River, Robert looked anxiously at the earthen breastworks on Coles Island, searching for signs of Rebel activity.

"I'll be damned," said Lt. Edward Speck, the white naval officer in charge of the scouting expedition. Speck, about the same age as Robert, was clean-shaven except for bushy sideburns that ran to the jawline. He and Robert liked each from the moment they first met.

"Smalls, you certainly knew what you were talking about. Looks like Johnny Reb has rolled out the welcome mat to the United States Navy."

The *Crusader* landed a small party of Marines. They approached the fort with caution and disappeared behind the parapet. A few minutes later they ran toward the ship to give a report.

"No sign of the Rebels," yelled the sergeant in charge. "Looks they skedaddled and took everything with them."

The Marines re-boarded the *Crusader* and both boats continued up the river.

"Charleston's only about five miles from here," Robert offered. Speck whistled softly.

"I can't wait to let the commodore know about this," he replied.

They rounded a bend in the river, where a company of Confederate soldiers gaped at the Union vessels. The Rebels did not hesitate before they ran into the woods.

The Union foray got as far as Legareville, a small fishing village, before Lt. Speck said he had seen enough. Robert turned the *Crusader* into the current and led the *Lance* back to the Atlantic Ocean. Not a single shot had been fired, but Robert felt victorious.

As the boats steamed back toward Port Royal, Speck clapped Robert on the back.

"Well done, Smalls. If we can get back to Coles Island with a regiment of soldiers, we can establish a base of operations that could hand us Charleston in a month. Now, all I have to do is convince Gen. Hunter. I might need your help."

Robert laughed in delight at this young captain's enthusiasm.

"Tell the General I am at his disposal."

They sailed southward and arrived at Port Royal at daybreak, where a small company of Naval officers waited on the pier. Lt. Sullivan signaled for Robert to follow him ashore.

An officer wearing a captain's braid raised a quizzical eyebrow after returning Sullivan's salute.

"Well?"

"It's just as Smalls described," said the lieutenant. "The Rebels have abandoned their fort on Coles Island. The whole area can be ours if we move quickly, sir."

"The Commodore sends his regards," he said to Robert. "Your orders are to take a day of shore leave to be with your family and then report to the commodore tomorrow."

* * *

A Union soldier knocked on Lydia's door mid-afternoon. He requested Robert to follow him to the general's headquarters.

"I thought I was to see Commodore DuPont?"

"Change of plans Smalls," said the soldier. "The general got wind of what you and your boys did in Charleston. All the top brass want to talk with you. Follow me please."

Wanting to look official, Robert put on the smart, navy-blue uniform he wore on the *Planter* before the war started. It still fit.

As he and the soldier walked toward Hunter's office on Bay Street, onlookers cast curious looks at the men. On several occasions, black men pointed and shouted, "Dat be Robert Smalls" and "Well done, Captain Smalls."

Robert had never seen them before and wondered how they knew his name.

* * *

Gen. Hunter made the home of Beaufort's most prosperous merchant his base of operations. The owner fled weeks before, leaving behind two slaves and "go to hell" written in red paint on the parlor wall. An American flag hung from the doorstep, guarded by four Army soldiers, who gawked at Robert before allowing him into the house. He glanced into a mirror in the hallway to see if anything was amiss that would cause the soldiers to stare at him in such a manner.

A burly Army sergeant opened the door to Gen. Hunter's office and motioned for Robert to enter. A booming baritone voice welcomed him into the room.

"There's the hero of Charleston." Gen. Hunter jumped from behind a large oak desk to stride across the room and take Robert by the shoulders. "Look gentlemen. If we had more like this man in service of the country, we would have Johnny Reb on the run!"

Robert stood rooted to the floor, not sure how to respond. He glanced about the room and saw Commodore DuPont, three Naval officers and two Army officers lounging in chairs. DuPont gave Robert a friendly wave.

"Come. Sit down. Make yourself comfortable." Gen. Hunter pointed to a chair at the side of the desk. "We've been reading all about your exploits young man. You have created quite a sensation."

"Why, thank you General." Still unsure about the fuss being made over him. "I hope I haven't made trouble for anyone."

Gen. Hunter and the others laughed in unison.

"I wish we had more trouble of the likes you created," he said. The general grabbed a newspaper from his desk and brandished it in the air.

"Have you seen this?" he pointed. "You are on the front page of *Harpers Weekly*. Here, read it for yourself."

Robert felt his blood rush.

"Sir, I have not had the pleasure of being taught to read."

Color rose in Hunter's face.

"Oh, of course," he said. "Excuse my clumsiness Robert."

He pointed to one of his subordinates.

"Read this to Mr. Smalls," he ordered.

The officer stood and read *Harper's Weekly*'s account of the *Planter's* escape from Charleston. A drawing of the *Planter* and a sketch of Robert illustrated the article.

One of the most daring and heroic adventures since the war commenced was undertaken and successfully accomplished by a party of negroes in Charleston on Monday night last. Nine colored men, comprising the pilot, engineers, and crew of the Rebel gun-boat Planter, took the vessel under their exclusive control, passed the batteries and forts in Charleston harbor, hoisted a white flag, ran out to the blockading squadron, and thence to Port Royal, via St. Helena Sound and Broad River, reaching the flagship Wabash shortly after ten o'clock last evening.

The story went on to give more details about the escape. The officer looked at Robert as he read the next passage from the article.

Robert Smalls, with whom I had a brief interview this morning, is an intelligent negro, born in Charleston, and employed for many years as a pilot in and about that harbor. He entered upon his duties on board the Planter a few months ago and as he told me adopted the idea of running the vessel to the sea from a joke which one of his companions perpetrated. He immediately cautioned the crew against alluding to the matter in any way on board the boat, but asked them, if they wanted to talk it up in sober earnestness, to meet with him later, where they would devise and determine upon a plan to place themselves under the protection of the Stars and Stripes instead of the Stars and Bars. Various plans were proposed, but finally the whole arrangement of the escape was left to the discretion and sagacity of Robert, his companions promising to obey him and be ready at a moment's notice to accompany him ...

"Tell me Robert—What would you have done had you been caught?" General Hunter asked.

"We discussed that General and we all agreed we would rather die before surrendering," said Robert. "After we scuttled the ship, that is."

Hunter pulled two other newspapers from his desk and waved them in Robert's direction.

"You have become quite a sensation Robert," Hunter mused. "This story has spread like wildfire. I have ten telegrams already from Congressmen wanting to see you. They want to meet the hero of Charleston. There's not been much good news of late from the war front. Your deeds give all of us hope and support my view that black men should, and must, help in this fight. I'd like to send you to Washington on the next packet ship!"

"Ahem," DuPont sounded a polite interruption.

All eyes turned to the commodore, who puffed serenely on a pipe.

"Best hold your horses General. We have more pressing matters for Mr. Smalls," he said. "We have confirmed his report that the Rebels abandoned Cole's Island. I'm afraid we need this man's help in occupying that ground. Perhaps we could spare him for a few weeks after that."

"But Commodore," protested Hunter. "You know the trouble I've had convincing Washington to let me enlist negroes into my army. We should strike now, while public sentiment is high, and send Smalls to Washington. He would serve as a great example of the ability of the black man to act bravely and intelligently."

The commodore pondered the point.

"Yes, I see what you're saying David, but really, getting a foothold on Rebel territory so close to Charleston is of utmost importance. Let us help you take Cole's Island and then we can talk about lending our man here, to you."

He rose, walked to where Robert sat, and put a hand on his shoulder.

"Robert holds the keys to Charleston General. Within the week, I would like to have an expedition ready to invade and hold Cole's Island and then proceed as far inland of that point as possible. The waters there can be treacherous. I've been told, and I have reason to believe, that few men in the Navy know the waters there as well as young Robert."

He squeezed Robert's shoulder.

"Isn't that right Robert?"

Robert seemed dazed, overwhelmed by the rapid events that had unfolded before him. "Why certainly, Commodore." He recovered his wits. "It would be my great pleasure to be of service to you and the General. The sooner we can get back to Cole's Island the better, suh."

Gen. Hunter went back to his desk and plopped into a leather seat. He turned toward Commodore DuPont and conceded, "Cole's Island, Commodore. But then, Washington."

Chapter 41

Port Royal, May 25, 1862

Robert was unprepared for the reception he received upon return the from Cole's Island. The *Harper's Weekly* article grabbed the imaginations of millions of Northerners. Every major Northern newspaper picked up the story. The *New York Daily Tribune* and the *New York Herald* instructed their war correspondents to obtain more details. Almost overnight, Robert Smalls became a household name, particularly in New England where strident abolitionists pointed to his deed as proof that colored men not only yearned for freedom but had the courage and intellect to pursue it.

* * *

French sat in Pierce's office in Port Royal reading the latest packet of the day's newspapers.

"Listen to this Edward. The *Trib* says, and I quote:

If we must still remember with humiliation that the Confederate flag yet waves where our National colors were first struck, we should be all the more prompt to recognize the merit that has put into our possession the first trophy from Fort Sumter. And the country should feel doubly humbled if there is not magnanimity enough to acknowledge a gallant action because it was the head of a black man who conceived, and the hand of a black man who executed it. It would be better, indeed, become us to remember that no small share of the naval glory of the war belongs to the race which we have forbidden to fight for us; that one has recaptured a vessel from a Southern privateer, and another had brought away from under the very guns of the enemy, where no fleet of our has yet dared venture, a prize whose possession a Commodore thinks worthy to be announced in a special dispatch ... his skillful and brave exploit is a justification for Gen. Hunter's assumption that in the class to which Small belongs in South Carolina, there is some intelligence and patriotism worth appealing to.

Pierce drew a deep breath.

"Well that should be some consolation to Gen. Hunter," he said. "In light of the fact that the President countermanded his order."

When word reached Washington, D.C. that Hunter had emancipated the slaves in South Carolina, Georgia, and Florida, Lincoln became livid, he considered the preservation of the Union his top priority. President Lincoln believed the action would cause border states to tip the scales in favor of the Confederacy, and he issued a commination to the general.

I, Abraham Lincoln, President of the United States, proclaim and declare, that the government of the United States, had no knowledge, information, or belief, of an intention on the part of General Hunter to issue such a proclamation; nor has it yet, any authentic information that the document is genuine—And further, that neither General Hunter, nor any other commander, or person, has been authorized by the Government of the United States, to make proclamations declaring the slaves of any State free; and that the supposed proclamation, now in question, whether genuine or false, is altogether void, so far as respects such declaration.

Pierce threw another copy of the *New York Tribune* into French's lap.

"This man Smalls has become the darling of the North. They are calling him a hero and a credit to his race."

French read a section of the paper out loud as Pierce puffed on a cigar.

... If each one of the generals in our army had displayed as much coolness and courage as he did when he saluted the Rebel flag and steamed past the Rebel fort, by this time the Rebellion would have been among the things that were. Smalls represent a race of blacks—a nation of slaves—many of whom are watching, as he did, for an opportunity to get away from their oppressors. He did not believe the rumors, got up by his masters, that the Northern people desired to catch the negroes and sell them to defray the expenses of war. On the contrary, hearing a faint whisper of Gen. Hunter's emancipation proclamation, he had confidence in his promise of freedom; so he looked death squarely in the face, and then started on his perilous errand ... He has added new proof to the evidence that negroes have skill—and courage and tact, and that they will risk their lives for the sake of their liberty ...

French continued reading, then exclaimed, "Did you see this on Page two Edward? Congress voted to give Smalls and his crew half of the value of the *Planter* and its cargo. A congressman from New York wants to make Smalls military governor of South Carolina after it's defeated!"

Pierce shook his head in amazement.

"This is a pretty remarkable set of events," he said. "Have you met Smalls?"

The minister shook his head.

"No, I went to Beaufort last week to arrange a meeting with him, but his wife told me he had sailed back to Cole's Island on DuPont's orders. I hear he's back though. Are you thinking what I'm thinking Edward?"

"Yes," replied Pierce. "This isn't the first I've heard of Smalls. A number of the plantation superintendents tell me the coloreds talk about Smalls constantly. He's become a folk hero to them. It would be worth our time to ask the Commodore if we can borrow Smalls for a day or two. I'd like to take him on the tour of the plantations, show him off, so to speak, and see what he can tell us about our current problems."

Work on the cotton plantations slowed. The former slaves were reluctant to go back to the fields, even when promised wages. The best efforts by Pierce, French, and the Gideonites led South had failed in large part. Only about half of the cotton fields were under cultivation. With more than 800 prime field hands conscripted into Gen. Hunters black regiment, most of the fields were in terrible condition, unplowed, and full of weeds. One superintendent had grimly forecast that this year's crop would be only a third of the previous yields.

"The coloreds don't trust us," the superintendent of Ashedale Plantation had written. "It's difficult to even communicate with them. They speak some infernal tongue called Gullah. I can't make heads or tails out of it."

"Mansfield, I have only a few more days before my commission in Port Royal expires. I've learned Gen. Saxton will be taking over my responsibilities. I would hate to leave knowing our experiment is in jeopardy. Let's get Saxton and Smalls and take a final survey before I leave," Pierce suggested.

"I love the idea Edward," French agreed. "I'll write the Commodore and Gen. Saxton today and try to arrange a tour of the plantations by the end of the week."

Chapter 42

Port Royal, May 28, 1862

The sound of laughter greeted Pierce, French, and Gen. Rufus Saxton when they climbed out of the skiff that transported them from Port Royal to St. Helena Island. They walked toward the sound of the merriment and found Robert with a dozen other black men gathered around a small fire.

"What's he saying that's so funny?" asked French.

"I have no idea," replied Pierce. "He is talking to them in Gullah. I understand a word here and there but not the gist of it."

They waved to Robert.

As they approached, Robert said something to the colored men and the laughter ended. Several of the men removed their hats and looked downward as the white trio came closer. Robert said goodbye to those in the little circle and went to meet his companions for the day. Introductions were made. Robert saluted General Saxton, then shook hands with Pierce and French.

* * *

Robert learned a great deal about the two Northern philanthropists during conversations with black ministers in Beaufort. Both men had built solid reputations for being honest and compassionate. Yet, the colored people they had come to serve held them at arm's length, still unsure about their true intentions.

Opinion of Saxton, who had arrived in Port Royal only a week earlier, had yet to be formed, but Robert felt an instant connection. A tall man, almost six feet in height, he carried himself with great dignity. Saxton was handsome, with a full, black beard and mustache, flecked with bits of gray, and thinning hair. His deep-set eyes gave Robert a glimpse into the man's character. Deep blue and curious, they gazed at Robert in a kind way, as if to offer a warm welcome. Little laugh lines at the corners made Robert feel relaxed, for the same type of crinkles lined his own face. Something about the general's demeanor told Robert he had found a kindred spirit.

* * *

Saxton had a good first impression of Robert. He was unlike any colored man he had ever met. Trim and athletic, Robert cut a fine figure in his new uniform. Clean shaven, except for a small mustache and goatee, Robert had the whitest teeth and a genuine smile.

Saxton was most impressed by his new acquaintance's bearing. Most of the black men he had met avoided eye contact. They look downward with dull eyes, answering only when asked a question. Robert broke the mold. He was confident and affable, willing to carry on a real conversation with his white counterparts.

"It's a great pleasure to meet you Smalls."

"The honor's mine general," said Robert. "But I would be more at ease if all of you would call me Robert."

Pierce and French had mapped out a plan to visit three plantations with a prolonged stop at the nearby Brick Baptist Church. The first stop at Tombee Plantation required an hour-long ride. The white men used the time to pepper Robert with questions.

"Why did the men stop laughing when we had arrived?"

"You have to remember Mr. Pierce that black folks aren't used to talking with white men," he said. "When the white masters ruled here, a black man could be beaten with a whip if they talked first. That's why the black slave is never off guard. He has become an expert at hiding emotions, never offering an opinion. A lot of time when he laughs, he is simple covering up his grief."

Robert chuckled. "And don't forget that the white masters told the slaves that the Northern soldiers would either eat them for lunch or send them to Cuba! A lot of them were scared to death when the 'Lincom Sojers' marched in."

"I see what you're saying," said French. "On numerous occasions I have had to scold men and women for not doing their work properly. They just laugh and say, 'We do betta' next time boss man, and then keep on doing the thing that I found offensive in the first place. It's so frustrating."

"Keep in mind Mr. French that the slave system has ingrained submissiveness and terror into the hearts of my people. Let me tell you a story ..."

Robert told about a slave who had been charged with stealing corn. He was innocent but he was so frightened with punishment that he ran away into the woods. The plantation overseer told the father he would not punish the boy if he came back to the plantation at once. The father convinced his son to return, but once back on the plantation the overseer had the slave tethered to the ground and given 200 lashes. It was a terrible beating and the boy died.

"Now, as a father, would you have wanted to rise up against the overseer?"

White faces stared back in indignation, unable to find words to respond.

"The father was helpless. Had he uttered any outrage at being betrayed, he would have been beaten too. He was obliged to say to the overseer 'he deserved it' and smile though his heart was breaking. Gentlemen, although you have come as liberators, you are white, and the black man has an inherit distrust of you."

244

French broke the silence, "I understand the distrust, but we came to free the slaves. Yet, I don't see an outpouring of happiness, nor gratitude. Especially among the plantation coloreds."

"I think you paint with too broad of a brush, Mr. French," said Robert. "Black folks have been hoping and praying most of their lives for deliverance from bondage. When I was in Charleston and heard that Gen. Hunter had freed the slaves, I knew I would have done anything to bring my family to the promised land. And, there are thousands and thousands of black folks that feel the same way. Just look at the black folks pouring into Port Royal from the countryside. Some of them faced hardships far worse than did I.

"But you ask why the freed slaves are not more passionate about their deliverance from their masters? You must remember that for those on the plantation, there was no hope of escape. I remember a slave named Toby. He got in trouble and ran for his life. But there was nowhere to run. He had no knowledge of the outside world, no familiar landmarks, no sanctuary. They killed him.

"The people you came to comfort grew up on an island, a prison without bars but with no way to escape. So, they put their faith in God. To you, they may seem ungrateful. They may not express it correctly, but they are thankful for what you are doing here. And, they want to do whatever it takes to help. You will find that they give God the credit for answering more than a century of prayers."

* * *

Jasper Fox, the white superintendent of Tombee Plantation, met the foursome and walked with them through the grounds. The majestic, two-story plantation house towered over the fields. When they visited the freshly white-washed, slave cabins, several elderly black men and women came to meet them. One of them spotted Robert.

"Is dat Mr. Smalls?"

Assured that it was, the elderly man turned to a small boy and whispered in his ear. Soon, more colored men and women appeared until a small crowd had gathered.

"Do you mind if I talk with them alone?" Robert requested.

The men obliged and walked toward a nearby field, leaving behind Robert amid a gaggle of excited voices.

At lunch, in the big house, Robert rejoined the white men. Talk soon turned to the cotton crop, or lack thereof. The superintendent said most of his best field hands had either been impressed into Hunter's new black regiment or hid in the woods. He had twenty-four people left to work more than 200-acres of cotton.

"To tell you the truth gentlemen, I had concerns about this year's crop even before Hunter plundered my men," he said. "We offered $1 per 300 pounds of cotton. A fair price. But very few of the negroes seemed enthusiastic about working the cotton."

"What do you think about that?" Gen. Saxton asked Robert.

"Can't say I'm surprised," said Robert. "People in the North love our cotton. They must, 'cause I haven't seen a single bale so far. I suppose it's all been collected and sent to market. Now, the North has sent folks like you to make sure there will be more cotton next year.

"You love cotton, but most people of my race despise it. How could it be otherwise? To the slave, cotton stands for agony and torment, for beatings and death. They worked from sunrise to sunset, threatened with punishment if they did not totally submit to their master's every whim.

"You have come here with pure hearts gentlemen. And we appreciate what you offer," Robert continued, "But the way you do things up North won't work in the South, not at this time. You asked the black man to do an honest day's work for and honest day's pay. Seems reasonable. But what you want for the black man isn't what the black man wants. Colored folks want land. They want a little piece of property where they can farm, raise a family, and be self-sufficient. They aren't asking for a handout, gentlemen. What they want is a chance to be free, able to make their own decisions, and reap the rewards of their own labor. I have never been up

246

North, but I reckon that's what folks there want, too. I hope I have not offended you."

"Quite the contrary Robert." Gen. Saxton cleared his throat. "I, for one, appreciate your candor. I think we have fallen victim to our own agendas, without taking into consideration those of your people."

"In every sense, Port Royal has been an experiment for those of us hoping to help our colored friends," Pierce added. "The object of our experiment was indefinite, the method and means untried. It was simply a generous and ready response to a cry for help."

Lunch concluded and the four travelers returned to their carriage for the short trip to Ashedale Planation on Lady's Island. As the coach drew from the big house, a young black girl raced to catch up. She offered a woven, sweetgrass basket to Gen. Saxton.

"Mr. Sojer," she said. "Here some baked sweet taters fo' yo' ride. It's all I gots."

"Dear girl," said Saxton. "You need them more than I do."

"Oh no mista' Please take 'em. It be a present for bringin' de sojers to free us po' peoples."

"Let me give you some money," said the general.

"Don't want no money. Jes wanna thank you for comin' all dis way from up Nawth to come and take care of we, when we be so po'. We don't know nothin' but Jesus. He all we got and nothin' else. You eat's dem taters now. Bye y'all."

Gen. Saxton put the basket of baked sweet potatoes on the floor of the carriage.

He looked at the others, speechless.

"Still think the colored folks don't appreciate you?" Robert's smile caused his face to beam with pride.

Chapter 43

Port Royal, Evening of May 28, 1862

The four men toured the Fripp and the Woodlands Plantations before a late afternoon visit to Brick Baptist Church. The situation at both plantations mirrored that of Tombee. Superintendents felt angry that Gen. Hunter had jeopardized their operations by conscripting their best men without prior notice. The former slave quarters on all three plantations were renovated and had freshly-tilled gardens for the occupants.

At Woodlands Plantation Robert gazed over a narrow channel of water and saw a familiar home. "That's Ashedale Plantation." He cleared his throat. "My former master owns it."

"Would you like to go visit?" asked French.

Robert shook his head.

"No, a lot of unpleasant memories der Mr French, I do want to meet Miss Laura Towns at the Penn School, though. My people speak so highly of her."

* * *

On the return trip, Robert used the time to ask questions that weighed heavily on his mind.

"Why did Mr. Lincoln overturn Gen. Hunter's order freeing the colored folks? I thought Father Abraham loved his black children."

"Let me try to answer that one," said Saxton.

"Robert, the President must walk a very fine line when it comes to the question of slavery. Like all of us in this carriage, the President considers slavery an abomination. Yet, he considers saving the Union his most important work." The general weighed his words. "People living in the border states, Missouri, Kentucky, Maryland, West Virginia, and Delaware remain very divided on the question of slavery. The President fears coming out strongly against slavery might cause the states to take up the Confederate banner. This is something he cannot allow to happen. It's too risky and that's why he considered Gen. Hunter's order to be out of line."

Robert considered the explanation.

"But where does that leave the colored folks Gen. Saxton? Are we entirely free? If we are not, are we to be a serf, or a paid laborer? Can we own land? Can we fight for the Union? Can we vote? Can we hold office? Do we have any rights like white folks? Pardon my language, sir, but what the hell does Mr. Lincoln think of us? These are some of the things my brothers and sisters want to know."

Pierce raised a hand.

"Robert, that's exactly why the Port Royal experiment remains so important," Pierce removed the delicate veneer of the situation. "There are many white people in the North, perhaps even some abolitionists, who fear giving black men their freedom outright. They don't know what will happen if negros are turned loose on white society. Some believe you will refuse to work. Others fear that the entire black race will flee North when liberated, filling up their cities and putting white men out of work. Many of those sent from the North to Port Royal came with the belief that the negros are not prepared for the full privileges of citizenship. That is why our teachers, superintendents, and ministers are here to help guide your people."

"We all shared your joy and excitement when Gen. Hunter freed the slaves in the states under his command," added French. "For a few days, until the President countermanded the general, we had a clear path for preparing our colored friends to enter society. Robert, I am convinced God will show the President the wisdom of emancipating all slaves. But we must be patient a while longer."

Mollified, but not satisfied, Robert replied, "We have been waiting for freedom for many years. I, too, believe the day of deliverance is at hand. I wish I could tell Father Abraham to free his people now."

Gen. Saxton looked at Robert. "Perhaps you will get that chance, one day, young man."

"Thank you for being truthful with me about your feelings," said Robert. "There's another thing I'd like to ask you about. This Col. Reynolds. He's been causing the black folks a lot of grief. He not only took all the cotton off the plantations, he's been taking all the livestock and furniture and 'bout anything that ain't nailed down. Then, he sells it back to them at high prices. All of the colored folks is scared of him. How long is he going to be here?"

"Reynolds came down with orders to confiscate last year's cotton crop and sell it to help finance the war." Saxton relayed in an aggravated tone. "Frankly, he has overstepped his bounds and I have had to call him in to my office on several occasions to question his activities. Last week, for example, his agents confiscated all of the books at the Beaufort library and sold them to a book company in Boston. Those books should have stayed here."

Pierce gave French a meaningful look.

"Actually Robert, things could be a lot worse," said the Treasury agent. "When I first came to Port Royal, Reynolds was already here and trying his best to get permission from Gen. Hunter to lease the plantations from the government. We fought tooth and nail over that because Reynolds would have kept the coloreds on Port Royal in a state of bondage, even if they were not technically slaves. Thank God, Gen. Hunter took our position on the matter. But if the people we have brought in from the North don't produce a good cotton crop this year, everything will be in jeopardy."

"I've got my eye on Reynolds, though," added Gen. Saxton. "One more outrage and he will be sent packing."

* * *

The sun had set behind the tall live oaks when the carriage rolled onto the grounds of the Brick Baptist Church. The sound of gospel hymns spilled out the windows into the crisp, spring air. On the lawn, dozens of black children laughed and frolicked. Two women, one white and one black, emerged from the two-story church and waited on the steps.

"The one on the right is Laura Towne and the other one is Charlotte Forten," said French.

The women were acquainted with French and Pierce and knew the general by his reputation as sympathetic to their cause.

French introduced Robert and their eyes grew wide with excitement.

"Is this the Mr. Small who pilots the *Planter*?" Laura drew out her words as if to savor the moment.

Robert smiled and bowed.

"The one and the same."

"We are so delighted to meet you," said Charlotte, a beautiful negress in her early twenties. "The people have been telling us about you. They are so proud of you Mr. Smalls."

Laura had arrived in Port Royal in April. The 37-year-old, who held strong anti-slavery views, had been sent to Port Royal by Philadelphia supporters of the Southern experiment in social change. Charlotte, 20 years Laura's junior, also from Philadelphia, was the daughter of an influential family there. Both women were devoted to educating the former slaves of the Sea Islands.

"Our work has only begun," Laura cautioned the visitors, "But we would be happy to show you our school."

The men walked into the Brick Church. Once a church for whites, it was given to the freed slaves in 1861. The men saw nearly sixty black men and women in front of a chalkboard. A petite, brunette woman used a ruler to point at letters of the alphabet. She pronounced each letter, then listened for her pupils to repeat it. She glanced up from her work and waved at Laura and the guests. Her eyes stopped on Gen. Saxton, then looked away demurely.

Charlotte whispered to Saxton, "That's Matilda Gordon. She's only been with us two days, but the coloreds seem to love her already."

Robert looked over the large hall with interest and asked, "Miss Laura, where are your younger students?"

"Oh, why they are out on the lawn. You saw them playing as you came in. They have finished their classes for the day. The people you see here are their parents and grandparents. They thirst for education even more then, their children. Many of the men walk five miles after their work in the fields to be with us. Others prefer to learn with the adults because they are embarrassed to be in the same class as the children."

Pierce complimented, "When I leave Port Royal, I will do so with the knowledge that of all the things we have tried to accomplish here, we have found the most success with our teachers. Wherever they go, even to the most distant of the Sea Islands, we receive the same report about this hunger the freed men and women have for learning."

"More than three-hundred children and a growing number of adults attended the newly formed classes at Brick Church." Laura beamed.

"We hear from teachers on other islands that the coloreds are just as eager to learn there," Charlotte added. "They learn very quickly and what is most encouraging is that everyone becomes a teacher as soon as they learn their letters. There is a great thirst among them to be able to read the Bible."

Robert squirmed. He knew numbers on nautical charts, but the intricacy of reading had escaped him. His last lesson had been with Alex Rhinds, more than ten years earlier. Since then, there was no opportunity to be taught, and he felt determined to remedy that.

"Mr. Smalls, we have encountered a problem that you could help us with," Charlotte interrupted his thoughts. "The colored people speak an unusual language called Gullah. It makes it difficult for us to be understood. And, there are times when I have no idea what they are trying to say to me. When time permits, would you be willing to teach us to speak Gullah?"

Gen. Saxton left the group and walked toward Miss Gordon.

"Perhaps we could walk outside and talk with the children," Robert said. "I could get you started with a few basic words in Gullah. Would you like to join us Mr. Pierce?"

Laura and French went to a room that doubled as an office and supply room while Pierce, Charlotte, and Robert walked toward the exit.

The door burst open and a black man rushed in. Behind him an orange glow on the horizon.

"Samuel, what is wrong?" Charlotte's voice was filled with concern.

"It's the Yankees," blurted the black man. "Lincoln's sojers is burnin' down Jerome's store!"

Robert and Pierce raced down the steps to the carriage, told Samuel to get in, and whipped the horses into a gallop toward flames. Within minutes, they arrived at a small, wooden structure, partially engulfed in fire. Six Union soldiers stood in front of the store, their bayonets pointed at a crowd of negroes milling about.

Jerome gestured to an officer in charge of the small company of Union soldiers. Pierce hopped from the carriage and ran to Jerome's side. A short, stocky figure smiled indifferently at Jerome's pleas for help.

"Reynolds, what's going on here? Why are you preventing this man from saving his store from the fire?"

"Mr. Pierce, he set de fire!" wailed Jerome.

"Is that true?" Pierce was incredulous.

"Of course, it's true. This nigger stole government property and tried to sell if from this shack he calls a store. Now, kindly remove yourself Sir."

Robert moved toward the cabin, he thought it could still be saved if the men could be organized into a bucket brigade.

Reynolds saw Robert and yelled to his men, "Shoot that black monkey dressed up like a sailor if he makes one more step."

Jerome tugged at Pierce's sleeve.

"What the man say ain't true Missah Pierce. All dat stuff in de store come from the teacher womens dat come in last week from up Nawth. Dey brought a big load of clothes and boots and shoes. Some molasses and salt. Soap, hats, and bonnets. Dem sweet womens told me I was to sell it fo' a fair price to de colored folks."

"You son of a bitch! Get out of my way!" Pierce shoved past Reynolds.

The officer sidestepped and caught Pierce off balance. Reynolds swung and his fist hit Pierce behind the ear, sending him flying to the ground.

Robert pushed Reynolds aside and ran to Pierce, shielding him from the soldiers. Pierce shook his head and stumbled to his knees. Blood trickled down his face. Robert helped him get to his feet.

Light from the fire showed the snarl on Reynold's face.

"You goddamn nigger lovers have gotten in my way for the last time," he screamed at Pierce. "Haven't you learned by now? These darkies don't want you down here. You ain't gonna have a crop this year 'cause you're too soft to make them work. Those Southern crackers had it right Pierce. Niggers ain't nothin' but animals. You want to work them, you gotta' use the whip."

His eyes moved to Smalls.

"You assaulted a Federal officer nigger," he growled. "That's a killing offense."

He motioned to his soldiers.

"Kill that nigger." He pointed at Robert.

The soldiers stood with mouths agape, unsure of how to respond.

"I said shoot him!"

The soldiers raised their rifles and aimed.

Robert closed his eyes.

Pierce stepped between him and the soldiers.

"If you kill him, you'll have to shoot me, too," he said calmly.

"Seems fair to me. You love them so much, you might as well die with 'em."

He raised his sword in the air.

"Stop!" a loud command echoed from the back of the crowd.

Reynolds looked up and saw Gen. Saxon walking toward him, trailed by Miss Gordon, Laura, and Charlotte.

"Lower your weapons men." Saxton was calm.

The soldiers complied with great relief.

Reynolds offered no resistance when Saxton took his sword. "Col. Reynolds, I believe your work here is done. Consider yourself under arrest and report to me in the morning. Sergeant, escort the colonel to his quarters."

"You okay?" Saxton moved toward Robert and Pierce.

Pierce nodded.

"Doing fine now General," Robert's voice shook. "Sure am glad to see you sir."

Saxton laughed. "The pleasure's mine sir."

Chapter 44

Robert could never have imagined how busy life would be after he brought the *Planter* out of Charleston and into the Union lines. Commodore DuPont and Gen. Saxton played tug-of-war with Robert's time that left few, precious moments with his family in Beaufort.

Lydia and Hannah enjoyed each other's company and worked well together. Robert's salary as a pilot in the Army, assigned to the Navy, provided a steady stream of income.

After Pierce returned to Boston, on the same ship as the disgraced Reynolds, Gen. Saxton sent Robert to the Brick House on St. Helena's Island as often as possible to work with the Gideonites. Robert and Charlotte had begun a Gullah lexicon and plantation superintendents often relied upon them to help resolve disputes.

His military duties consumed even more time. Shortly after Pierce's departure, the *Planter* participated in the liberation of Edisto Island, one of the largest of the Sea Islands. The Federal troops met a light resistance from Rebel forces. White plantation owners fled and left several thousand slaves to fend for themselves. Nearly 800 of them sought protection at Port Royal and the *Planter* transported them to the safe environs of the military outpost.

DuPont also called upon Robert and the *Planter* to transport troops to James Island to support maneuvers along the Stono River. Thanks to intelligence provided by Robert following his escape from Charleston, the Union now possessed the abandoned Rebel fort on Cole's Island. Gen. Hunter hoped to advance on Charleston by the end of June and capture the hotbed of the secessionists.

Within three weeks, Commodore DuPont's fleet, led by the *Planter*, shuttled nearly 6,000 Union troops to Cole's Island without resistance from Southern forces. Even Gen. Hunter, who anticipated a counterattack from the Rebels, seemed surprised by the ease his forces established a foothold.

The incursion into Southern soil didn't go unnoticed. Federal scouts reported several forts erected and fortified along the Stono River. The largest was near a small hamlet renamed Secessionville, in honor of the rebellion that began in Charleston.

Gen. Hunter put Gen. Henry Benham in charge of securing the Union's foothold. He gave strict orders not to advance on Rebel positions until reinforcements arrived. Despite a large presence on Sullivan's Island, the ever-cautious Hunter wanted to double the size of his army before it advanced on Charleston.

Events in Northern Virginia stymied his plans. Gen. George McClellan refused to send additional troops to Port Royal, saying they were needed to bolster the army he commanded that protected Washington, D.C.

Then allow me use of my black regiment, wrote Gen. Hunter to Secretary of War Edwin Stanton. His pleas fell on deaf ears and the opportunity to capture Charleston began to fade.

The delay upset Robert as much as it did DuPont.

"Why is the general waiting?" Robert asked Commodore DuPont during a supply run to Coles Island to look at the new federal fortifications.

"It's complicated Robert," the Naval commander replied. "Lincoln has given McClellan orders to advance on Richmond and capture the Rebel's capital. But McClellan refuses to follow those orders until he believes he has an army large enough to overrun Lee."

"I see that," said Robert. "but I also see thousands of black men at Port Royal who would be eager to fight for the Yanks. Hell, Commodore, I would be one of the first to fight."

DuPont gave Robert's shoulder a squeeze.

"I know you would, son. But the Navy needs you worse than the Army at this point. I agree with you that raising an army of freed black men would help Gen. Hunter's efforts to capture Charleston. But you also have to understand the President's position. If he allowed black men to fight for the Union, it could infuriate those in the border states."

"Well, it's a damn shame, if you don't mind me saying so Commodore. If the Union struck now, the Bluecoats could be in Charleston within a week."

Commodore DuPont sighed.

"Point well taken Robert."

* * *

A week after returning from Cole's Island with DuPont, Robert gazed over the *Planter's* deck, which was covered with wounded men. He couldn't believe how quickly the fortunes of war had changed in just a few days.

On June 15th, Gen. Benham defied Gen. Hunter's orders and attacked the Rebel batteries on James Island. Although the Union soldiers fought valiantly, Confederate forces under the command of Col. T. G. Lamar repulsed the assault. Benham ordered a frontal attack at daybreak on the fort held by Lamar's 750 men. The Union lines faltered after slogging through the knee-deep mud that protected approaches to the Confederate fort at Secessionville.

At one point it appeared the Federal assault might succeed. Blue-clad soldiers reached the fort's parapet before Rebel reinforcements arrived. After fierce, hand-to-hand combat, the Union troops retreated. Two more assaults were ordered. Both met similar results before Gen. Benham ordered a general retreat.

258

The *Planter*, docked a mile from the battle, received casualties after the outbreak of the hostilities. Robert's concern mounted as a trickle of wounded turned into a torrent. Blood stained the decks as the wounded cried for help.

By 9 a.m., the battle ended. The North's window of opportunity to end the war in South Carolina, closed with 689 wounded and 107 fatalities. Confederate forces, emboldened by success, pushed Union forces back to a narrow strip of land near the mouth of Stono River before Hunter ordered the evacuation of James Island.

Bad news plagued Gen. Hunter for the remainder of the summer. Without approval from the War Department, his efforts to form two regiments of black soldiers languished. He had no authority to issue commissions and no money to buy uniforms or guns, so he disbanded the regiment he started and sent 800 men back to the Sea Island plantations.

Ten thousand of his enlisted men went North to bolster Federal forces that suffered heavy losses in the Seven Days Battle in Virginia. He was left with a skeleton force to maintain control over South Carolina, Georgia, and Florida.

His long friendship with Lincoln was on the ropes. Repeated letters to the President produced no help. Lincoln adamantly refused to allow black soldiers to carry arms. Instead, the Commander-in-Chief wanted to send freed slaves to colonies in Central America.

Gen. Saxton encountered difficulties with the colored population on the Sea Islands and it became obvious the cotton crop would fail. Able bodied men, drafted by Hunter, returned to fields overrun with weeds and insects. Black men who avoided the draft, still hid in the woods.

The Gideonites enjoyed limited success during the hot summer days of 1862. Schools flourished throughout the Sea Islands. However, efforts to instill New England values of free labor, thriftiness, and self-reliance had not caught on with many of the colored people. Some of the white superintendent and missionaries questioned if the Port Royal experiment was destined to fail. More than three dozen white volunteers had already gone back North, unable to cope with the scorching South Carolina summer.

As the dog days of August descended on Port Royal, Gen. Hunter called an emergency meeting of French, Gen. Saxton, and Commodore DuPont. Saxton sent a special invitation to Robert to join the group at Hunter's headquarters in Beaufort.

A dispirited Hunter opened the meeting.

"I feel as though Washington has conspired against us at every turn. The eyes of the nation are on Port Royal and Pierce's grand experiment. What chance do we have when President Lincoln prefers to send the negro to their own colonies? I wonder sometimes if he has ever met a black man!"

"Don't be too harsh general," said DuPont. "The war isn't going well. McClellan won't cooperate with Lincoln. He must appease the slave states still in the Union and deal with the anti-slavery lobby. Our problems in Port Royal must pale in comparison."

French bemoaned the fact that donations for the Gideonites had slowed to a trickle. The Baptist New Yorkers and the Unitarians of Boston bickered without pause. Neither group could pay their workers past September.

"Out of sight, out of mind," offered Gen. Saxton.

"What was that?" Hunter said with disbelief.

"I'm just saying, David, that there's a whole lot to the old adage: 'the squeaky wheel gets the grease.' We can sit in this office and moan and groan all day, but if we want something done, we must be heard by those who can help. I think all of us have forgotten that we have a national treasure right here in Port Royal."

He pointed to Robert, who was caught off guard by Saxton's comment.

"Robert Smalls is known throughout the North for the courage he showed in sailing the *Planter* to our fleet. He has worked closely with his people since then and knows their fears, and needs, better than most. Furthermore, I feel certain the President would like to meet the hero of

Charleston," Saxton assured the group. "I propose arranging a meeting between our man and the President."

All four men turned to Robert, who looked back in astonishment.

French was excited by the idea. "While we are in Washington, I could take Robert to Philadelphia, Boston, and New York. I think he would be quite a sensation, get people excited again about our efforts here."

Robert had yet to weigh in on the plan. He wasn't sure how to respond.

Gen. Hunter slapped his hand on the table.

"Pack your bags Robert. You're going to Washington!" ordered Hunter.

"Uh, uh, uh," stammered Robert. "Yes sir, General Sir."

* * *

They voyaged by steamship to Washington, D.C. French prepared Robert for many hours to meet with the President. Once Robert learned more about Lincoln's view of slavery, his initial optimism began to fade.

Chapter 45

Washington, D.C., August 20, 1862

Robert was accustomed to heat and humidity, but the waiting room in the White House was unbearably hot. An occasional whiff of a breeze blew through the open windows to provide a temporary respite. A few soldiers and men dressed in business suits, fanned themselves with hats, folded newspapers, and anything else available. The conversation was as still as the air.

Robert looked at Mansfield French, seated to his right. The preacher seemed unperturbed by the heat. He read placidly from the Bible, noticed Robert's stare, and gave his friend a comforting smile.

"It won't be long."

Robert, dressed in his blue dress uniform, tried to get comfortable in the chair but a million butterflies flitted about in his abdomen. His leg twitched nervously as he closed his eyes to calm his nerves.

The door to the President's office opened and an officer motioned to French.

"The President will see you now."

Robert's heart leapt into his throat. He followed French, unaware of the stares from the others in the waiting room.

Sunshine spilled in from a large window and lit the small, richly-appointed room. Two men stood, one behind the desk, the other in the shadows near a curtain. Secretary of War Stanton sat in a side chair but rose to acknowledge the newcomers to the Oval Office. Robert recognized the familiar face of Abraham Lincoln, and the man in the shadows looked vaguely familiar. French walked with an outstretched hand toward Lincoln.

"Hello Mansfield."

Lincoln's voice was more high-pitched than Robert expected. He thought a much deeper voice would emanate from such a large man.

"Mr. President, it's so nice to see you again. Gen. Hunter sends his regards."

Lincoln smiled.

"I hope the general is faring well in South Carolina. I'm afraid we have been at cross-purposes these last few months. He was, and I hope, still is my friend."

Robert, yet to be introduced, watched in fascination as the President and French exchanged pleasantries. Lincoln, at six feet, four inches, dwarfed Mansfield. He was thin, almost gangly. The man's face intrigued Robert. He had been told the President was ugly, "practically an ogre." Lincoln couldn't be considered handsome, yet, his craggy face beamed with kindness and benevolence. Robert's nervousness vanished.

"Mr. President, I'd like to introduce you ..."

"I know who this man is." His grey eyes twinkled with merriment. "The Secretary has told me all about Mr. Smalls. Welcome to the White House young man. I can't wait to hear your story. By the way, have you met Mr. Frederick Douglass?"

Douglass stepped out of the shadows.

Robert thought Douglass was the most handsome negro he had ever seen.

Not as tall as Lincoln, powerfully-built with broad shoulders, Douglass' presence filled the room. His long black hair, streaked with gray, swept back from his face revealed riveting eyes with a stern countenance.

If God is black, this is what he must look like.

"It's a pleasure to finally meet you," Douglass' voice was deep and rich in tone. "We've been reading about your exploits in the newspapers. You are an inspiration to our race."

Lincoln sat at his desk and leaned back in his chair, his hands propped behind his neck. He sat and looked at Robert with expectation. "Start from the beginning and tell me everything."

For the next half hour, the men in the room listened intently as Robert described his childhood in Beaufort, his work in Charleston as a waiter and street lamp lighter, his love of the sea and his career as a riverboat pilot. He explained the events of May 13, the details of how he managed to pass the Rebel sentries without detection. When he got to the part of the story where the *Planter* raised a white flag before reaching the Union blockade, Lincoln stopped him.

"It sounds like that may have been the most terrifying moment of the journey."

"No sir. I was scared most when we went to pick up my wife and children. They mean everything to me. When I didn't see their signal, I thought I would die."

The President looked puzzled but motioned with a wave for Robert to proceed.

Robert continued to speak about the joy he felt when he delivered his family and crew to his former home in Beaufort, about the good work being done on the Sea Islands on behalf of the former slaves, and about his disappointment that U.S. troops had not captured Charleston after securing a strong foothold on Cole's Island.

"I guess that's about it, Sir," concluded Robert. He looked around the room to see if anyone had questions.

Lincoln rose from his chair and reached his arm toward Robert.

"I'd like to shake your hand sir. You acted with great courage and skill. I wish we had a dozen more just like you."

Robert shook the President's hand. "But you do have a dozen like me Mr. Lincoln. A dozen, dozen. Hundreds of dozens. Thousands even—all just waiting for your call to action!"

"Well put Mr. Smalls." Douglass released a genuine laugh. "That's exactly what Mr. Lincoln and I were discussing before you arrived. Unfortunately, the President isn't convinced the black man will fight for his freedom."

Lincoln, taken aback by the fervor in Robert's voice, looked pensively out of the window.

"I admit I do have reservations about arming negroes," he finally said to Douglass. "I'm not sure we could do much for the blacks. Indeed, we do not have enough arms to equip our own white troops."

The President reiterated what most of the men in the room already knew. Preserving the Union remained his primary concern. "If I could save the Union without freeing any slaves I would do it, and if I could save it by freeing all the slaves I would do it; and if I could save it by freeing some and leaving others alone, I would also do that. What I do about slavery and the colored race, I do because I believe it helps to save the Union."

Douglass' eyes blazed with fury.

"You are being obstinate." His roar caused the others to look at him in astonishment. "Lincoln, you have always considered the negro an inferior race. I've heard you say it time and again. You direct too much attention to the border states. You fear giving the black man his freedom will provoke them to join the rebellion. You tell us you want to preserve the Union, yet, you refuse to hit the South where it would hurt most, by freeing their slaves."

The outburst stunned Robert and French. The President, however, listened politely.

"Would my word free the slaves when I cannot even enforce the Constitution in the Rebel states, Douglass?" he said without a trace of rancor in his voice. "Is there a single court, or judge, or individual that would be influenced by it there? I recently signed legislation from Congress that offers protection and freedom to slaves of rebel masters who come into our lines? Yet, I have not learned that the law has caused a single slave to come over to us."

Douglass looked at the President in amazement.

"You haven't heard of slaves fleeing to freedom?" Incredulous, he pointed to Robert. "You are looking at a man, Sir, who risked death, and the death of his children, to seek freedom. What kind of proof do you need, Mr. President?"

For the first time, Secretary Stanton entered the conversation.

"Abraham," he was calm, but firm. "There are other considerations we must take into account when discussing the negroes who have been liberated in the South. After our losses in Virginia, we face a serious manpower problem. Recruitment isn't keeping pace with our casualties. As Robert has told us, there are thousands of black men in Port Royal ready and willing to fight on behalf of the Union. As our forces advance into rebel territory, thousands more will rally to the Union flag, but, only if you allow it.

"In my view, negroes are like other people. They act upon motive. Why should they do anything for us, if we will do nothing for them? If they stake their lives for us, they must be prompted by the strongest motives—even the promise of freedom."

Deep in thought, the President pulled his beard. After a moment's silence, he asked Robert, "Why did you risk everything? I need to know."

Robert took a deep breath and gazed into the President's warm, grey eyes.

"Mr. Lincoln, on the trip to Washington, Mr. French told me you recently lost a son."

Lincoln nodded.

"I have a son, too. His name is Robert Smalls, Jr. and I love him as dearly as you must have loved the son you lost, and those that still live. Although we have never met, Mr. Lincoln, I know in my heart that you would do anything for your children, even if it caused you great grief. When I put my family on the *Planter*, I did so with the full knowledge that I was putting them in harm's way. I also knew that if I stayed in

266

Charleston, they were also in peril. My wife had a good, kind master. But the law in the South gave him the right to sell my children if he so chose. That knowledge hung over me like a sword, Mr. Lincoln.

"When word came to Charleston that Gen. Hunter had freed the slaves, it felt as though God himself had sent an angel to Earth to show me a path to freedom. I would have beaten down the doors of Hell to follow that glorious path.

"I am so saddened that you lost a son, Mr. Lincoln, but if you take a stand against slavery, you will gain many more sons who will call you father. Your colored sons and daughters will love you, they will respect you, and they will fight for you. Because, Mr. President, you will offer them a kind of salvation second only to that given by God. Give my people hope, Mr. President. You will never regret it."

Drained, Robert sank into his chair..

Lincoln looked at him with sadness, then compassion. He turned to French.

"Well, Mansfield, I suspect you came to Washington with something in mind?"

"Why yes, Mr. President. Gen. Hunter asks again for permission to recruit and arm a regiment of black soldiers to aid in the defense of Port Royal."

"Unfortunately, I have other plans for Gen. Hunter," Lincoln replied. "Isn't there another General in Port Royal? Saxton maybe?"

French confirmed Gen. Saxton was the military commander of Port Royal.

"Mr. Smalls speaks eloquently," interrupted Douglass. "You have the moral imperative to listen to him Lincoln."

The President didn't respond to the abolitionist, instead he addressed Stanton.

"I have not decided against a proclamation of liberty to the slaves, but I hold the matter under advisement." He stood to indicate the meeting was over.

"I can assure you the matter of slavery and what should be done with those we free is on my mind, by day and night, more than any other. Whatever shall appear to be God's will, I will do. Goodbye, Robert. Thank you for traveling this long distance to be with me today. Perhaps we will meet again. Safe travels, gentlemen."

* * *

A week later, Robert spoke to a large crowd of abolitionists in New York. He returned to his hotel room to pack for another engagement when someone knocked on the door. Before Robert could open it, French burst into the room, a letter clutched in his hand.

"The most incredible news!" Elation filled his voice. "A letter from the President. He has given Gen. Saxton permission to recruit the first black regiment in the United States. We've done it Robert. We've done it."

* * *

Their efforts bore fruit when President Lincoln read the Emancipation Proclamation, which freed those in bondage in the Southern states. For the first time, black men could legally enlist in the U.S. Army and they responded in great numbers. The 1st South Carolina Volunteer Infantry Regiment officially mustered January 1, 1863 under the Emancipation Tree at Camp Saxton. Robert attended the ceremony as a dignitary and his heart swelled with pride.

Chapter 46

After he met with the President, Robert spent two months in New England with French. He was paraded before dozens of prominent abolitionists eager to meet the man who commandeered one of the Rebel's most prized ships. Donations poured into the relief efforts on the Sea Islands.

The popularity and fame he enjoyed in the North settled uncomfortably on Robert's shoulders. As he moved from one meeting to the next in cities like New York, Boston, and Philadelphia, Robert became more confident in his ability to inspire large audiences with his story and testimony about the willingness of colored men to fight on behalf of the Union.

Robert missed his family. He hadn't seen Hannah or the children in weeks. As a special surprise, French arranged for Hannah to sail north with baby Robert in October to participate in a special celebration. Lydia agreed to care for Elizabeth while Hannah was away.

Tears of joy flowed when Robert greeted them when they disembarked from the steamer in New York City.

Hannah's face glowed with pride as she looked into Robert's eyes.

"We've heard so much about yo' work in the Nawth, and dey say you seen Mr. Lincon, too. Honey, we all be so proud of you."

Robert snuggled with Robert and marveled at how much he had grown. Hannah giggled when Robert articulated the details of his meeting with the President.

"My heart was beating like a drum, when they called us to go into the President's office," Robert perspired at the memory. "Thought it was going to pop right out of my chest. Then I remembered what Mr. French has told me about speaking in front people. He said, 'just close your eyes and pretend like the people in the audience are in their underwear.' So, when I first saw Mr. Lincoln, I tried to see him in his long john's. Didn't work though. I was about to faint before he spoke, but when he did, I knew everything was gonna be alright!"

They rode in an open carriage, and Hannah gawked at the tall buildings and streets that teemed with people of various colors.

Michael Clemmons, a prominent New York businessman, volunteered to host the Smalls family. Clemmons, and his wife Bobbie, met the Smalls at the mansion's door.

"Welcome to New York!" Mrs. Clemmons kissed Hannah on the cheek and asked to hold Robert.

* * *

After lunch, Robert met French in the parlor of the Clemmons' home. The little minister seemed exceptionally animated. He hurried Robert and Hannah into a carriage bound for Shiloh Church at the corner of Prince and Marion Streets.

When the carriage stopped at the destination, French told Robert to wait while he went into the large, brick church. He emerged a minute later and motioned for Robert and Hannah to join him at the door.

"Robert, a grateful people welcome you."

He swung open the double doors to reveal hundreds of black and white parishioners who stood in Robert's honor. A signal from the church's preacher caused the room to erupt into deafening cheers. Dazed, Robert allowed French to lead him, Hannah, and the baby to the front of the church. As they walked down the aisle, people jostled one another just to touch Robert and shout words of appreciation.

The Rev. Henry Highland Garnet met Robert at the altar and hugged him. He caught Robert's hand and raised it high into the air, a gesture met with exuberant cheers. The minister motioned for an assistant to come forward with an elegant leather case.

Rev. Garnet raised his hands to quiet the crowd. "Robert Smalls, of Charleston, SC, the colored people of the City of New York cordially welcome you as a representative of the loyal people, comprising four-million black Unionists, now living in the Rebel or semi-Rebel states. You have nobly represented this loyal population by achieving your own liberty and that of your wife, children, and crew.

"The act of seizing the gunboat and passing successfully the six forts of Charleston harbor demonstrated a capacity for military and naval conduct excelled by nothing which has occurred in this present war. Our brother Smalls has by this one act proven beyond any man's dispute the safety, the justice and the easy possibility of the government giving immediate and universal emancipation."

Rev. Garnet removed a gold medal emblazoned with a depiction of Charleston Harbor with the steamer *Planter* and Fort Sumter in the foreground and the Union fleet in the background. The reverse side read,

Presented to Robert Smalls by the colored citizens of
New York, October 2, 1862, as a token of their regard for
his heroism, his love of liberty and his passion.

Robert signaled Hannah to his side. They turned together to receive more thunderous applause.

"God bless you, Mr. Smalls," came a shout from the audience. A chorus of 'amens' followed as Robert basked in the love and admiration of his people.

Chapter 47

Port Royal, December 1862

Robert and Hannah returned to Port Royal in time for Christmas.

Admiral DuPont stopped by the Smalls home to welcome his pilot back. "I hope the Northern abolitionists haven't spoiled you and turned your head."

"Admiral, my head was turned the entire time—to Port Royal," he chuckled.

* * *

In January of 1863, every man, woman, and child in Port Royal lined the shore to watch the arrival of five Union ironclads: The *New Ironsides, Passaic, Montauk, Patapsco,* and the *Weehawken.* Sent by Secretary of the Navy Gideon Welles, they represented the vanguard of a fleet of the new, powerful ironclad boats put under DuPont's command. They came with instructions for DuPont to enter the harbor of Charleston and demand the surrender of all its defenses.

With an election looming, Lincoln was desperate for a military victory to recover fading public support. Confederate forces under Robert E. Lee remained firmly in control of Richmond. In the West, the Union advance had run into a roadblock at Vicksburg, Miss. Lincoln needed a victory as symbolic as the fall of Charleston, where the rebellion had started.

To reduce the Confederate forts, the Navy sent almost every heavily-armored warship in its fleet to Port Royal. Maps of Charleston Harbor draped the walls of Admiral DuPont's war room aboard the *New Ironsides* four months later. The admiral, surrounded by the captains of nine ironclads, poured over a hand-drawn map of Charleston harbor. The mapmaker, Robert Smalls, pointed to a shoal on the southern approach to the Rebel bastion.

"The main channel will be a tight squeeze." Robert indicated a spot on the chart. "I remember having no problem laying mines across the length of it while the *Planter* was in Charleston. We had stretched nets across portions of the inlet to foul propellers. You will also find buoys that the gunners of Fort Sumter and Fort Moultrie use for sighting their guns."

He looked at DuPont, despondent. "It will be like piking a hornet's nest, Admiral."

Despite apprehension about the Navy's impending attack on Charleston, Robert felt elated to be back in Port Royal and engaged in military operations again.

Admiral DuPont stood on the deck of the *Wabash* with Robert by his side.

"Quite a sight, eh Robert?"

Robert whistled softly. "Hard to imagine how they float with all of that iron on them."

DuPont invited Robert aboard his flagship to review the pilot's knowledge of Charleston Harbor. Before he escaped the port city, Robert helped lay mines and other obstructions in the main channel leading into the harbor, but his knowledge was nearing a year old. However, the pilot knew of the harbor's tides and currents, two factors that could play an important role in the impending battle.

The four iron monitors made an impressive addition to the fleet in Port Royal, but DuPont remained dubious about the warships' ability to overcome a well-built Rebel fort. In March, he sent the *Weehawken* and several gunboats to attack Ft. McAllister, an earthen fort near Savannah, Georgia—the results were suboptimal.

The *Weehawken's* two smooth-bore guns blasted holes in the fort during the day. By night, the Confederates simply filled the holes and the whole process had to be repeated the next day. The Admiral fretted about the *Weehawken's* slow rate of fire. It took seven minutes to reload the cannons and the portholes became vulnerable to return fire from the enemy.

DuPont sent three other ironclads to assist in the attack on Ft. McAllister, but the Rebel bastion repelled the invaders. The *Weehawken* hit a mine and only the quick action of its captain kept it from sinking.

* * *

In late March, four more monitors reached Port Royal. The *Catskill, Nantucket,* and *Nahant* filled out the compliment of Passaic-class warships. All had single turrets containing two cannons. The Navy's new, experimental monitor, the *Keokuk*, created a stir with its twin turrets. Long and narrow, the *Keokuk* looked sleek compared to the squat little boats that made up the Passaic-class ships.

Robert followed DuPont and a group of senior officers to the wharf where the new ship berthed. All were eager to go aboard and explore the experimental craft. The ship's captain climbed down from the helm atop the forward turret and saluted the Admiral.

"Capt. Rhinds at your service, Sir."

Robert couldn't contain his excitement. He rushed past DuPont and jumped onto the *Keokuk*, wrapping his old friend in a firm embrace. Alex returned the hug, looking over Robert's shoulder at DuPont with amusement.

"You're commanding this tin can?" Robert laughed.

"The honor is mine," Alex chuckled.

DuPont cleared his throat.

Robert wheeled around to face him.

274

"Welcome to Port Royal Capt. Rhinds," said the Admiral. "That is a fine ship you have. Very unusual in design, I must say. What do you think of her?"

"Come take a look, sir." Alex moved to one side to let the curious visitors aboard.

Alex proudly gave the men a tour of the ship. Each of the two, massive turrets contained an 11-inch Dahlgren gun. Each gun revolved on a circular track, which could be aimed from any of three armored gun openings. Fully-loaded and carrying a complement of ninety-two officers and men, the *Keokuk* could make nine knots, twice the speed of the other monitors in the fleet. Commissioned only a month earlier, the ship still smelled of fresh paint.

DuPont examined the armor that stretched to the waterline of the ship. The new design called for alternating horizontal iron bars and oak, sheathed with sheet iron, at a thickness of almost six inches.

"We're giving up some armor to gain speed." Alex noticed the Admiral's critical look. "The ship is quick, and I think she will do well in battle."

"Well, she has a good captain," replied DuPont. "I know a pilot who has a lot of time on his hands. Think you may have room on board for a no-good, fast-talking rascal?"

Robert and Alex looked at each.

"You wouldn't be referring to my nappy-haired friend, here would you?" Alex tried to keep the laughter out of his voice.

"One and the same," said DuPont. "Smalls, would you like to go back to Charleston? You know they still have a price on your head?"

Two days later, the *Keokuk* steamed out of Port Royal with other advance elements of the invasion fleet. Her new pilot could only grin.

Chapter 48

Charleston, April 7, 1863

Robert couldn't see. Thick blue smoke enveloped the *Keokuk* making it impossible to navigate through the viewing slits in the forward turret. The smoke cleared without warning and bright sunlight brought the enormous bulk of Fort Sumter into sharp focus. A blossom of orange erupted from the fort, followed by an explosion that rocked the *Keokuk* from bow to stern. Sunlight streamed through a five-inch hole punched near the turret's base.

"Shit, we're in trouble Robert," Capt. Rhinds shouted above the sound of the raging battle.

The federal assault on Fort Sumter took place nearly two years after it fell to the rebels. The battle began abysmally and went downhill from there. Admiral DuPont's plan called for a two-prong attack that commenced when the tide turned. As the sea rushed from the harbor, it would make it easier to steer. In addition, any ships disabled during battle would drift seaward instead of further into the harbor.

The squadron carried thirty-two guns, the most powerful attack force ever sent by the U.S. Navy against an enemy force. It faced three rings of forts bristling with smaller, but extremely accurate cannons. Fort Sumter, alone, had eighty guns guarding the entrance to the city.

In advance of the attack, Capt. Rhinds, with Robert's direction, placed buoys marking the main channel. By midday, preparations were complete. The order of attack called for the *Weehawken* to lead the column, followed by *Passaic, Montauk, Patapsco*, and the admiral's flagship, the *New Ironsides*. Once in position, the remainder of the ironclads would follow with *Keokuk* bringing up the rear.

The morning of April 7th dawned clear and mild. The fleet rocked gently on small swells. From the observation platform atop the forward turret, Robert scanned the horizon with his field glasses. The Confederate flag and the South Carolina flag waved over Fort Sumter, with small regimental flags along the parapets. In the distance, he could make out the shapes of people along the wharfs and piers. The battle for Charleston had drawn an audience.

Admiral DuPont signaled for the attack to begin, but the advance ran into immediate trouble. The *Weehawken,* equipped with a raft attached to the bow, sailed first in line to detonate Rebel mines. The ship's captain, John Rodgers, had rigged the raft with grapnels to catch any obstacles in its path.

When the *Weehawken* attempted to weigh anchor, the chain caught one of the grapnels and fouled the ship's propeller. The crew worked feverishly to clear the propeller, but it took 90-minutes and delayed the operation.

The first wave made its way through the main channel leading to Charleston, two hours after DuPont gave the go order.

Aboard the *Keokuk*, Rhinds and Robert heard cheers from across the water in the direction of Fort Sumter as a band played *Dixie*

"They're ready for us." Rhinds gulped.

The ironclads sailed past the Confederate batteries at Cummings Point without incident and made a beeline toward Fort Sumter. The first shot of the battle came from Fort Moultrie, far away on Sullivan's Island. The cannon ball splashed near the *Weehawken*, spraying it with water.

As soon as the *Weehawken* reached a buoy, well-known by Confederate gunners, all guns from Fort Sumter, Fort Moultrie, Batteries

Bee and Beauregard on Sullivan's Island, and Battery Gregg at Cummings Point opened fire on the invaders.

The second wave of the squadron lined up behind the *New Ironsides*. From the vantage point atop the forward turret, Robert and Rhinds saw the devastation the Confederate forts poured on the lead elements of the attack force. Some cannon balls bounced off the heavily-armored monitors, but others pummeled the vessels. The *Weehawken* and *Passaic* stopped, then began drifting back into the channel, which caused the tight forward formation to become disorganized.

"Look, the *New Ironside* is in trouble!" Rhinds yelled.

The huge frigate, still a mile from Fort Sumter, weaved erratically, and made little headway against the tide.

"Maybe she has lost steam, or the steering is jammed," Robert offered.

As Confederate forces directed effective fire on the first wave of monitors, flags went up on the *New Ironsides* mast to signal she was out of action. DuPont ordered the second wave of monitors to join the attack.

Robert watched as the *Weehawken* finally fired its Dahlgren cannon, sending a 400-pound projectile toward Fort Sumter. The impact caused shards of brick to spray into the air. The second shot sprayed a column of water over the fort's ramparts.

As each of the monitors returned fire, they were enveloped in clouds of smoke. After several minutes, a slight breeze cleared the gunpowder vapor, and they fired again. For each shot taken by the monitors, the forts returned ten.

Catskill led the remaining Navy monitors into the fray. The battle raged for almost two hours and all the ships of the first wave experienced varying degrees of damage.

More than 150-direct hits put the *Passaic* out of action. Her crew scrambled to plug holes near the ship's waterline. The *Patapsco* ran aground, and Confederate gunners zeroed in on the hapless ship. The *Montauk*, still fired on Fort Sumter, but lolled in the channel, impeding the second wave.

The *Catskill* led the second wave past Fort Moultrie, but lost steerage when the Rebel gunners hit her just below the waterline. She continued to return ineffective fire while the crew struggled to clear the rudder.

Rhinds and Robert left the observation deck and took positions on the small bridge located near the *Keokuk's* forward turret. Narrow slits in the armor, about twelve-inches long and four-inches in depth, allowed the captain and his pilot to see the battle unfold. A young, white ensign manned the helm to Robert's right, awaiting orders from Capt. Rhinds.

As the *Keokuk* passed the *Nantucket*, he saw the ship's turret cocked at an awkward angle. Smoke poured from the gun ports and men inside fought a fire.

A shell bounced off the curved sides of the *Keokuk* and sprayed water over the ship's forward battery. Inside the turret, covered with five inches of iron—compared to the eleven inches on the other monitors—gunners looked up to see Capt. Rhinds. The ships guns stood primed and ready for action.

Another Confederate shell slammed into the *Keokuk*. Then another.

Rhinds peered through the little observation port. He could only see parts of the battle, so he directed the helmsman to make small course corrections from side to side to get a better view of his position. Robert scanned for familiar buoys and landmarks, with an occasional shout to the helmsman to keep the *Keokuk* in the main channel.

Through the smoke and disorder of the Union squadron, Robert saw a clear path to Fort Sumter at the same time as Rhinds. The captain ordered full-speed and the *Keokuk* sprinted toward the rebel fort.

Officers in Fort Sumter saw the *Keokuk* and ordered gunners to give her their full attention. The very foundations of the fort shook as dozens of heavy guns fired on the double-turreted boat as it approached through clouds of smoke.

Shells whistled through the air and pummeled the *Keokuk*.

"Stay on course," ordered Capt. Rhinds.

On his command, the gunner in the forward turret opened the porthole and pushed the cannon's muzzle through.

"Fire!"

The *Keokuk* shuddered against the recoil, then continued its relentless forward progress. Gunners drew the cannon back, closed the porthole and began the laborious reload. They cheered when Rhinds announced the shot hit Fort Sumter.

The ship passed through another thick cloud. Robert was confident, despite zero visibility, that nothing stood between the Keokuk and the fort. When the smoke cleared, Fort Sumter filled his view port.

"We are on top of her!" he screamed to Rhinds, just before a Confederate shell punched a hole in the forward turret. Bolts that affixed the armor ricocheted around the interior like buckshot. The detritus broke the arm of a gunner, but the gun was spared.

Rhinds gave the command to fire the Dahlgren again. At such close range, less than 200-yards, the shot was a direct hit. When the smoke cleared, Rhinds saw a three-foot crater in the face of the fort.

A shower of canon fire rained down on the *Keokuk*. The ear-shattering blasts resulted in more holes in the turret.

The crew alerted the captain, "Some shells penetrated the hull!"

Sailors scurried to plug the damage.

"This is suicide Captain," the panicked helmsman beseeched. "Shall we retreat?"

"Hell no, Smathers!"

Light shined through seven new holes in the turret. Two other gunners, wounded by shrapnel, lay on the floor while other sailors from the inactive aft turret streamed forward to take their place.

Rhinds ordered the gunners to open the gun port facing Fort Sumter.

As they fired, an incoming shell made a direct hit on the *Keokuk's* bridge. The concussion knocked the men to the ground.

Robert slowly rose. He rubbed the sting from his eyes. The helmsman was sprawled out on the deck, beside him, Rhinds stirred.

The anguished cries of sailors came from below.

"Are you okay Alex?" Robert yelled over the roar of battle.

Rhinds pushed to his knees, then stood.

He reached to help Robert to his feet. "Take the helm," Rhinds ordered. "I'm going below to see how bad it is."

Robert looked through the view port. The *Keokuk* stood close enough to the fort for Robert to see the faces of the Rebel gunners and hear the officers direct fire on the ironclad.

Rhinds stuck his head through the hatch between the bridge and crew quarters. "It looks like Swiss cheese down here. Holes everywhere."

The captain hung his head and looked up in resignation.

"The ship is sinking. Can you get us out of here?"

Robert gave orders to reverse the engines as the *Keokuk*, weighted down with tons of sea water, slowly turned from Fort Sumter and clawed its way back to open water. Guns from Fort Sumter continued to hit the ship as it retreated.

A sad procession of Union ironclads filed out of Charleston Harbor as the sun begin to set. They remained under power, though severely damaged. The *Keokuk* sat heavily in the water, listing to port. Below, Rhinds rushed from one part of the ship to another to order the seamen to plug holes that peppered the hull.

"Say a prayer. It might hold." Rhinds half-joked as he returned to the bridge, exhausted.

Tenders from other ships in the squadron joined the *Keokuk* with the much-needed supplies to reinforce temporary patches. Robert and Rhinds walked on the deck, taking measure of the damage.

"I count ninety-two hits."

"The Lord was with us Alex. There's no way this ship should be floating. We took a hell of a beating."

Robert stiffened. A subtle shift in the wind put his senses on high alert. "And, it's not over."

* * *

A storm rolled off the coast creating waves five feet tall. The *Keokuk*, in its weakened condition, took on water. Despite valiant efforts to save her, the *Keokuk* sank shortly after Robert managed to bring her out of Charleston Harbor. All hands survived to fight another day.

Although the *Keokuk* sank in shallow water, Federal engineers deemed the vessel lost. However, under the cover of darkness, Confederate engineers miraculously managed to salvage the valuable canons two weeks later and put the weapons back into service against the invaders.

Chapter 49

Port Royal, June 2, 1863

The fleet's dismal failure had serious consequences for Admiral DuPont. Upon his return to Port Royal, the admiral engaged in a spirited correspondence with Navy Secretary Welles. The admiral wanted to launch a counteroffensive the day after the defeat; the captains of the ironclads persuaded him the attempt would be futile.

"The Rebels have too many guns. We are sitting ducks," said Capt. Rodgers of the *Weehawken*.

DuPont submitted his resignation soon after.

* * *

Robert resumed his duty as pilot of the *Planter*. Rhinds received a promotion and transferred to the USS Commodore McDonough. The *Planter's* new captain, James Lee, treated Robert with diffidence, yielding to the pilot's superior knowledge of the Port Royal waterways.

A steady flow of former slaves sought sanctuary at Port Royal. Three times a week the *Planter* picked up fresh arrivals in Beaufort and transported them to St. Helena. Gideonites welcomed them and assured they received placement at surrounding plantations.

The *Planter* was taking on supplies for another run when Robert, Capt. Lee, and others on the ship watched in amazement as a tiny colored woman led a column of seven hundred black men, women, and children to the wharf. Robert used his field glasses to get a better look.

"We'll I'll be pickled and smoked," he exclaimed to the captain. "That's Harriet Tubman!"

Robert met the little black woman, who barely reached his shoulders, shortly after she came to Port Royal. Already famous for her exploits in leading fellow slaves to freedom, Tubman developed great respect among white soldiers and her kinsmen. The skilled nurse treated men with dysentery and malaria with medicine she made from roots and herbs. Her remedies accomplished more than the Army's could.

The fearless woman also spied on behalf of the Union. Like a ghost, she slipped through Confederate lines to report on troop strengths and provide maps of the enemy terrain. On several occasions, Tubman entertained Robert on board the *Planter* with her adventures and close escapes. She matter-of-factly told him about leading more than seventy slaves to freedom, including members of her own family. The people called her "Moses."

As the *Planter* tied off at the wharf to collect the passengers, Tubman gave Robert a friendly wave. Her face shone with joy. She wore a bright red, checkered scarf around her head and an ill-fitted, green dress, that appeared to be torn in several places.

The hundreds of colored people looked in awe at the *Planter* and meekly followed Tubman on board. As soon as the ship got underway, they spread out on the deck and broke into joyful spiritual songs.

Tubman climbed into the wheelhouse and gave Robert a hug and a little half-salute to the captain.

"Thanks for comin' to get these chilluns." She had a deep voice and still spoke in slave vernacular.

Tubman stood about five feet tall. She had small, lively eyes and a firm, round chin, and a convex forehead. She confided in Robert that the deformity came as a result of an overseer hitting her in the head with a brick when she was a child. "Almost died right den and der."

Curious, Robert asked, "How you come to be in possession of hundreds of negros?"

She laughed and told of a Yankee expedition she led up the Combahee River earlier in the day. Tubman steered three Federal steamships involved in the raid past the river's mines. She scouted the area a few days prior and alerted those living along the river to go to a bridge spanning the Combahee when they heard a ship's whistle.

Federal troops went ashore and destroyed several plantations, seized food and supplies. As the white owners fled for their lives, their black slaves rushed to the designated meeting place.

"I nebber seen such a sight," laughed Tubman. "Here you'd see a woman wid a pail on her head, rice a smokin' in jes as she'd taken it from de fire, youn' one hangin' on behind, one hand roun' her forehead to hold on, 'tother hand diggin' into de rice pot, eating' wid all its might, hold of her dress, and two or three more down her back, plus a bag with a pig in it.

"One woman brought two pigs, a white one an' a black one. We took 'em all on board, named de white pig Beauregard and de black pig Jeff Davis. I nebber see so many twins in my life, bags on der shoulders, basket on der heads, and young ones taggin' behind, all loaded; pigs squealin', chickens screamin', young ones squallin'."

In the middle of the chaos, Col. Montgomery, military leader of the expedition, said "Moses, you'll have to give them a song."

So, she lifted up her voice and sang.

Of all the whole creation in the East or in the West,
The glorious Yankee nation is the greatest and the best.
Come along! Come Along! Don't be alarmed
Uncle Sam is rich enough to give you all a farm.

Her voice reassured and calmed the escapees clamoring to get on board the Yankee gunboats.

"Dey all look at me to see what to do next. Dey reached to thank me and dat' how I got dis torn dress Robert. But dat's okay 'cause de' Lord have showered dese people with freedom. Praise God, Robert. Praise Jesus."

Chapter 50

Morris Island, July 1863

The Army launched a new offensive to capture Charleston and the *Planter* began transferring thousands of troops from Folly Island, across Lighthouse Inlet, to Morris Island. The routine of the deployment operation took a dramatic turn on July 8th, when Robert inched the *Planter* to a jetty off the island. The sound of fife and drums filled the air as a white officer, mounted on a black stallion, led troops around a bend in the road.

Robert's heart swelled with pride as rank after rank of black soldiers, dressed in Federal blue, marched in perfect step toward the boat. The brass buckles on their uniforms sparkled in the afternoon sun. Solemn, the men moved with apparent pride.

The 54th Massachusetts formed into companies and awaited the orders of their commander, Col. Robert Shaw, who watched with a satisfied smile.

The sight of an assemblage of black men, prepared to fight, swelled Robert's heart with pride. He recalled the tribulations Gen. Hunter and his own promise to President Lincoln that the freed men would fight on behalf of the Union. These black soldiers, assembled in front of the *Planter,* represented the fulfillment of a dream. As the regiment boarded, Robert stood proudly at the helm, and saluted every soldier.

The last rays of the summer sun bathed the deck of the *Planter* in soft hues of orange and pink. Robert asked Capt. Lee's permission to talk with some of the 54th Mass soldiers. He went from one group of soldiers to the next to express gratitude for their service. They all responded warmly, called him 'sir,' and assured they looked forward to the upcoming battle.

A tap on Robert's shoulder caused him to turn.

"Moses, what in the world are you doin' here?"

Harriet smiled. "Der's someone I wants you to meet."

Robert followed Tubman to the rear of the ship. Along the way she explained that she received permission to tag along from Col. Shaw.

"De men who come back from dis fight gonna need nursin'," she explained. "I wanna' be der for dese brave boys."

The colonel gazed into the *Planter's* wake that glittered in the setting sun.

"Col. Shaw dis be Robert Smalls, de one I was tellin' you 'bout. He de one dat sailed dis here boat out o' Charleston."

Without hesitation, the young colonel reached for Robert's hand.

"It's a great pleasure to meet you Lt. Smalls. Moses has been telling me about your exploits. I hear you have brought many black men into the Army to join the fight."

Shaw's boyish good looks told Robert the officer couldn't have been more than twenty-five years old, young even for the times. Shaw's intelligent brown eyes and calm manner exuded confidence. About the same age, the pilot of the *Planter* felt overshadowed by Shaw's erect, military bearing.

The disparities between them melted away when the colonel asked, "Tell me your story Robert."

For the next hour, as the *Planter* paddled slowly toward Morris Island, the two men shared their unique war experiences. Shaw smiled appreciatively as Robert told him about the escape from Charleston. The young colonel seemed especially curious about Robert's meeting with the President and his efforts to recruit black soldiers into the Army.

Shaw told Robert about his initial reluctance to assume command of the 54th Massachusetts. Though he was a firm abolitionist, Shaw questioned the ability of the black race to fight in battle. It was only at the encouragement of his father that Shaw accepted the assignment. Since assuming command, his attitude changed, and a great respect developed toward those in his charge.

"When it comes to it, I believe they will fight. Don't you, Robert?"

He took the colonel's hands into his own.

"Col. Shaw, I believe with all of my heart that your soldiers would follow you through the gates of Hell, if you needed them to. Yes. They will fight. They will fight gallantly for you, for their race and for the glory of freedom."

* * *

The initial assault by a regiment of white troops, on the heavily-defended Fort Wagner, failed. The result was 127 Union deaths.

Capt. Lee ordered the *Planter* to take a position off the coast of Morris Island to participate in the bombardment of Fort Wagner and support the second assault, led by Col. Shaw's troops. Robert, Alfred, and several other black members of the crew climbed atop the wheelhouse to get a better view of the battle.

The 54th Mass formed in long blue lines about two-hundred yards from the fort's sloped walls. Confederate soldiers on the ramparts taunted them to come closer

At the sound of a bugle, the ranks of blue moved forward in trot. Naval ships involved in the action ceased fire. They did what could be done to soften the fort's defenses.

Cannon's atop the fort fired, creating gaps in the ranks of the black soldiers. The formations quickly reformed and pressed the attack. The front ranks passed out of sight as they waded through a deep moat protecting the fort.

Regimental flags climbed the sandy walls of Fort Wagner. The bombardment had collapsed part of a rampart and federal soldiers streamed through the break in the wall. Screams and the roar of cannons floated over the water to where Robert watched in awe.

He grabbed the ship's field glasses to get a better view of the battle. He caught sight of Col. Shaw, surrounded by his soldiers, fighting their way to the top of the rampart. Shaw raised his sword at the summit. Robert saw him shout to his men, then the officer went down—he didn't get up.

The battle raged on, but Robert stopped watching.

"That fine young man is dead," he said as the others watched the assault unfold.

An hour later, Capt. Lee ordered Robert to the wheelhouse.

"We need to go back to base on Morris Island." Sadness filled his eyes. "There's going to be a lot of casualties."

Robert piloted the *Planter* southward, then glanced back at the fort. Motionless blue uniforms filled the beach and the slopes of Fort Wagner. The Confederate flag still waved in defiance.

* * *

Hundreds of wounded men awaited transport to the hospital on Folly's Island by the time the *Planter* reached the staging grounds. Stretcher-bearers brought the worst of the wounded aboard the ship. Soldiers limped up the gangway, bleeding and hurting. Robert watched Tubman moved from one soldier to the next, dressing wounds and offering comfort.

Robert assisted her with a man whose leg had been severed.

She looked at Robert, despair gave her face a taunt appearance. "We saw de lightnin' and dat was de guns. Then we heard de thunder, and dat was de big guns. And then we heard de rain falling, an dat was de drops of blood falling. And, when it came to get de crops, it was dead men dat we reaped. But Lawd, dem po' black boys did put up a fight. I know Col.

Shaw be in Heaben, sittin' right next to Jesus, sayin', 'Good job boys. I be's mighty proud of you.'"

For the first time since he had known her, Moses cried.

Chapter 51

Lighthouse Inlet, December 1, 1863

Capt. Lee's stalwart conduct during the Morris Island campaign caught the attention of his superiors. It came as no surprise when the he received a promotion to command a larger ship in the Port Royal fleet. The *Planter's* pilot hoped Lee's replacement would be of similar caliber.

Robert arrived at the *Planter's* berth near the Beaufort waterfront in high spirits. After weeks at sea, he cherished the few days of leave to celebrate the holiday with his family. Hannah and Lydia cooked a feast to feed the black crew members of the *Planter*. Robert's $50 a month salary provided the little family with a better lifestyle than most.

Robert made his way to the wheelhouse and opened the door. There stood the replacement captain looking over a nautical chart. The new captain turned toward him, and Robert's heart nearly stopped.

"Hey nigger, remember me?"

Robert stared into the beady, black eyes of Festus Rhinds. The fat little boy Robert remembered from his childhood had grown into a tall, thin man sporting a full beard. The cruel set of the mouth remained the same, as did his arrogance.

"G-g-ood morning Captain," Robert managed to stutter. "Welcome aboard, sir."

Rhinds gave a dismissive laugh.

"I guess you're surprised to see me. It's been a long time since you tried to kill my brother. But I haven't forgotten. Funny the way things have turned out. Me a captain and you being my little nigger errand boy."

Robert didn't try to correct Rhinds' lie.

Festus turned back to his charts. "Get this piece of shit boat underway."

Festus Rhinds' career in the Navy had been as lackluster as Alexander's was stellar. The younger brother rose quickly through the ranks while Festus stagnated in a series of desk jobs in Norfolk. He never lost his love for the Navy, nor his aspiration to be a ship's captain. Repeated requests to have command went nowhere, perhaps because of his ability to alienate every superior with whom he worked.

When a position opened on the aging *Planter*, Rhinds jumped at the opportunity to become captain of the steamer, famous for being sailed to the Union blockade by a person he knew quite well. Festus boiled with fury when he thought about the fame that went to Robert, instead of to him. The *Planter* wasn't a ship of the line, but for Festus Rhinds, it represented a start—an opportunity—to prove himself a capable commander.

While Capt. Lee allowed Robert complete control of piloting through tricky waterways, Rhinds hovered and questioned almost every change of course. Frustrated, Robert quit trying to reason with the man.

"I'm back to just being another nigger," he told Alfred one night as the *Planter* waited at the Port Royal wharf for war supplies to be loaded.

"Jes be patient Mr. Robert. We been through worser den this."

* * *

The *Planter* stood near the entrance to Lighthouse Inlet, which separated Folly Island from Morris Island. Robert had piloted her through the treacherous waters of the inlet many times before, but on this day, he advised Rhinds to wait until a thick fog lifted.

"You're such a ninny. I've got orders to get these supplies to Col. Sorbet's outpost and I'll be damned if I will let a little bit of fog stand in the way. Take us in, damn your black hide."

Robert signaled Alfred to inch the *Planter* forward.

She crossed the bar and pushed slowly against the ebbing tide. The ship passed tall sand dunes. Robert gave a sigh of relief. Soon, the dunes gave way to the ghostly outline of cypress trees lining the banks of the inlet.

Rhinds gave Robert a triumphant smirk.

"Captain, I still don't like this. Why don't we weigh anchor until the sun cuts through this fog? These waters are tricky even in full daylight."

The captain gave a grunt of disgust and ordered Robert to take the *Planter* further into the inlet.

Instead of lifting, the fog got denser as the steamboat paddled forward. A creek appeared to the port side of the ship and Robert gave it wide berth, knowing the water got shallow near its mouth.

The *Planter* inched further up the narrow inlet. The waterway forked again, Robert turned the wheel right, but Rhinds pointed to the map and instructed the pilot to go left.

"I don't think so, Sir."

"Turn to port! Now!"

Against his instincts, Robert steered in the direction commanded by Rhinds. Through the haze, the pilot went against the flow of the inlet for thirty minutes. The fog enveloped the ship in a white blanket. Unable to see the bow, Robert had enough.

"Captain, this is ridiculous. We've got to set anchor for now."

Rhinds slapped Robert with the back of his hand, "Dammit, when I give you an order you damn well better obey." He grabbed the chart of the river and waved it in Robert's face. "Just follow the damn map Smalls. Hell, stand back, I'll do it myself."

Robert wiped a trickle of blood from the corner of his mouth. He brought a fist back and slammed it into the side of Rhinds' face, causing the captain to buckle over the ship's wheel. He looked at Robert, his eyes bulged with shock.

"You...you...hit me! A damn nigger hit me." He lunged at Robert in an attempt to lock him in a chokehold.

Robert sidestepped and pushed the captain to the floor of the wheelhouse. He kicked him hard in the ribs.

"You son of a bitch, the time has passed when you can hit a black man and get away with it," Robert said between clench teeth. "You ain't never gonna hit me again Festus. Not here, not now, not ever. Now get up, I'm stopping this boat."

Robert stepped over Rhinds and signaled for Alfred to bring the *Planter* to a full stop.

"Turn around," Rhinds growled as he pulled his pistol from its holster.

Robert faced the coward who pointed the barrel of the gun between his eyes.

Robert shut his eyelids and waited for the shot. Instead, Rhinds shoved him aside.

"Oh shit!" Festus screamed.

Robert twirled and looked out of the wheelhouse window. The fog had lifted and the barrels of four cannon's pointed at the *Planter*. The pilot realized they had sailed past the Union camp and now confronted the big guns of the Confederate fort at Secessionville.

A blast from the fort sent a cannon ball whistling past the *Planter's* smokestack and kicked up a shower of water aft of the boat. Rhinds screamed in terror and turned the ship's wheel hard to port.

"We've got to get out of here!" he cried.

The ship made a slow turn.

The ship was too long for such a narrow channel and Robert braced for impact. The bow buried itself on a sandy beach, less than four-hundred-yards from the Rebel fort.

Robert pushed Rhinds away from the wheel and signaled for Alfred to reverse engines. The steamship's twin sidewheels churned ineffectively, kicking up great clouds of water and mud.

Robert shouted to the engineer, "Is that all she's got?"

"Dat's it Mr. Smalls. Can't do no mo',"

Another cannonball screamed toward the *Planter*, now a stationary target for the Rebel gunners. Someone from the fort shout, "It's the *Planter* boys. Don't let her get away."

The federal soldiers on the *Planter's* deck raced for cover. Sgt. Strong directed his company to seek protection in the ship's hold. A crew of Union gunners pointed the forward cannon at the Rebel fort and fired. They struggled to reload as a shot from the fort hit the bow of the ship, bits and pieces of the men flew into the water. The Parrott rifle pointed toward the sky. The blast blew the gun off its carriage.

Rifle fire sprayed the *Planter* from the ramparts above, none of the shells hit the boat before the waterline, but they wreaked havoc on the bulwarks protecting the ship's engines.

From the corner of his eye, Robert saw Rhinds reach into a cabinet. He pulled out a white flag and waved it through the wheelhouse window. Robert jerked his arm back into the cabin and hit him hard with his free hand. Rhinds went down and cowered in the corner.

"We have to surrender," Rhinds blubbered.

A shell hit the wheelhouse, an enormous explosion rent the air. Robert turned from the blast as something hit his head, and everything went black.

* * *

Rhinds recovered and got to his feet. The wheelhouse had been rocked by the enemy shell. Sections of the walls disappeared. The captain's bladder turned loose and stained his pants, when another shell hit the side of the ship.

In a panic, he jumped onto the deck of the ship and scrambled below.

The negro crew and Sgt. Strong's soldiers stared in disbelief.

"All is lost. I can't take it anymore. I won't lose my life for a bunch of niggers," he shrieked as he ran into the ship's wood bunker.

* * *

Alfred climbed out of the engine room to look for Robert. He found his friend lying unconscious in the remains of the wheelhouse. Blood trickled from several cuts in Robert's scalp.

Alfred held Robert in his arms. "Wake up Mr. Robert. For Gawd's sake wake up!" he cried.

Robert's eyes fluttered.

"Oh, thank You Jesus!" shouted the black man, holding Robert in a desperate embrace. "You ain't dead."

Robert struggled to his feet and leaned against the ship's wheel.

A nightmarish spectacle met his gaze. He saw the barrel of the ship's forward cannon tilting toward the sky. The ship's bow rested on a sandy beach. Four hundred yards farther loomed a large earthen fort. A tattered Confederate flag whipped in the wind over the ramparts. Orange-blossoms of fire followed by ear-splitting explosions erupted from the fort and the high-pitched scream of cannon balls passed overhead.

Alfred explained that Capt. Rhinds abandoned his post and hid in the ship's wood bunker.

"How about Sgt. Strong?"

"Dey still here but below stayin' away from all dis gunfire."

* * *

Robert convinced Sgt. Strong and his men to resume defensive positions atop the *Planter*.

"The boat is stuck in the sand. That's why we can't reverse," he explained to Alfred. "I want to try to wiggle us out. On my command, reverse the starboard engine. Then, when I say, stop the starboard engine and reverse the portside engine. Keep doing this until I order otherwise. Got it?"

The engineer nodded and ran to the engine controls.

Robert raced back to what was left of the wheelhouse. Cannon fire ceased to give advancing Rebel soldiers a clear path to capture the *Planter*.

"Good." He saw debris float downriver. "The tide has turned. God, please give us some time."

Sgt. Strong's squad returned fire on the Confederates. He saw one grey coat fall. Others dropped to their knees and took aim at the soldiers on board.

Robert yelled to Alfred, "Starboard engine!"

The paddle wheels turned slowly in reverse and picked up speed.

"Port engine!"

As the starboard paddlewheels slowed, those on the opposite side spun furiously in reverse.

Robert thought he felt a slight movement in the ship.

He repeated the orders twice more. On the third round, he felt the *Planter* move. Filled with hope, he shouted, "One more time Alfred."

With a sucking noise, the *Planter* lurched sideways and pulled itself from the sandy prison. The last turn of the starboard paddle wheel propelled the *Planter* toward the Rebel fort.

"Reverse Alfred. Full reverse on both engines!"

The Confederate soldiers watched in dismay as the *Planter* pulled back with the tide and out of range of the cannons.

Sgt. Strong yelled, "Smalls! Watch out behind us!"

Two Confederate picket boats emerged from the bank of fog. The boats teemed with soldiers and small cannons powerful enough to disable the *Planter*.

Robert watched the gunboats approach, numb, unable to think of another move.

Thunder erupted from the fog and one of the Rebel gunboats burst into flames. A second clap sounded as the other gunboat split in half, throwing the soldiers into the water. As they struggled to swim to shore, the prow of a large naval ship poked through the fog.

"It's the *McDonough*," exclaimed Sgt. Strong.

His men jumped up and down, excited to see the Union sailors. The sidewheeler, much bigger and better armed than the *Planter*, lobbed more fire into the Confederate fort as both ships pulled away. The *McDonough's* guns put up a protective screen while Robert pivoted his ship and steamed to safety. Once out of range of the Confederate fort, the *McDonough* joined the *Planter* in its retreat to the Atlantic Ocean. Crewmembers from both ships cheered and shouted for joy as the *Planter* pulled up alongside the *McDonough*.

"Is that you Robert?" a voice from the *McDonough's* wheelhouse shouted.

Robert, shirt in tatters and face smudged with gunpowder, peered closer. The *McDonough's* captain stepped out of the cabin and waved. Robert fell to his knees in the remnants of the *Planter's* wheelhouse.

"Alex," he mouthed. "My brother."

Safely over the bar of Lighthouse Inlet, Capt. Alex Rhind boarded the *Planter*. He gave a low whistle when he saw the damage.

Robert clambered down from the wheelhouse and ran to embrace his friend. Soldiers waved their hats and saluted him, shouting "thank you" to Rhinds and the men aboard the *McDonough*.

"How did you know we were in trouble?"

"I've been keeping an eye on the *Planter* since learning that Festus had taken command. We were on patrol duty off of Morris Island when I thought I saw the *Planter* enter the inlet. You disappeared in the fog. I was wondering what the hell you were doing taking the ship into that kind of soup."

"I heard gunfire coming from the direction of Secessionville and worried you might be in trouble. Just as the fog lifted, two Rebel gunboats emerged from the creek in front of us."

"You saved our lives. Thank you, Alex."

Alex grinned.

"By the way, Robert, did Festus make it out alive?"

"He alive Alex. Once the action got hot, he ran below and hid in the wood bunker. I had Alfred lock the door behind him."

Alex laughed until his belly hurt.

"What do you want me to do with him?"

"My brother Festus? Leave his ass locked up until we get back to Port Royal!"

* * *

Upon returning to Port Royal, Gen. Gilmore, who replaced Gen. Hunter, met the *Planter* at the wharf. He came aboard the heavily-damaged steamer and asked Robert for a report. When the pilot told the general about Festus Rhinds' deportment during the fight, the general's eyebrows shot up.

"Where is he now?"

"He's down below, sir. We thought he'd be safest there."

The general ordered for an aide to bring the disgraced officer to the wheelhouse.

Rhinds stood before Gilmore, his head hanging low, his uniform covered in soot.

"Look at me!" barked Gilmore.

His uniform in tatters, hair in disarray, Rhinds looked at the general with bloodshot, defiant eyes.

"The nigger did it!" He pointed an accusing finger at Robert.

The general gave a snort of disgust.

"Rhinds, you have disgraced yourself and the Navy. Consider yourself under arrest." He motioned to a lieutenant. "Escort this man to the brig. Rhinds, I am recommending a court martial for cowardice and dereliction of duty."

The soldier motioned for Rhinds to move and escorted him off the boat.

Gilmore appreciated Robert and knew the pilot's reputation.

If any man deserves the command of the Planter, it is this one.

He smiled at Robert. "Young man, by the power invested in me as Commander of the Department of the South, I promote you to Captain of the *Planter*. I believe, Sir, you now have the distinction of being the first negro to ever hold such a position."

The general spied Festus Rhinds' Bell Crown cap on a peg and put it on Robert's head.

"Fits you well," he said with great satisfaction.

Chapter 52

Charleston, April 14, 1865

The *Planter* steamed slowly past the ruins of Fort Sumter. For all practical purposes, the bloody war that threatened to tear the United States in two, had ended. Gen. Lee's Army of Northern Virginia surrendered to Gen. Ulysses S. Grant April 9, 1865 at a farm house in Virginia, ending four years of resistance by the Rebels.

On the fourth anniversary of the opening shots of the Civil War, the President chose the *Planter* to lead the Union's ceremonial return to Fort Sumter.

Captain Robert Smalls, the first black man to hold that rank in the service of the country, stood beside the ship's pilot, as the *Planter* approached the same wharf it berthed before its delivery to the Union blockade. The irony didn't escape Robert, or three of the original crewmembers still serving on the *Planter*.

"Doesn't seem that long ago," mused Robert.

Two years of constant work had left its mark on the *Planter*. Despite Alfred's loving care, the engines needed an overhaul. The Navy wanted to turn the *Planter* into a coal-burning ship rather than one fueled with wood. In May of 1864, Robert sailed her to Philadelphia for repairs.

He made good use of his six-month stay in the City of Brotherly Love. Anti-slavery societies often called upon him to speak. He took advantage of the time away from the war and hired two free black men to teach him to read. By the time the *Planter* was ready to sail back to Port Royal, Robert formed the habit of reading the city's newspapers daily.

Excitement permeated the air at Port Royal when the *Planter* made its eventful return in November. Although Charleston stubbornly resisted occupation, Gen. William Tecumseh Sherman had hammered his way through Georgia. Atlanta fell while Robert was in Philadelphia. Savannah, just thirty miles from Port Royal, could not hold out much longer.

As the federal forces approached Savannah, thousands of negroes fled to Port Royal. They came destitute, a few meager possessions that could not fill a gunny sack. Gen. Saxton had the *Planter* shuttle the newcomers to tent cities set up on several Sea Island plantations to provide temporary relief.

Savannah fell on Christmas Day, 1864. A month later, responding to cries for help from freed slaves, Sherman issued Order 15, which set aside the Sea Islands for settlement by the freemen. Each freed black family was allotted forty acres of tillable ground. Later, the triumphant general added a mule to the deal. Transporting thousands of negroes from Savannah to Port Royal kept the *Planter* busy.

Sherman spared Charleston from the torch and the city surrendered in February. Pounded by federal siege guns for more than a year, not many buildings remained. What the great fire of 1861 had not ravaged, the bombardment had. In April of 1865, Robert received orders to transport Gen. Saxton and other high-ranking officials to Charleston to assist in the occupation of the city.

Robert ferried fresh troops from the 54th Massachusetts at Morris Island to occupy Charleston after Rebels evacuated the city. He also brought Gen. Saxton's black regiment. Confederate sympathizers that remained looked sullenly at the black soldiers who patrolled the streets, giving them a wide berth. The bravado that filled Charleston with rebellious fervor four years earlier had evaporated.

As Robert neared the Southern Wharf, throngs of people waved and cheered the *Planter*. In the vanguard stood Gen. Saxton, and Robert Anderson, the commander of Fort Sumter before surrendering it to the Confederacy. Now a general, Anderson stood tall and erect, his dress uniform dripped with ribbons and medals. He carried a folded flag under one arm.

The crew tied the *Planter* to the wharf, Robert, also outfitted in his dress uniform, hurried to greet the dignitaries as they boarded the ship. He gave a crisp salute to Gen. Saxton. When Gen. Anderson approached, he asked Robert, "We met before, haven't we?"

"Yes sir. We met briefly four years ago on this very ship. Under much different circumstances.

Recognition lit the general's eyes.

"Of course. But you were just the wheelman then. Now, I see you are captain!"

Robert invited the two generals to join him in the wheelhouse.

They watched as those who wanted to participate in the ceremony at Fort Sumter came aboard. Colored and white men, women, and children filed onto the *Planter*, chattering with great excitement. They filled all three decks, the hold, and climbed atop the wheelhouse and. Robert estimated at least three thousand people were on board. Concerned about the boat's stability, he signaled for soldiers on the wharf to close the gates.

A soldier argued with a black woman at the gate, before she darted through a small opening in the gate and ran toward the *Planter*.

Hannah.

Robert ordered the gangplank lowered and smiled with delight as his wife fought her way through the crowd to join him in the wheelhouse.

"I thought you weren't coming." Robert enveloped Hannah in a tight embrace.

She looked at him, eyes shining with pride.

"I wasn't going to. You know how I hate crowds, Baby."

She sniffled, "But you know a woman has de right to change her mind."

Robert ordered the pilot to back away from the wharf and the *Planter* turned slowly toward the jetty in Charleston Harbor.

As the *Planter* neared the fort, Robert felt mixed emotions. Fort Sumter, a symbol of Southern defiance, guardian of slavery, had also propelled Robert into a position of great influence. He recalled the anxiety he felt passing under the fort's big guns on the morning of the escape. He vividly remembered staring out of the viewports on the *Keokuk*, the fort's guns firing at point blank range, knowing he was about to die.

It seemed only days ago that he talked with President Lincoln, encouraging the great man to send black troops into battle. Such a meeting would have never occurred, thought Robert, had he not passed Fort Sumter. He thought sadly of brave Robert Shaw, the colonel who led his black regiment against Fort Wagner. The men didn't take the Rebel bastion, but tales of their valor inspired thousands of black men to enlist and fight for the Union.

The fort, so entwined with his life, had been reduced to rubble; as broken as the Southern culture that enslaved more than four million people of African descent.

Surely, a new day has arrived.

As they moored at Fort Sumter, Robert and Hannah said goodbye to their guests, electing to stay on board alone together. They listened as bands played and speeches resonated off its broken walls. A United States flag, the one Anderson took with him after the fort was surrendered, climbed up a flagpole and waved again over Fort Sumter. Batteries in forts Moultrie, Wagner, Ripley Johnson, and Cummings Point fired salutes.

Robert stood behind Hannah, his arms around her waist, and leaned his head on her shoulder.

Emanating from the fort came the sonorous voice of the respected abolitionist, the Rev. Henry Ward Beecher.

"It is not the same flag," Beecher said. "When it went down four years ago, four million people had no flag. Today it rises and four million people cry out, behold our flag! No more slavery!"

They gazed lovingly at the red, white, and blue flag fluttering above Fort Sumter.

Folded in Robert's arms, Hannah raised her chin to his face. "What happens now?"

He looked at her lovingly. "I don't know, Honey. The old ways are in shambles, like this fort. But a new world awaits. I want to be part of rebuilding it, Hannah. The South wanted my head, but I will give it my heart."

Epilogue

Hannah and Robert returned to Beaufort. The reward Robert received for delivering the *Planter* into Union hands, allowed him to purchase the McKee's home on Prince Street. Mrs. McKee, left destitute by the war, lived with them for the remainder of her life.

The day after Robert transported passengers to the dedication of Fort Sumter, an assassin shot and killed Abraham Lincoln at Ford's Theater. Robert felt as though the plans he made were shattered, but he continued to fight for his people and country by serving as a state senator and a member of Congress.

During Reconstruction, he faced death and financial ruin. Always a firm believer in the power of education, Smalls introduced legislation establishing the first free education system in South Carolina.

Capt. Ferguson managed to buy the *Planter* back two years after the war ended but died a year later of yellow fever. In 1876, the *Planter* foundered at sea while she pulled another ship from a sandbar and sank without loss of life.

In 2016, researchers found remnants of the *Planter* near Cape Romaine, SC.

Made in the USA
Columbia, SC
18 February 2020

88105303R00186